PS
3570
.H453
G69
2008

GOWANUS CANAL

HANS KNUDSEN

S P U Y T E N   D U Y V I L
New York City

copyright © 2005 Tod Thilleman
ISBN 1-933132-00-0

Portions of this novel appeared in *The Brooklyn Rail* and *Surface-to-Surface*.
Special thanks to Tsipi Keller.

Library of Congress Cataloging-in-Publication Data

Thilleman, Tod.
Gowanus Canal, Hans Knudsen.
p. cm.
ISBN 1-933132-00-0
1. Gowanus Canal (New York, N.Y.)--Fiction. 2. Obsessive-compulsive disorder--Fiction. 3. New York (N.Y.)--Fiction. 4. Missing persons--Fiction. 5. Actresses--Fiction. 6. Theater--Fiction. I. Title.

PS3570.H453G69 2005
813'.54--dc22   2004019377

Printed in Canada

Letter from Rev. Robert Knudsen
St. Paul's Lutheran Church
Knowlton, PA

IN AN EFFORT TO HELP OTHERS we have finally, after much time, decided to make public our son's notebook entries, partly because they illustrate the troubled soul and plight of young men and women who have lost their way in this nation. The disappearance of our son caused us much grief, but we hope that through our grief others might learn how to keep their children away from harm.

Our son's malady seems to have come about upon moving to New York City, where he mingled with various artists, and worse—criminal types I suppose you could call them. I am not casting judgment upon these people, but what I mean to point out to you is that our son, Hans, held on to his dreams too long. That our son rebelled against God. Whether this was his intention none of us really know—it remains to be seen between the scraps of journal entries he left behind and the righteousness that is God's love.

We are especially indebted to Tod Thilleman, the editor at Spuyten Duyvil, whom we sought out, having heard good things about his publishing company. The care and attention he has had for Hans's journal entries, and the insights as to the order of their presentation, and the hours spent explaining his reasons to both me and Hans's mother, have been invaluable.

It is our faith, of course, that helps us with our grief. We know our son is in heaven, wherever he might be, or will be one day, living or passed on, or staggering blind in a dark place ... We also know and believe in our hearts that others are with him.

(signed) Rev. Robert Knudsen

"To all those responsible for finally re-opening the old flushing tunnel, May 13, 1999." Hans Knudsen

I now live between Bond and Nevins, right over the Union Street bridge. I was not born in Brooklyn. I have one window, faded and flecked of old paint. Out below me—
 the Gowanus Canal. And my life began and ended with one thing—
 God.
 And even though I was born in Pennsylvania where I was to finish my teachings in school I suppose alongside the Catechism of Luther—
 it is precisely this heap of humanity where I find that exact essence of religious practice, servitude and artful brain-warp to be of utmost measure! That there actually exists in our world something so degrading to the intellect, something so foreign to the winds of soul and mind and—
 Birth AND Death—
 Ergo—
 I am being rushed into death, knowing I cannot stop it. Actually spitten out.

In sum—

all the time men, women and children have spent in church, or paying lip-service to church or religion in general, raising its vain and trite head in the midst of a baseball game a badminton backyard bungalow bull's-eye match a ping pong hell in the head a trafficked intersection a construction site a fifth floor walkup—

must feel shame like the real shame that goaded poor Eve and Adam in their absurd jungle habitat.

Ever a beginning and ever an end. This place. Again. The window, its dirt and grime, its fallow luminescence.

Therefore—*Ergo*—*Ahem!*

But then what of all this that has come to pass? What would this stagnant oily mass of lifeless water down below me be? The pure and just?—

Hippolyte, the young actress?

None such like, I say, in my halted English, homage to those that came and those that still do come here. Did they merely pass through or did they stay? The window, again, gives its only response, late in the day. Late.

So—

smelling the winds off the old Gowanus plantation (those protestants and beggars from slippery ships, setting sail for what would be a hell and always, may I attain naught but the insurrection of this lifeless and watery slash-of-an-inlet in South Brooklyn.)

—Finally—

the bridge rises out my window.

Finally, one day, I saw it rise and let a tug-boat into the last definition of the canal.
The gears creaked. It was late. The body (mine) was tired, and I approached the window only to see *its* wood and metal filings where once there had been a street.
How quaint, I thought—
one little tug-boat, one little unused canal at the end of the world and the blank face of its oily water.

—Ergo my eyes look to the sky to define the world—
just that little blue I have to crane my neck to at the window-ledge of lead exhaust-dust and death-fuzz in the glass—
a godless amen.

—

HIPPOLYTE (how parents can be so utterly devoid of responsibility: It's a man's name!—*)*
came from a small suburb in Nassau County.
How stagnant are *her* waters? Do they rush after a rain or do they merely rise? Are her eyes the color of mud? Does light ray from the glassy substance?
Does she speak with the dead or the living?
Does she inhabit space or was she meant only for brief time?

I won't be able to visit that bar and that theater again, where we met.
I haven't felt like visiting any of the buzzing little bee-

hives past 3rd Avenue, past 4th Avenue, 5th, 6th, 7th, 8th, up the slope into Prospect Park, here in Brooklyn—

Broken Land.

I can't bring myself to suffer all that indulgence, all those non-attentioned people, gathered and oozing like honey into a matrix of wax. I can't face it.

Maybe I was destined to live here in this recently converted warehouse, in Brooklyn, before the rents arose.

And they *are* rising. More and more people are moving into these dilapidated, industrially monstrous buildings. Converting them.

I would go to the bar—

and I remember now why the East Village, downtown Manhattan, had seemed so peaceful then—

I discovered a haunt, like they say, few people had known. And I could sit for hours, drinking, looking out the one window onto 4th Street and 2nd Avenue, Manhattan, and smoke.

And when the few little girls would come in I could ignore them. Or shout something stupid and cock-eyed at them! (They had no idea where they were anyway.)

It was a *new* place. There hadn't been anything like this that I could remember (experience of ten adult years in New York City).

My own bar!

Until it became popular, that is, and began to be inhabited.

But that was a little later—

always, a little later—

the just-around-the-corner of bourgeois existence. One

day things are all grease, sweat, toil and useless difficulty, then come the conveniences, the conveyances, the inventions of a multitude to keep the honey dripping into the comb, silent, sweet—
the end.

The names remain the same and song was never sung. As it must, apparently, be—
rapping knuckles on the brick wall of this soon-to-be converted room I sometimes manage to keep out the past as well as the present.

And from my window, where I now approach in stockinged feet, there is no tale, no wonder, only water beyond the dirty sill.

That is the action to the plot as it begins to unfold here night after day after night.

Making faces at the girls while I got drunk was a great luxury. And there were very few people to witness, therefore to stand in my way. And so I continued to frequent the bar after its daily opening—
about four in the afternoon.

I'd get tipsy, make a face, and then head to the meeting with Richard and Sara on the third floor, above the bar.

The bar was on the second floor above the stage.

On the third floor: a performance area, which we used as our office, our weekly meeting and strategy room.

On the fourth floor the actual administrative office was housed, where Richard and Sara held court and began to worm their way into the beginnings of a sordid partnership with the building's owners. Richard, who had inherited some money from a dead relative, was persuaded by Sara, his wife, to assume the daily activities in the running of this particular theater. She probably thought they'd be in a position to, then, own the bar; and, maybe, produce Richard's inheritance to support their position; and, coupled with their influence on the aesthetics of the theater and performance areas, purchase the building from its mysterious owner(s).

(Maybe I'm making too much of their relationship to that building and its theater but I can't find any other excuse in their anatomies. One wants control, attention and all the other conveniences the good life has to offer. And so it seems that Richard and Sara had always wanted nothing more than the only stage of the only building they, seemingly, inhabited day in and out. We were all obliged to follow.)

Art is theater and theater life. The simple facts played themselves out in a simple building in a simple city full of simple people.

In the bar they also held court late into the evening, as the crowds of young drinkers and actors began to tumble in and ruin my little chapel, my little dwelling place of spirit (that would soon become a synonym for the early tragedy of the Balkan Peninsula half-way around the world, the news of which rambling out over radio and television seemed to isolate all other news that could be fit into a sense of domesticity; to vilify and condemn all of us onlookers and listeners into the surreal worldliness our former game of solitaire never meant to become). Where, also, my writings and memories would soon become Hippolyte's and Hippolyte's alone—

Word had spread, that is.

No need for much advertisement—

Manhattan is crawling with people, young and old, looking for a "scene" to get in on, star in, move within.

As for me, I had stumbled on the theater and later the bar while looking for a place to perform (with the help, I had hoped, of a company of actors) my own plays and short dramatic sketches—

and clumsily worded poems.

Of course I knew at the time there would be others seeking out a like place for like dramas and like wishes within a like world. But I had arrived first (or so I was meant to feel) for, after showing some of my material to them, Sara approached and asked if I would like to become a member of their ensemble.

Behind the bartender, a large mirror trimmed in ersatz medieval filigree (c. 1900 a.d.)

Sitting there, with Sara, I began to lose touch with reality. It wasn't the booze and soda (placed before me, beginning to bubble in thin tall strands of rising oxygen) but the fact that her eyes, looking right into my own, seemed to sense nothing from me. I was helpless to her advances and made no pretense to ward them off.

And they *were* advances. I saw—

I definitely saw *that* then. But I was confident my own disarming nature (or what I took to be disarming and affable) would even and flatten our conversation and nothing more need be said later regarding her forwardness.

"Are you currently under arrangements with any other company?"

Her question startled me. I thought my demeanor made

it obvious this was a first for me, that entering the world of the theater was something I had, until recently, never really considered.

"No not at all!" I remember saying.

"I'll get Richard to handle this part of the deal."

"Yes but."

"We should really sit down and talk with Richard if you don't mind because I'm not sure how to handle your material." She touched my arm. "You are *really* a *very* good playwright."

"Thank you," I sweetly said, not sure why that both pleased *and* irritated me. "It's basically my intention to join three different ideals into one."

"We'll sit with Richard and discuss the limits of the contract and such and then be able to proceed."

"Contract?" I asked.

"And other things that we can quickly get out of the way and then proceed we'll get everything moving forward. Forward is good you should keep that in mind."

She had been coming on to me, that's why I was irritated. She paused and pivoted at the bar stool. The windows behind her, overlooking Fourth Street, showed a curious, livid, unwashed translucence—

something in her pause betrayed her own better self. It wasn't merely a snapped, broken logic she was portraying for me—

a logic that no doubt she made herself a home in—

but it was her willingness to enter that place, as if she meant to show how comfortable she was with me in spite of her broken logic.

But I had never really thought my poems and plays

would take such a short time to produce such dramatic effect.

I smiled, feeling a swelling pride at the unusualness, what must have been the absolute genuineness, of my material, to her.

"I'm glad you like my work but would it be a conflict of interest if we that is you and others were to perform my—"

"Excuse me," she said, again touching my arm, "did you hear that?"

"No. What?" And I cupped my ear to the empty bar and toward the empty staircase out the second floor door.

I remember thinking this is merely the way people feel when they are on stage, when they are displayed in front of others. That, and nothing more.

She looked into my eyes again and I began to get dizzy. She actually began to put me under a spell. She paused and took a deep breath—

"Would you consider letting us use one of your scripts for an upcoming showcase?"

She was deadly serious at this point. One of Sara's traits—

she could turn on the thin dime of the Real and become deadly serious, narrowing the atmosphere to the point of her broken logic. Until you too snapped into its empty focus.

"Of course." I laughed. "That's why I'm here!"

The absurdity of it makes my skin crawl even now. I'm sure my skin was crawling then, too. But I shrugged it off, like I said.

Again, I had never wanted to get involved with the theater. Well, I certainly had never entertained the idea, except in the face of sermonizing for my Father's Parish.

—

PICTURE YOURSELF in the throes of an oncoming and infamous Jim Beam inebriation. The red walls of the second floor bar beginning to tell in every detail your fuzzy, but happy, brain, any cares you care relate to. Surely, other actors and drinkers are there at the bar with you, but you're trying to zone them out, and you're not doing too badly at that. You're concentrating on your third bourbon and soda. You're not wondering if you have a drinking problem (not yet anyway) and besides, that is completely irrelevant to my story.

What is relevant, however, is the young actress: Hippolyte.

I thought I would have to spend the better part of a year at this particular theater trying to get my plays accepted by the directors, so I somehow felt compelled to follow up on the initial interest Sara had quickly given my work.

Upstairs, they had a different plan, a plan for a performance, for a series of performances, none of them defined as conventional. And so I guess I was ready to ascend to the unconventional, to convene my small talents with other small talents in sight of a small world.

And maybe I shouldn't be telling this to you right now (I find it more than ironic to be goaded forward by memory in this notebook) but I have of late come to realize that if I am to have any love left in my life I must look to the general love of my time. Without calling into the equation any elaborate philosophical scheme, I am trying to find out why it is that I

am continuing. It's a simple proposition—
Why should—
I—
exist? Furthermore, literary fame, the concept, completely eludes me.
And that's what tempted me to relate the story of the young Hippolyte. My story intertwined with hers—
A swish in the headwaters of the canal. An echo. A crack of night's whip?
The dim buildings asleep in the void. Lights having gone out long before I arrived.

I thought if I were to reveal what happened in that time, and, indeed, continues to happen in my own time, I'd have to reveal Hippolyte completely. Hence I haven't held back her name, haven't given her an alias.
I am offering her wholly and solely in the person and name that her parents gave her lo some twenty-nine years ago this coming July.
I met her when she was twenty-five. That is to say, I met her very briefly when she was twenty-five. I wasn't allowed much more than a brief, few moments of time in eternity for the pleasure (and now pain) which transpired.
Does this mean the entire history of my life's love is still in the stealing power of Sara?
And yet the relativity of my infatuation with Hippolyte still bears upon this philosophy of love. And yes, what I am seeking to capture is a kind of philosophy of love. I'll admit that much.
Richard's wife, Sara, kept us apart.

Sara turned to the others (as we sat in the empty bar) who were trouncing up the stairs, and, seeing that they were continuing on up those stairs toward the third floor and beyond, she called to them.

"Excuse me."

She stuck her head out into the hall and whispered.

Sara then invited me upstairs. When I walked into the office on the fourth floor there stood a couple of young girls, blandly dressed, faces lacking make-up. And there was Richard behind his desk. And there also the young Hippolyte, demurely beaming her youthful blush. We shuffled our way between the stacks of old magazines and junk piled everywhere, past the walls lined with books and old theater memorabilia.

"What *was* this place?" I asked, to the room.

Sara, without stopping to shuffle, mumbled something then laughed, then sat at her desk, a small table with a phone and papers and newspapers heaped into one corner. Next to Richard's equally cluttered set-up.

"Did you call the *Post*?" Sara asked of Richard, who paused, reflecting.

"Welcome to the pulse the." He searched for the words with a half-smile on his slightly bearded, youngish face.

"So this is the center of operations the production office." I finished his sentence for him.

"Richard did the *Post* call?"

"The *Post* let me see the *Post* did call they."

"I just wanna find out if the ad was placed for next week's showcase otherwise I'm gonna have to call that Yugoslavian bitch and she's *not* gonna like that but I can't see as I blame her I mean we all need publicity without publicity we can't have an audience or a theater now can we?" And Sara turned and smiled at all of us with a garish and mocking mask-of-a-smile. Her dirty blond hair suddenly twinkled, as if motes of dusty resin were flashing through the pores of her scalp.

"Oh that yes that was done yesterday," stated Richard, reclining and finally relaxing in his beat-up, antique silver and grey swivel-chair.

I turned to the girls who had sat next to Hippolyte on the couch—

"Are you actresses?"

"Actresses," they communally muttered.

"Actresses yeah?"

"Actress-es-ess-es"

"Writer," I said, nodding. Nodding. Nodding.

Sara rather quickly approached Hippolyte and took her by the arm. The other girls and I watched her lead Hippolyte into a small side room just beyond the desks where they proceeded to whisper.

I laughed, and smiled, at the girls, but they cast their eyes down to the floor, their arms straight down their drably clothed sides, their faces conscious but only in the fact that they had no expression on them, as if in a perpetual waiting for that face to arrive.

"So Hans I wanted to thank you for the," and Richard addressed the girls on the couch, "were any of you at the readings the auditions downstairs this afternoon?"

They shook their silent heads, a pause, then they said: "No we're here for." And they motioned to where Sara continued to whisper to the young Hippolyte.

"Well Hans is our new playwright."

"You mean I'm the *only* one?" I said, approaching his desk. He ceased and leaned forward, glancing toward the side room.

It was then I saw the graph paper on his desk.

He leaned back in the swivel-chair and took a deep breath, "No but well at *this* point in time."

"Make him sign the contract before he leaves!" Sara bellowed from her whispering somewhere in the small and, from what I could see, extremely cluttered side room.

"Here Hans let me she's right."

Sara poked her head in from the side room, smiling, "Sorry I mean please Richard see if Hans would like to sign the contract." Then she disappeared again.

"Is a contract necessary?" Even at this early time (exactly at the beginning!) I was very suspicious. A contract meant something I was not prepared to accept. I mean, we were only doing silly plays. All the rights were mine anyway, it said so on my scripts and poems with that symbol (©).

"Take a look at these and if you have any problem with them we can talk about it later."

"WHY DON'T YOU HAVE HIM SIT AND READ IT NOW!" Sara blasted from the side room.

"Sorry." Her head appeared again. "Richard why don't you have him sit right here and read it and that way we can have this done today you know it's already 11:30."

There was a pause. Then she said "Please honey" and smiled a big broad smile so that all her teeth were exposed.

"Well if he wants to take it home then."

"Fine. Hans you just sit there and read that if you can it would really be great if you could. But if you can't of course we understand." She had fully emerged from the side room and now tried to physically re-position me on the couch with the actresses.

"No problem," I interjected, affably, "I'll read it I'm actually curious as to what it might have to say I'm not really sure this is necessary though."

"Oh it's necessary!" Sara called out, having disappeared once again within the side room.

She continued to speak with Hippolyte in low tones while I cozied in with the girls and began to read.

After a few minutes, Richard, I guess from not having anything to do, said—

"When you sign this agreement it's basically an agreement."

All went silent in the side room.

"Then we can start the group meetings and try to get other people interested and with enough people we might be able to attract some attention."

"Honey! Let the man read it first!" Sara suddenly now sweetly sang from the side room.

It was beginning to get warm in the office so I told them I would have to get running, what with work and all that afternoon. I had to prepare an inventory for the restaurant and make sure all the portions were in serving order and—

"I think she's right I mean if you can just take a couple of minutes to read this then we'll be able to have you taken care of and be able to get down to business."

"Listen," I said, "I'd very much like to be part of this theater performance group I'm very much into the idea especially now. I have a lot of poetry I'd like to set to music and."

"Music?" Richard stood up. Sara appeared at the doorway.

"Well not music per se," I stumbled on, "but a sort of many-voiced arrangement that would take into consideration the actual sound of."

"You would have the audience involved?" Richard was curious, and sat back down at his oversized desk, a dwarfed official in a very unofficial place.

"Well sure the audience a lot of people. I was thinking maybe an entire field we could film it with video cameras and show it in the theater downstairs."

"Richard?" Sara suddenly wanted to change the subject. "We would like to rehearse our piece now."

She was talking about Hippolyte, and, I presumed, the two girls sitting on the couch, their ankles surrounded by books and other debris.

"Listen Hans." Then Richard turned and addressed the girls, "Why don't you all go down to the theater."

"I thought we were going to use the bar before it opens?" Sara snapped.

"Hans," she said, "you stay here and we'll be right back."

"I'll be right back too," said Richard, "they have to rehearse it's something we might use for the."

"That's enough Richard," Sara scolded.

She called to Hippolyte, "OK we're ready!"

Hippolyte emerged, walking into the open as if on eggshells, a slender, transient young beauty with dark all-seeing eyes. She seemed to be in some sort of trance, yet very aware of her surroundings, as if she knew the office, the fourth floor, intimately.

The girls stood up from the shabby couch. Richard sat

back down, his eyes on the procession, as if he didn't want to acknowledge my presence.

As they were filing past, Sara first, then Hippolyte, then the two girls, I said, "Do you need a trumpet player?"

Sara was smiling, but, an odd thing, she was staring off into the distance. She stopped, and let Hippolyte pass behind her, shielding my view of her.

"'Cause if you need a trumpet player then I'm your man," I bumbled on after their exiting processional.

The girls blushed. Hippolyte began to giggle. Sara, still looking straight ahead, turned that head, just as it was the only thing left of her over the fourth floor landing.

She began talking to Hippolyte, "The next thing you say to him should be—"

and her head disappeared, just as Hippolyte's had done a second earlier, as did the girls' heads a second before that.

Richard was again bowed at his desk, reading. I had expected him to say something but he was silent, and in our collective silence we both continued to read.

The agreement I had before me was trapped in a legalease that seemed to have nothing to say as regards my part within the theater. It merely stated that in case of accident the theater, its employees and owners, would not be responsible and no civil or legal action could be taken against any of them in case of injury. Since there was no reason to suspect anything dangerous would happen, and feeling its framework had nothing to do with my own writings, I signed it.

Just then a crash was heard below and Sara came rumbling up the stairs and into the office.

"Did you sign it?"

"Yes well I."

"Good. Now," she announced, a little out of breath, "if you would be able to come back tomorrow we can have our first group meeting I'm sorry but you understand we have to rehearse."

"Oh I understand. I'm on my way out now."

"Good." She smiled and shook my hand. "We will see you tomorrow then!"

"I was just wondering," I said, but Sara began talking—

"Richard dear would you know where the broom is?"

"What?" Richard had been drawing on the graph paper at his desk and appeared not to have even heard the crash.

"The broom dear would you know where it might be?"

"What for?"

"There's been an accident that's what for."

"John'll clean it later," Richard returned to his drawing.

"Johnny will not clean it later! We have to rehearse Richard you know we only have a few more days before the show!"

Richard looked past her toward me, standing by the door that led to the landing. I had been admiring the books and posters on the shelves. There were old pictures from what I took to be the early twentieth century, of acting troops, group shots, individual characters in even older period costume.

Suddenly I sensed more silence.

"If you'd like to come watch us rehearse you may," Sara said, with her back side facing me.

"You're talking to me?" I asked.

"Yes," she said, slowly turning around, her face very expressionless, but then breaking into a sour smile. "Yes *you* would you like to stay for the rehearsal?"

"No no like I said I gotta get going." I put my foot onto the landing, reached and felt my pockets, to see if I had forgotten anything.

"Why don't you stay Hans," Sara said.

I paused and looked back.

"Why don't you stay for the rehearsal."

I brought my foot back.

"Come on we're running late enough as it is you might as well have a look at this but do promise me you won't take any of our ideas with you."

"She means don't steal any of their ideas," chimed Richard, coming out from behind his desk, clutching the piece of graph paper.

Slowly Sara turned to Richard. Then she turned to me as if I were to lead us out.

I began to move but Sara took a giant step in front of me. She walked slowly, as if to bring forth the creak of the wood of the landing with every step. I see now it was all just a dance for her.

—

WE CONTINUED DOWN the stairs at the same pace and stopped in front of the bar door.

"Excuse me for a minute," Sara said, and vanished into another side room off the second floor landing.

Entering the bar I noticed the two girls and Hippolyte, interrupted in mid-rehearsal. Animated gestures flew off their lines. When they saw Richard and I were going to stay and began taking seats out from under some of the tables they had moved to one side, they ceased.

The cheap chairs made creaking sounds as we sat.

"Hello," I sheepishly intoned, and noticed clearly, Hippolyte. She giggled and went to sit 'neath the green and grimey window. The others watched intently.

"Hans is going to stay for a while if that's OK," said Richard, "he's our playwright."

"Well not the *resident* I hope!" and I addressed the young Hippolyte, who even then, many years before the big time (you know which show she now appears in, so I won't name it, just to say that this was in the early 1990's) was an obvious beauty, ultimate attraction for not only my eyes but something within. "Isn't there someone else writing for all of you I mean?"

And Hippolyte, whose ribbed, long-sleeved and form fitting shirt seemed to move in time to what she was about to say, "We're all writers we yes," she blushed, "we're all writers now that—"

"What she means," said Sara curtly, walking into the room, "we've been working on this piece for quite some time now Hipp have you met Hans? He's going to be our new playwright."

"I was just telling him," she answered and quietly approached to shake my hand, "we're all playwrights." Her softness held me for a brief moment as she returned to the window.

"Well we're all not really writers now are we?" said Sara, searching Hippolyte's face.

"No," said Hippolyte, "I guess not." And she let her eyes droop playfully.

"Now," said Sara, "enough time wasted let's try this again from the top let's get into position. Girls I want you to try and do everything you can to move this piece along quickly." She paused and studied them. They were eagerly nodding. "Do you understand?"

"Yes yes yes."

Sara went to Hippolyte and took her by the elbow and brought her to a back room behind stacks of liquor bottles and an old wooden bar-top, only slightly visible behind a velvety black hanging. This was their offstage area for the rehearsal, I took it. Sara began to whisper and speak in low tones to Hippolyte. There was something mentioned about posture and other issues related to the fashion industry. Then Hippolyte spoke and her voice was more audible than Sara's. She had difficulty, however, maintaining a complete sentence, and even though she was rising to the moment she lacked the nouns and basic predication of a communicable language to create an obstacle to Sara's constant ordering. But she managed to do her best with what little came out of her mouth.

"Your....important....said....," I heard Sara say.

"Even if...standing I guess...like this...or like this...would be the....," I heard Hippolyte say.

"When ......the.......certain shifts in balance....," said Sara's voice.

"When I enter then you're saying...." countered Hippolyte.

"You should...gowns.....night.....within......," topped Sara.

"...Place!" concluded Hippolyte.

Then Sara emerged and approached the two actresses at

the wooden bar.

"If you cannot you know sustain any kind of momentum just let her know and you should be able to get through the business. OK? Faces up. *Tense character. Release and flow.* OK? Sustain for as long as."

Then she backed away, telling the girls they could begin the scene whenever they were ready. But Sara backed up toward me and there remained throughout the scene so I had to crane my neck around her ass to see all the action. After a few minutes I gave up, and contented myself with the sight, for the most part, of the two girls. Her young Hippolyte was blocked from our view.

Except when she entered from behind the bar. But this did not occur for quite some time at first.

Then finally she made her entrance, energetically. All the things I'd heard about posture weren't there, but it probably wasn't applicable to the scene. She came running, hysterical and pulling her hair. She was obviously possessed of an acting ability, an ability at any rate belied by demure charm. Yes, she was full of spitfire, and I began to see what was underneath this young girl right from the very first day.

Sara told her, "Try the entrance again but this time more energy. *Tighten. Control. Length of Tension. Eye Surprise. Maneuver Number One.* Start right at the beginning of our exercises Dear that should get you through. But try *Eye Surprise. Length of Tension.* And *Tighten Control.*"

I saw Hippolyte absorbed in thought as she made her way back to her starting position.

Squirming in my seat at this point, but I remember not wanting to say anything. After all, I was beginning to see another side to this young woman, a side I was sure she'd be able to get out into the full light of day, such as it was, in that bar, and deliver something interesting. I mean interesting not in any artistic sense. I could care less about the scene they were doing (which was, by the way, some old French dramatist's text, presumably reworked by Sara).

I hadn't quite approached the fall that occurred a few days later but was engaged nonetheless by Hippolyte's evident beauty. She was very pretty, like I said, and young, and this youthful beauty so entirely untapped, it seemed, was beginning to come to the surface. Like witnessing a wild animal in a forest or jungle—

you can't believe you're there, and that such a creature actually exists, and you know that creature has an unbounded intelligence but you can't quite put your finger on it. Magical, primordial, totally indescribable.

Hippolyte entered again and again only to advance a few seconds further into the scene, then drop out of character.

Like I said, I was beginning to get bored. But it was not because of Hippolyte (what little I was allowed to see of her) it was the scene itself. Hippolyte held me spellbound. She kept pushing herself that much closer to some ultimate realization of her person.

But her person was, like I've written, demure, shy—

and yet this was her fiery appeal; her flame always licked you awake. When Sara did move to the side (as she did reluctantly) I would, it seemed, be given a glimpse, not only of that whole evolving person but her body, so magnificently young and in the prime (past!) the prime of some sexual flowering.

The fact was she was in heat and I could smell it.

Eventually Sara turned to me and said, "I guess you

should be on your way.

"Girls! Girls I think this is all we'll have time for today. By the way Hans thank you for showing us your work."

A silence fell amongst the girls.

"Thanks again and we'll see you tomorrow," she concluded.

As I was leaving I heard her run through her directions once again. "*Tighten Tragedy. Lengthen Tension* until midway then *Full Stoppage*. Do you understand?"

They giggled, all of them, but I heard Hippolyte's giggle, in particular, above all.

—

SOMETIMES THINGS HAPPEN very quickly, other times they take forever to develop. If I had just been patient, I would not have found myself rapping at the office door on the fourth floor of the theater bar shortly after two in the morning. Sometimes desire is a good thing, but more often than not it leads to the truly unwanted.

"Anybody in? Hello!"

There was a rustle from behind the other door on the landing, the door that led to the cluttered side room next to Richard and Sara's makeshift headquarters.

"Anybody there?"

More rustling. Then—

"Come in!"

I recognized Sara's use of the command and quickly opened the door.

"Hans would you help me with this I'm in here."

Odd time, I thought, to be cleaning the side room, but I was willing to help.

Sara was indeed in the side room, but she wasn't cleaning anything. Just the opposite— she had dropped most of her clothing and was now offering the back of her bra for me to unsnap.

I *was* startled, but you see, her back was facing me, so I was able to enter and proceed to undo her bra without really bearing witness. Indeed, she continued to keep her back to me, her panties a little worse for wear, overly stretched and a bit dingy.

"I'm glad you're here I was just thinking about you," she said, now beginning to lay aside the dress she had taken off and pulling on a pair of jeans. Of course her enormous breasts (Sara was almost six feet tall, with an ample bone and muscle structure) shook as she hiked on the bluejeans.

"You don't mind do you?" she turned her head to me, now pretending to cradle her bosom in protection from my intruding sight.

"Huh?"

"You're a man aren't you?"

She dropped her arms and walked toward me, her half-gallon dugs leading the charge.

"You're a man. *Aren't* you?" She picked up a loose fitting t-shirt off the cluttered shelf near the entrance I was standing under and slid her head through it. She paused before gathering the tourniquetted shirt above her breasts. I was looking at her breasts, of course, but doing the polite thing too—

that is, trying to listen to what she was saying, trying to flatten my gaze, to narrow it into the center of her voice. To show I was listening, not wantonly watching.

She pulled the shirt down and walked past me to Richard's desk, shaking a cigarette loose from a pack of Marlboro Lights and lighting it. She tossed back her hair and found some slippers near the couch and stepped into them.

"Well so much for that show I'm glad you weren't there to see it."

"What show was this?" I asked, sliding a cigarette out for myself.

Sara went behind Richard's desk and creaked down into his swivel chair.

"Well you saw the rehearsal the other day."

"The adaptation?" I asked, sitting on a stool in front of her.

"You don't mind if I show you my tits do you?"

I smiled. That was *my* mistake, I should never have smiled. Sara was attractive but only if you were from the farm. I mean, she had a half-washed sense about her. Not only the way she wore her clothing but the fact that her hair was a dirty half-blond, always fatigued, the waves generating a sense of disappointed, hard-working curls that never found their rightful place on that head. She also had a slight case of acne, probably from stage makeup. And when I smiled, I'm sure she thought I enjoyed seeing her semi-nude.

"I mean Hans you know we're going to be working together and this kind of thing happens." She took a drag off her cigarette and exhaled. "What am I saying," she laughed, "of course you know it happens. Listen to me. Honestly sometimes I ain't got no sense."

I laughed too, hearing her mock herself. But I was

laughing at the absurdity of the situation, her trying to manipulate the situation into a more comfortable, and what I would learn later (that night and for the next week or two) a more lucrative situation.

My bigger mistake came that night, as you probably guessed. That is, Sara and I ended up sleeping together. First, we were on the couch, lapping up each other's wet kisses. Her mouth was sloppy, which was desirable enough, but at the same time I couldn't shake the feeling she probably hadn't brushed her teeth in a long time, the saliva just kept coming. Before I knew what I was doing, I was following her home, out the office and into the streets, my exhausted frame too willing, already, to perform for her what she unabashedly desired. She was doggedly adamant about getting me back to her apartment so that we could, to use her own words, "Let's do what the big dogs do." Or some such strange Sara expression. I kept seeing dogs and their owners on the street as we walked to her place, wondering if they knew what we were up to. I always thought passion was something a little less unkempt, but here I was with a would-be queen of off-off-broadway, and who better to know about the backstage.

I'm not saying that the sex was bad, or that she was entirely unclean, you know, down there. It wasn't anything like that. I mean, it was good. Sara had long legs and her huge bosky triangle (endless hair, hair that spread and, I thought, are those bits of paper, toilet paper caught and nested there?) fed and seemed to rejuvenate me. But, of course, one night of that kind of thing is enough. To go on with it, that's where the terrible conceit enters. There, precisely there, between those long legs, her scheme wrapped and

wetly held my promise until—
"Well, ejaculation, of course."
"Richard's not going to be back until tomorrow," she said, taking a drag from her post-coital cigarette.
"Not that I really—"
"Of course you don't care but I do."
"Strange way to act then isn't it," I said, trying to find why she so readily took me into her East Village bedroom.
"You have to realize Hans I needed it."
"Who doesn't? There's always a sense of relief that comes from."
"Well I need more than most."
"More than."
I felt her breast fall toward me as we lay there in bed.
"Richard you know has all my money."
"I guess that's."
"No you don't understand," she continued, "Richard inherited a large sum from his aunt last year. That's why we're here."
"I think I'm about to inherit some of it myself. Wait. You mean it's *you're* money?"
"What's *that* mean," she exhaled, testily, pulling away, crushing her cigarette out on the floor, then placing it on the bedside table.
"Hell I don't know I just say things sometimes. But that's OK," I said, dragging authoritatively on my cigarette, "there are three things that really get me going. Like I told you when we first met."
"When was that?"
"You know. The other day."
"What other day?" she seriously questioned.

"One," I continued, "reality, how incredibly un-interesting that is. And."

"You just *say* things? And. And *reality*? What is."

"What's reality? Simple. What's this?"

"This? You mean us. Here? Well buster if this is reality then I think you landed on a gold mine because."

"Oh I know you've got money. Or will have *some* money. That's interesting but it's not reality. That's imagination pure and—"

"Simple," Sara added, appropriately. "But what," she continued, "is so simple about the imagination? It's mysterious. Total mystery my dear. I have veins running through my head and I know which are imagination and which are not. Whatever they are. We're involved with each other. Now. But you see there are corners. Things just come to life without knowing."

"That's my third point: reason."

"Reason?" Sara intoned, absent-mindedly.

"*Knowledge* you just said. Knowing. Reason. Deduction. Induction. Ways of influencing what we already know to continue that knowledge."

"Not only do you just say things you have no idea what's happening do you?"

"And that's my second point: art. Or in our case I suppose theater. Theater."

"I've always known that we were artists." Sara sat up. "Us actors. I knew it was not right to be thought of as some sort of whore. Like in olden days. You know."

But Sara was a kind of whore, it appeared, glomming on to her husband's money, and now the theater as a way of becoming someone big in a big city.

"I am not," she continued, to the walls, "a whore. Do you hear me world? And I will not be lectured to by anyone who even has the remotest idea that that might be the case."

"That's not so bad," I thought I'd allay her fear. "Most actresses were always thought of as whores. Long ago."

"Like I was saying."

"And they were! Much sought for because of their 'low' position in society."

"But that's history," Sara barked, "I don't care if anyone wants to seek me out. That's your problem I suppose."

"History. They were forced into it if you like—"

"You just continue blabbering that's OK but I'm still not a whore."

"But to my second point," I continued, "art *and* theater are a whore. Art's the whore. And that's OK. So you see," I wanted to summarize, "we keep falling from something. Maybe we're falling right now, tpgether in a work of—"

Sara pulled herself up out of bed and into the bathroom. The tap ran, a stream, then it stopped. She then pissed, wiped herself, and turned on the shower. Rumbling and muffled screaching sounds sprang out of the plumbing in the walls.

I finished my cigarette and began dozing, or trying to. I didn't want to think about the day eventually turning nightward and me with it.

Sara appeared again and sat next to me. Her hair was pulled back. She started rubbing me. A slow, silly kind of rub, but I warmed to the idea. Too quickly, of course. I closed my eyes, and soon felt her saliva, and an incidental sucking noise, very sloppy, perverse, yes, but very strange, with teeth and wetness awkwardly placed on my member. I began to harden in spite of her technique. Which took a little concentration. I just kept trying to concentrate on my desire to sleep and that seemed to help.

Then she stopped.

"Let's shower."

I opened my eyes, a little surprised.

"O—"

and she pulled me up out of bed—

"K."

—

—Down they went and down they still go, to the East River and the boarded-up and abandoned docks of Brooklyn where Verrazano once turned a corner and spied paradise—

turned out to sea, the vast Atlantic, the waves—

too many, torrential freedom, downpour—

puritanical, blasphemous mice loosed from the belly of a beast—

a force-thrown-up-destiny within the natural wildfires of the night of a dark and untouched continent—

the completion of the world—

a place more powerful than any of their Gods, any belief, any ethic, any temple in service of commerce—

than any—

that every other force in the known universe is hooked into idiotic belief, put there from the time of the founding of nations, planted in the very crotch of one's progenitors.

Mankind *does* live in the presence of the unknown and unknowable. This is a fact a verifiable fact!

More than fact—

it's my own isolation and reality. I'm of a form they call the real. The place of all?

The real!

—

WHEN MY FATHER, at the pulpit of his parish in, oh, it must have been 1967 or so, mouthed a sermon for the first time, that (I guess you'd have to say) was the beginning of eternity for me.

And so the entire wilderness of the ancient past that was (and still is) under all this concrete, a city of machine-like desecration and filth and corruption no picture of imaginary infernal realms comes close to, looms and takes over my own imagination to conjure the present day in the form of a mouse, or one of these rats at the garbage bags left in the street too long opposite the laundromat downstairs.

And, lest I forget, the old, fat, greasy lady with the leg wounds whose brother lets her sit out front because he owns the joint—

To find the eternity of *the real eternity* is my only wish.

Because I know reality corresponds with Hippolyte, with her reality, her real life, a life that began in a little house out on Long Island. A little girl whose existence came into my own, soon to be used by Sara and her useless husband, Richard.

But this is an admission better stated in the chronology of my leaving the Lutheran religion to take up the Catholic, then, not finding a suitable Catholic school, the Episcopalian Seminary where I enrolled in nineteen hundred and eighty. AD.

Long after my Father was given a church of his own to run (near the Delaware Water Gap) I was faced with the prospect of following in his footsteps.

I had even delivered some of my own sermons and read from the Gospel a few times in my early teens (rare for a Lutheran church, but not taboo by any means—
the Lutheran religion being very loose in its rules).

It had all but been decided I would continue in those footsteps, my interest in religion being considerably intense enough at that age to foster an assumption in those around me that I would rise up in the so-called chain of belief.

It was all bookish, I saw later.

It related to the naive learning, entrenched in my Mother and Father and the other members of the congregation; for, from that first reading in the Bible I had unwittingly opened the pages to my own fate, as it were. Their condescension seemed to burn into my own supposedly free conscience and harbor the choice for me. Such is praise when visited upon the young of heart.

I had not the wish, however, to continue in my Father's religion. Suffice it to say, my Father's adherence to religion in general and to his specific religion was so vastly different from my own, even then, that it would have been folly for me to merely sleepwalk in his keeping. In the religion of his sleep.

An episode within the chronology might help to elucidate:

Lighting the candles in the church one winter I had failed to perform the proper ritual, having done it a hundred times before, and having been influenced to a very egregious degree by one of the other altar boys (actually all of them)—

if they could let one candle remain unlit during the upcoming service, then so could I.

(This reminds me of where my people come from. How they got here. In that far away Europe of centuries past, in between populations, in mountainous terrain between states and potentates my people were thrust, along with their God, into the dark earth of survival. Once Luther lit a fire in the minds of his country folk, his brethren, and touched upon the center of belief as personal, the boundaries between states, mountains and potentates and princely warriors began to move. Actually, they began to disappear and then reappear without warning or rumor. One minute we were supplicating to the Holy Roman state of things, paying tribute and centering around churches here and there, and the next we were persuaded to pay allegience to those centers of reform that had previously seemed so heretical. In our words, leading to acts and deeds, the fire that Luther had lit inhered. So that next minute it was the Lutheran Church we gathered around, took our food and customs to and from. Then Calvin had his say and Princes and Feudal boilings-over grasped the Calvinist crown to further divide and conquer the appearing and disappearing boundaries. Add to that famine and decades of war between kingdoms and interests that bore little in common with us and we were pushed into crevices of self and mountainside until they became one and the same with our religion and quickly evolving origins. Sensing this, the protestant world, whose ambassadors and Queens and political allies knew we would be lost and sacrificed bloodily to the new world order, and that they would be held responsible, immediately gave to us passage to the new new world. We were chattel, of course, and all one could do with chattel was get them into the stream of commerce, there to mingle with the flotsam and jetsam of other merchandise. The European powers, whose might began to stretch over the globe, could only treat their God with a tribute of riches, and so we were added to the pile, no longer representative of poor Earthly wonder, the clay from which our souls sought communion. Up and out we went to the new new world as if we hadn't already done that from a crack in old Europe's earth. Dream time took us off course, way off course, and so we continue to this very moment.)

But as I was saying, it wasn't unusual for many candles, not only in the nave but in the foyers and vestibules of the church, to sometimes go unlit throughout the entire Sunday Service.

A stricter, simpler adherence to the proper rite before the entire service began would have eliminated this error. But my Father was very lenient when it came to us altar boys. Our gowns were often unwashed for weeks, our faces dirty, and our clothes sometimes inappropriate. But that was unimportant to him. For him, the congregation and its families existed as the soul of the church, under his direction, and so he allowed for a dialectic, a give-and-take within the figurehead of authority which was his (so to speak) and his alone.

In the Sacristy, where we put on our gowns, Father

would sit at his chair before the service and banter with us boys:

"You say it's the Tigers this year Louey 'cause I thought you fellas had a darn good team last year."

"No one can beat the Tigers they got Mark Whechsler!" said little Louis Bendtsen.

"Wechsler huh?" said my Father with a wan smile, no heed as to the service about to commence, stage right, just five minutes away.

"*And* they got Uzinger *and* Jones y'know *and* Karlfeldt y'know Carl Karlfeldt!"

"Is he their quarterback?"

"He's everything! He can pass *and*."

"He can throw the bomb easy!" said Eric Drummond, as he searched for his rod and snuffer—

"*And*," continued Louis, bending down to roll up his gown so as to expose his jeans and sneakers.

"No no that won't do," I interjected, having already donned my gown properly, and assumed position beside my Father's chair, the wine chalice and holy wafers spread behind me on the counter. I had made certain they were on the clean linen and that extra packages were open and ready to retrieve backstage, in case they were needed.

"*And* he can cut and run upfield," said Louis, without acknowledging me.

"Sounds like he gets the ball all the time," opined my Father.

"*And* he's middle linebacker!"

"Well. But you fellas have a chance you're how old now?" asked my Father as if he didn't know.

"Twelve," chimed both Eric and Louis.

"Yes. I can feel it this is going to be the Cardinal's year as long as you boys get some practice in with *your* quarterback."

"WE don't *have* a quarterback," said Louis, sadly.

"What about you?"

"ME! Haw no Mr. Knudsen that's not my position I play defense defense wins games nobody knows that though."

"No," said my Father, "nobody knows that that's right."

Very soon I discovered this attitude of leniency he so "ruled" with went far deeper than just the formalities of the Church but extended to his inability to discern between good and bad within the teaching of Luther's Catechism.

He did not instill in the children under his direction the proper role assigned to faith, thus allowing us to understand religion in general as the state we were to live under later, in the world at large.

I can only imagine what those little ruffians, both boys and girls from the Sunday School class, are doing now, out wandering the American frontier of pain and futility.

But it was just this figurehead that let souls slip by into the dark of night en route to Confirmation.

—

I HAPPENED INTO the fourth-floor office one Saturday Morning. Walked right in. There was Richard, slabbed out on the sofa, his eyes bleary and opening just as I knocked a few knuckle-raps on the couch's arm-rest.

"Do you sleep here?"

"Sometimes oh boy!" and Richard shook himself awake

and made his way to the swivel-chair behind the desk.

Once in position he was ready to think, I suppose. Outside that position behind the desk he had no alternative but to take commands or extreme inference from Sara. At least that's the way it seemed. A broken-down fax machine, a typewriter, various notepads, posters and schemata hung up behind his head between the two windows whose grime was literally half an inch thick.

A temporary workstation, beside the desk, had been carved from the books and debris and antique garbage that had been stored on this top floor since the late nineteenth century.

To the side of that was another smaller room (as mentioned before) crammed and stuffed with old theater posters, scripts, books, all of it covered in dust, waiting to be torched by an errant and still-smoldering match. I'm sure there was no insurance for the place.

I edged my step into the side room to take a peek. Piles of costumes and old brown books with gold lettering. The floor was wood, but it looked more like a tar varnish had been applied from years of wear and dust. Someone had attempted to clean the narrow window that also faced Fourth Street but stopped after a couple of strokes. Towers of brown books, old clothing and costume regalia, shoes and suspenders and hats and canes strewn upon the floor, some of it bearing dusty footprints. On the other side of the room a leaking lava lamp, a pair of scissors, a box from circa 1940, Q-tips, and, along a shelf against the wall, several mannequin limbs. Someone had also attempted to paint the wall in a fresh cream color but abandoned the brush and the rolling pan and the bucket after a couple of swipes.

Suddenly I realized Richard was standing behind me. He had a cup of coffee in his hand.

"We can use any of these things for props if you like what do you want?"

"Oh I don't need anything most of my work has nothing to do with props." Noticing the coffee I said, "How did you slip out so fast?"

"Magic." I knew he was joking of course, but his face, suddenly, held so much of his statement, as if it had been a true statement, that my eye was caught and carried by him as he made his way behind the desk again.

"What do you want Hans?" he said as he sipped his coffee.

I dropped a couple of scripts and my card plans for the graph paper performance project on his desk. He shuffled through the papers.

"What's all this?"

"Other writings but mainly I came up with a very good idea for the graph paper performance."

"The what?"

Like an idiot I scrambled through my bag to produce the graph paper that only a week before he and Sara had assigned to everyone in the group.

"You mean this?" He held aloft a copy from off his desk.

"That's it!"

"Well Sara and I aren't quite sure if we're going to proceed with this plan."

"If you do," I tried to sound amenable, always, never had a problem trying to smooth things out, "if you do I thought maybe the cards would come in handy as a device for generating non-actorly activity."

"Now I know we talked about that but."

"Well listen," I continued, "if it's a matter of funding the enterprise in any way it's not that expensive. You would save a lot of expense the way I have it figured."

Richard kind of swallowed what I had to say about money, then straightened his face out with his hand. "We're not determined solely by money Hans. But it's something we might have to determine later. The thing is to grow and."

"I understand completely about growth." I paused. "I completely understand about growth."

Richard was beginning to tire of my idea, and engaged his coffee.

"What I mean is—"

"I know what you mean Hans. We're very interested in any idea you have for the performance group. I am especially interested in activity that takes us away from the theater. Anything. I liked the thought you had about filming sequences from helicopters. Though that would cost some but not to worry about that it's the idea that counts. To get things started."

I pulled out a stack of notecards from my back pants' pocket and placed them on his desk.

—

This vile valley of cement and these floating, noxious, miasmic, oily, degenerative, obligatory, motionless, snapshotsssssss. Waters.

This place of car exhaust. This place of animal spirit hidden in the eyes of the few—

This place, this valley, has nothing whatsoever in common with what I am doing to survive.

It certainly had nothing to do with my involvement in theater.

To think I was going, almost daily, into a tiny theater on Fourth Street, Manhattan, attempting some sort of aesthetic conversion. As if to uncover myself? What had the writing already uncovered? The real, this place?

Meanwhile, this canal and this neighborhood endured the days and nights. I wonder if there isn't something wrong with me, something wrong with everyone who has entered a theater or museum for the express purpose of escaping all this dull and lifeless space. How could anyone view this with the romance of an eighteenth century sea-captain? We're land-lubbered in the strictly present century as if space and place mean history?

—

My Father, of course, was our head instructor in the Catechism. With the same lax attention he had for the candles in the church he had for myself and the rest of the children of his congregation. Questions unanswered and left waiting in the little child's head he *would* supply with answer, but not an answer that would lift the child toward the true essence of the Lutheran faith.

Bible stories he'd let wander into stories from his own youth, parabling the enigma that was his own self not so much as Pastor, but as John Q. Public. I think we learned more about Being than we did about Religion. We certainly learned more about the fallen man who was my Father (Bob, as he called himself in his stories from the days of a wayward youth).

One day, in the basement of the church, my Father unfolded a map of our town, Knowlton, PA:

"OK boys and girls I want to show you something," said my Father, placing the map on the table we were seated around. He took his hands back and stuffed them into his pockets, the same wan smile directing our gazes toward the map and he, of course, never looking anywhere but at it. "You might recognize this," he said.

"It's our town," I quickly said noting the name KNOWLTON, PENNSYLVANIA printed on the bottom.

"That's right but what I want to show you is: over where Lynn and Tracy are sitting is the farthest city limit today."

We all looked at Lynn Thomsen and Tracy Anderson.

"And where Paul is is the other limit."

We all looked at Paul Christiansen.

"And where I'm standing is another."

We all looked at my Father, Bob Knudsen.

"And where Becky here is is yet another."

We all turned to look at Becky Yount.

"And the rest of you too are at the other limits of Knowlton, our fair town," concluded my Father, laughing a bit, prompting the rest of the class to break into hysterics.

"But what I wanted to show you," my Father finally resumed, "was where the city limits were when I was your age."

Murmurs went up from the kids.

"Now do you see this here," my Father said, leaning over the map. The children stood and also leaned over the map, hunting for the figure under his finger—

"This is the direct center of town. The population of the town used to stretch this far. No farther than that all around. Do you see that?"

"Yeah," everyone murmured.

"Well do you see the difference between where it was then and where it is now?"

"It's further out," said Paul Christiansen.

"Much further," said Becky Yount.

"This is where we live and my dad said he bought our house later when they re-zoned the street," said Eric Drummond, excitedly.

"That's right," approved my Father.

And everyone began talking and scrambled to find where their houses were on the map.

"OK OK," said my Father, standing erect, plunging his hands into his pockets then leaning back in his stance.

"I want to trace for you the route my first car would travel on hot summer nights."

"To the river!" shouted Louis Bendtsen.

"Yes the Gap that's where you still go isn't it?" my Father asked.

"Down by the recreation area," Lynn Thomsen correctly concurred.

"We took a raft there once," added Louis.

"Well we all've done that dope," admonished Tracy Anderson.

All the kids laughed.

"But I remember when there weren't any piers down by the recreation area and the highway wasn't as built up as it is now," mused my Father. "In fact," he laughed, "we used

to take our dates down there—
you know—
you can't do *that now* can you?"
"No no I guess we can't," everyone agreed.
"We used to have drag races! Can you imagine that! How could you do that *now*! Down there! By the river!"
Everyone was silent.
"Let's all open the Catechism. I want to talk to you— and I used this to illustrate a pair of Lutheran concepts— Transubstantiation. Is one. Consubstantiation the other."

—

Just out my window, here over the Union Street Bridge. Over the Gowanus Canal. Sunken city thrown to the guard dogs and the casket makers and hub-cap collectors!

It's as if the valley, suddenly put to sleep by nothing but its vacant self, just as suddenly woke to the sound of commerce—

What did I do to deserve this place?

The work-a-day world guarded by hounds in protection of property that exists in ownership somewhere else—

always the abuse of this place by its own structure, its own placement. From the base currency of history burning with jealousy out of the confines of some other place—

with unknown rage not here, not present and accounted for—

acceding to the power of some sort of vacant judgment.

This is the rule of cement and my hole and home therein—

the humming and metallic vitality come sometimes over what was a swamp, now tar and cement—

pictures, people, presentations of the slow stampede. I can smell all of it and all of them in oily fumes over the canal whose course seems now that of my ancestors and every poor weak animal that was thrown down here.

Here! Damnit, right here—

the place of places!

—

ONE DAY I WENT TO THE CHURCH a good hour or so before the service was supposed to begin. No one was there; no Sunday School classes were being conducted downstairs. My parents had let me out without checking to see where I was going. If they had known me better, they would have understood that on a Sunday church was all I cared to think about, and that I would not be joining any friends out in the neighborhood streets and yards.

To be honest, I think they thought of me one day and then forgot about me for the rest of my young life, always referring to me as Little Hans Brinker, as if that were enough to bring me around to their way of thinking. In their minds my own name, Hans, always illicited the image of that famed skater of holiday tv classics. That, coupled with the fact they assumed I enjoyed going out to play with the other little kids in the neighborhood.

Anyway, I walked into the church and immediately had

the urge to light all the candles in the Nave, the Refectory, in the entrance hall to the bathrooms outside the church proper—
everywhere.

I had dug out all the candles from the storage closet in my Father's office, replacing the old with new to ensure a long burn.

I proceeded to light them. At one point, towards the lighting of the last few I noticed out of the corner of my eye that the church was lit solely by the warm and golden light of my candles.

I approached the aisle and made my way to the center of the church at the foot of the Cross in the Nave. As I got closer, the light seemed to magnify in my sight. That is, I knew I was getting closer to the candle but something else, something within my own eye multiplied that light sending its multiplication back toward the candle-source, then back at me, and so on, growing and growing. Until I passed out.

I didn't really pass out. I was still conscious. I had suspended my life in a moment of candlelight. And I lay there on the floor under the benches knowing no one would be coming into the church for still some time.

It was very peaceful. The carpet was red and padded and very comfortable. The light continued to fall down from everywhere within the hall of worship. I closed my eyes and then opened them. Under the pews my view stretched into at least half an hour. How had I fallen precisely here? I rehearsed all the shuffling that would be going on later down there. Nothing would compare to this candle-lit service, however.

I must have begun dozing. Two shoes paused before me

under the pew. A voice, attached to them from above, kept repeating my name.
"Hans are you OK Hans Hans is that you?" And so on.
I finally answered, yet remained on the red carpet.
"Hans what's the matter?"
"Oh nothing nothing I'm OK."
The shoes moved a stutter-step to the left.
I knew who it was, of course. But that didn't really matter. I wasn't about to suspend my euphoric encounter with the church and its floor for him. Come to think of it, I wonder why he hadn't made any effort to help me up? He must have felt I was enjoying myself. I know he was enjoying my handiwork, the candles, because the shoes did a 360 degree turn and the voice attached uttered a quizzical sigh.
"Don't worry you can leave them lit I'll clean it all up later after the service."
"You sure you're OK down there?"
"Yeah I'm fine don't worry just do what you gotta do I'll take care of everything later."
"Well I wasn't going to do anything Hans I just saw the lights and wondered if there wasn't a seance going on in here."
"No seance no science. Ha! that's a good one don't you think that's a good one?"
Shoeshift.
"No nothing's going on I."
"Good. You alright down there?"
"Oh yeah I'm fine just getting to know this place is all."
"Huh! Well if you need me I'll be in the."
"Yeah I know I checked the toilets before I got here and everything's all set and ready to go"

"You *checked* the bathrooms? Anything else I should know about or can I just as well get on home?"

"Well if you want to you could go home and I could take care of whatever."

"Do you even know how to."

"Oh I've watched you a hundred times I think I—"

I paused as the shoes shuffled over to the right, exposing the entrance to the nave in its golden glow.

"You think you could handle the clean up Hans?"

"Sure."

"Well just in case I'll be around after the service to help you out if that's OK."

"Yeah sure that's OK I'm just about through here now anyway. I'm sure I won't need any help though I can manage. Ha! I'll endure like the song says."

"Through? Through with what Hans what are you doing down there I know we've been *through* this kind of thing before with you but."

"I'm OK you just meet me after the service and I'll help you with whatever you need help with. It's not like I was passing through on my way anywhere special."

"You'll help *me* will you?"

"Yes sir don't worry."

"Oh I'm not worried Hans," and the shoes and its now chuckling voice pushed the swinging door open into the sacristy and out into the back hall that led to my Father's office.

Suddenly I knew what was wrong with me. And from that moment on I vowed to turn my back on Lutheranism and to one day join the true church, wherever and whatever it was.

—

I MENTION THE CANDLE story to highlight another, more important discovery, made only of late.

While I was in the theater bar I had the opportunity to sit and converse with Hippolyte. Her young and beautiful figure pertly propped on the bar stool. I had nothing really significant to say, but I spoke anyway. And she giggled. And then it happened: she was to say something to me but her eyes caught mine.

Really, a very trite thing, very much like they say happens, only, it wasn't usual because the candlelight from across the dark and red-painted room caught and glowed in her dark eye. Johnny, the bartender, thought it pleasing to put up a few candles behind the bar as the evenings began and the room waited for a population explosion.

She noticed the reflecting light too and began to slow her speech, until she finally said, frankly, she had forgotten what it was she wanted to say.

The candles set up along the bar's back mirror and in the corners of the room, on that evening after a weekly theater meeting, were indeed strange.

It was a moment of eternal bliss. Not so much because of the possibility of a romance between us—

it was the candle flame *in* her eye that sent me reeling.

But it was at that very moment, when the candle slowed her brain into dreamy stupor, mine was leaping in a previous life, as it were, re-lighting all those damn candles in my Father's church!

I leaned over the bar, slightly tipsy, and asked Johnny if he had lit all these candles by himself. He walked away and Hippolyte looked down at her glass. Suddenly, a young man, very good looking, approached the bar. He sneaked up behind Hippolyte, then they began to kiss. She was straining to act as if she had forgotten everything that had occurred between us just a moment ago.

But I was polite to him. Then resumed my drinking, ordering another bourbon and soda—

the moment had flat gone, pift! disappeared.

It was as if I had no past.

The bartender suddenly seemed pleased with his candles. He showed me the brand name on the box behind the bar and I asked him to spike my bourbon and soda a little more.

Either I would stay and have to confront Richard and Sara when they retired to the bar (their work at wrangling all the souls under their presumed authority soon concluding) or get up and leave.

If I stood to leave I would have the opportunity to say goodbye to Hippolyte. I decided it was the proper thing to do. I left the last of my money on the bar and shook her boyfriend's hand.

I wanted to savor the feeling that was burning in me. I don't even think I ate anything that night. I just walked into my shitty little room over the Gowanus Canal, unable to sleep until the very early morning.

—

A FEW NIGHTS LATER, I walked past the old theater bar after my restaurant shift (this was, oh, about the time of the beginning of the graph paper performances) and had every intention of getting on the subway for home but ran up the stairs to the second floor to see Johnny just in the act of closing the bar. It was a hot night.

Some of his friends, sloe-eyed, dressed in throw-back, ersatz leisure suits or parts of leisure suits, were waiting for him to close the bar. I quickly sat and he poured the usual bourbon and soda, taking his time about it, waiting for me to say something. There began the usual flurry of identification and empty banter through which I learned the theater was losing more money than it would be able to handle. These are the kinds of things one learns if one hangs on until closing time.

Johnny was afraid they'd close the bar for good. He had been asked to take on extra duties. He was trying to shut things down for the night when I walked in at one thirty, early for a Thursday night because tomorrow a large load of liquor was coming in and he was now the only one in charge of stocking the bar, all the managerial duties having passed quite unexpectedly into his possession the previous week.

"Don't get me started on G.," he said. "He's a nice guy and all."

I felt like I just blew into the eye of a storm (who the hell was G.?) "Something will happen. Don't worry," I said. "Some windfall or some such purse flying open will disgorge a pile of cash on you guys."

"It'll be here knock on wood it'll survive," Johnny quickly added. "Yep. That's right."

I just sat there holding my drink and nodding. The more I nodded the more he told about the bar, its history, its problems, his day-to-day duties, the further, I realized, I was being taken. For good or bad I couldn't tell. I liked Johnny. Another Long Island kid. Actually not that young, probably mid to late thirties, long sideburns, some kind of fashion consciousness gone through a hand-me-down blender: antique plaid high-waters, buckled leather shoes, black socks, a dirty burgundy colored shirt buttoned all the way up, an old silk vest. I can't quite get a grip on who or what he thought he was trying to be. His shirt matched the dingy red walls of the second floor bar, once a secret speakeasy, so I relinquished my perplexity.

The theater, downstairs and up, ran on a separate life-support. Johnny filled me with another B&S and I noticed his friends were still waiting.

So I left and down on the street it was one of those summer nights hot and irritable but less so than during the day. I thought I'd walk and maybe try to air my head. Who was G.? I wondered. But I suspected it was simply the usual nightmare: a small business, no cash-flow and all the rest. G. wasn't Richard, at least I didn't think so, unless he or Sarah somehow used another last name. But they weren't the owners. I assumed, I guess I had assumed from the beginning, that someone else owned the entire building. So maybe G. was simply the owner of the bar.

Past the domino players at the Boricua Bodega and at the corner of the Bowery I couldn't help thinking maybe the last several weeks had been nothing but a dream, or simply a waste of time. Why was I so drawn to the theater? Was it some latent desire to lie abed with Hippolyte that kept me writing out performance directives on 5 X 7 notecards? Where did this latency come from, and could I contain it, move it around, dismiss it as irrelevent and simply none of my business?

Over the Bowery and into the neon my head rose and descended. In the cement at the parking lot on the corner of Fourth and the Bowery I spied an imprint in the sidewalk's cement, possibly left by a leaf or some other detritus—

a capped head with feathery wings jutting out from the ears.

The red neon glow amplified at Broadway, the *Tower Books* illumination descending in a red and yellow webbing over the intersection.

The open door of the pub across the street and all the crammed bodies yelling and the music and the clinking of glasses. Outside that establishment a few young men and women were smoking. One of the girls wore a pink tank-top with very tight leather pants and high heels. Another girl was hiding behind a blackened half-wall that stretched to the glass front of the next building.

A man approached me with torn and filthy clothes. I turned as he passed and saw he carried over his shoulder a black bag. His pants rode down no farther than his exposed calves and ankles stuck inside some gray sneakers.

Past the neon warbles of reflected glass inside the *Tower Records* store, a boy with his hair tied up in a bun was browsing through CD stacks. Behind him an escalator carried a couple of girls, NYU students I presumed, wearing loose-fitting black tank-tops, up to the second floor.

At the edge of Lafayette and Fourth Street the night sky hung over the white of the far corner building an ambient blue. A car honked wildly and some girls screamed and ran across the street, narrowly avoiding being struck by a silver and black-topped limousine. The manhole cover in the middle of the street said *Made in China* on its outer edge and in its center was a five-pointed star.

Tiled entrance to the Law Library of NYU. A boy with heavy backpack was holding a glass door open for others who joined him and lit cigarettes as I passed looking down at the red-bricked sidewalk that lay under my next few steps. Then the concrete began again.

Steam was pouring out the front of a dry cleaners down Mercer Street. A line outside the *Bottom Line* was busy talking and waiting. The foot traffic at the entrance to Washington Square blocked the passage of cars, their headlights then breaking free and nearer.

Kid with a ketchup bottle turning off MacDougal onto West Fourth with several others after him. This the witching hour? What girls with those faces giggling into their white hands as a bottle rocket explodes back in the park.

Gangs of people shuffling and gliding over the intersection. One loner, two, another, crossing in the middle of Sixth Avenue to get to the other side.

A fire hydrant. A trash barrel and a sticker with the logo in green and yellow: WGM. Squeaking door of the restaurant I turn to witness then out of the flat-seeming corner of my left eye two dark people sitting in the shadows of their building.

The name plate on the front of the door unreadable. Terra cotta blues and asphalt blacks. Little bulbs like styrofoam balls over the windowed canopy of a bar and the chalk-board outside one woman no a man walks by with four others before him now stopping at Seventh Avenue and Sheridan Square the lights pouring down from cars recently released by the green light.

A tree with cobbles erupting from its ancient root.

Clamorous conversation. Silverware poured into the bus-boy's bucket behind a fake wooden podium at the street café.

Pitched cement and buckled curb. Short summer cotton dress with small yellow flowers if you watch long enough the orange glare of the night street lamp will show her outline as she passes but others will know of course at the corner everyone's just flat out awake to this.

—?

A historical plaque. Side-streets. Eighth Avenue. Gas station. Yellow sign. Traffic. Horizon above and beyond. Billiards. Drunks shouting in the triangular park and pissing in the bushes.

Then the steady push up the Avenue to Twentieth Street.

—

I ENDED THIS HAPHAZARD walk in Chelsea, at the old Seminary, walking around it entirely, even stopping to talk to a prostitute on Tenth Avenue as I approached the Garden entrance.

We were given keys when I was a student. The Garden ran the length of the back of the school spanning Ninth and Tenth Avenues.

Talking briefly, inexplicably (all of a sudden) forward with the slightly aged street-walker, staring at her almost non-existent short cut-offs over leather-tailored legs that both hid and yet outlined her figure, it occurred to me that maybe I could pick the lock and get into the Garden. And where did this Street-walker come from? It was as if she just rose up from underground, and, to accentuate this, her head was topped with a blond wig, strands of darker, natural hair malconcealed beneath it.

It wasn't very difficult to break in through the Garden door, actually. In fact, if it hadn't been for my quickly made new friend I could probably have figured out how to pick the lock myself.

A few squad cars passed but we were talking, or pretending to, and I guess that made it OK, from their point of view—

but, I mean, anyone could tell she was a prostitute. Made-up blunt features. Cheap, before she even spoke. Made by that quick assent through the earth's crust from its core, quickly molded and fashioned into the image of hips and legs and little else.

I noticed we'd left the garden door open. I moved to close it but just as I got there some creepy-looking fellow with an orange hunting jacket put his hand on it to stop it from moving back into place. I say creepy-looking mainly because he was slightly bald with long, stringy side-of-the-head hair and an unshaven face; he also reminded me of Professor Mickelmann!

Professor Mickelmann used to teach at the Seminary. He was the reason I finally dropped out. But he was taller than the hunter.

I knew if there were going to be a scene I'd better not be the one to start it. The short, balding, semi-haired man quickly looked at me (all the eye contact compressed into one little over-grown eye) and then motioned to the prostitute. His camouflaged pants tucked into laced black boots to complete the portrait of a hunter.

I slid back in the bench to see the Seminary buildings that enclosed the entire block with its paths and tennis courts and small children's playground. There were a few lighted windows. Someone would be calling the cops any minute. The good Professor himself didn't live there, he was in New Jersey somewhere. I wondered what he'd gotten up to as I sat on the Garden bench among the few headstones of early believers, the early settlers, the teachers, the masters. The masters?

Did he really believe all that crap he spoke of in class?

You bet he did. Of course he did. They all did.

The books came flooding into my memory. What the hell was I thinking trying to study philosophy? Mickelmann had me, of course, along with the curriculum itself, flat up against a wall. So I dropped out. Why should I continue to fight with a man whose only idea of my existence was perceived through his own existence, his own narrow understanding of that existence?

I dropped out about the time I discovered, of all things, Descartes' *Book of Light*. I thought Professor Mickelmann and I had a good rapport at the time and I remember approaching him about that book in particular. There was something so appealing in the simple way Descartes took the whole world into one thought, and then another, and then another. Reading him it suddenly made sense that what I was searching for in the church existed nowhere but in thought itself. And, once again, that thought led directly to my earliest childhood memories.

My eyes, blurry from the alcohol, searched for the spot in the Garden where I approached him:

"No no," he said, laughing, "not that again!"

"What do you mean? Isn't this a viable road? *Monde; ou, Traite de la lumière?*"

He snorted. "Ah the French language Hans what a discovery you must be the very first to—"

I see now all that talk was, for him, issuing from his students. He thought he could keep me in line. He thought he'd be able to head the devil off at the pass, a pass that had grown not from anything but those errant forces chasing souls out of Europe, the historical, a memorable categorical imperative, a new imperative brooding over the new world, brooding over water dank and oily and turned to stagnation at the world's end—

The Gowanus Canal. My home.

—

HOW COULD, I ASKED, LUTHER be so correct and divinely justified as to deny that the Holy Roman Church had not been the direct authority of God on this earth—

and in *his* mortal time, no less?

A routine enough question, mind you, but because my Father conducted our classes with so much of his own free will and not enough attention to the details of the points Luther himself makes—

that is, my Father had neglected to supply us with the proper historical frame in order to show us that Luther received most of his message of Consubstantiation from St. Paul's writings, with which we might then envision Luther gazing upon divine inspiration.

To tell you the truth, all I remember from those classes was my Father's discussion of Luther's wedding ring and the scandal this had invoked in the Holy Roman Church and the Diet at Worms. (Not even my Father, Lutheran Minister of *St. Paul's* Church, seemed to get it.)

I believe to this day most of the other children from Sunday School class have the same attitude toward wedding rings that I do: they are unduly magical; they pertain more to the swashbuckling romance of a pirate Luther than to the holy bond it means to represent between man, woman and God himself. A God that would later spread throughout Europe and into the souls of my own forebears landing in the new world, between jungles of death and desolation and the iniquities of a fathomless authority—

all of it (God-stuff, Time-stuff) buried in the self.

My Father always left God out of the equation—

any equation. And so he would leave history out too. And it wasn't just me who sensed I had dealt a significant blow to the teachings of Luther and the Catechism to follow, for the other children came to continually relate their own little lives in light of this incident.

They came to me as if they were little lost lambs in search of a shepherd, I the Pastor's son, the one who had immersed himself in the Catechism, to their continual delight. And so I played the role they seemingly wanted me to play. A game of marbles, for instance, turned into a holy occasion in the fields back of school on a Saturday afternoon.

The initial occasion I remember noting, a book on the Catechism footnoted the Imperial Diet at Worms in 1521 A.D.—

summoned Luther before their weight to be tried for having left unanswered a previous mercy proffered toward his heretical stance. Luther's stance insisted that the Church beg forgiveness for its corruption, for its taking of bribes in exchange for granting God's grace and forgiveness. It was decided Luther should recant previous accusations levelled against the Church's Simonizing ways. All would then be forgiven.

I was marked by the greater spread and character of the Reformation itself, civil, as well as divine. This is absolutely understandable, even at a very young age, the implementation of Democratic values blown into one's impressionable young state through every form of communication has always been the chatter we Americans use as currency. This, of course, marked me deeply, so that the edges of our little education became, for instance, not so much a Sunday School exercise, but a continuation of the five-day week.

I immediately made it known, in the basement of the Church one early morning during class, that this spread in divine education was what I saw in the teachings of Luther's Catechism.

My Father looked at me, stunned that I had, no doubt, read the Catechism book. The children, of course, had no idea what was going on, and, after having seen the look on my Father's face, and having watched him pause within my grasping knowledge, they had only but to speak with me in the playground and mention "The Worms," and fits of laughter and spells of uncertain dictation issued from forehead to toe.

"It's a city in Germany," I remember calmly telling the few boys gathered about me, before the marble courts at the back of the public school the following Monday.

"Dja hear that! Ha! He says worms are da city of Germy!"

"You ever been to Germy Hans?"

"Of course not. But Luther was!"

"OK OK what *did* dese worms do to him. And how come you know so much 'bout it?"

"If you'd read your homework you'd know. You wouldn't be surprised by cities called Worms or by Transubstantiation within the two-fold semblance of Faith—

Luther's faith—

the faith of the Lutherans."

"Listen to him! Boy! What a 'cyclopedia!"

"Nonsense like a 'cyclopedia too!"

"You not very smart ha are ya Knudsen?"

And they all laughed and rolled in front of me at the marble courts, before getting in a few games at recess.

Of course my lessons to them in the ways of Luther's faith only strengthened my resolve to seek out new venue, as it were, to expand my scope and influence within the neighborhood. If I were a complete idiot to them, then that was the message I would convey, in excelsis.

"Hey!" a voice would say at a corner or in a nearby field, "Hey dat's dat Luter guy!" And I'd trot up to their playful meeting and introduce myself as Luther.

Other times I'd steal right into their action, steal their ball or something, and run away until they tackled me.

"For a Pastor's kid you sure don't play fair!"

"Who says the spirit's fair?" And they'd fall silent. You say things like that at the right time and you've got them within your grasp.

I had their complete attention the moment I mentioned anything from my readings. Those pauses turned into spells, which turned into the filip I'd need to burn through some more of the Catechism, or the biography on Luther my Father had in his office.

"Who says the spirit's fair? I'll tell you. The time it takes to figure your faith as having fallen from the sky the actual sky above my friends."

Their little heads broke in movement to gaze at the blue sky, probably for the first time.

"You should notice the sky more often."

"Yeah we know dat Luter."

"Yeah hey! What you our Mudder?"

"No he's Luter look at him!"

"Luter luter pooter dooter."

"Mudder Fadder Mudder Fadder."

"Silly Luter pooter wit his stupid rooter tooter."

"Yeah hey he says things all da time like tooter pooter rooter!"

"Rooter for da pooter poo-poo. Ha ha ha ha!"

"Poo-poo pooter Looter rooter!"

"Mudder Fadder rooter pooter poo-poo!"

"How 'bout poo-poo pooter Looter....rooter!"

"Or rooter pooper hee hee!"

"How 'bout dis how 'bout dis: poo-poo poo-poo poo-poo."

"Now you have it!" I'd cheeringly filip their youthful madness, "that's the spirit I was talking about. That's it!"

"And dis Looter poo-poo pooter he trying tell us look da sky see God for Chrite's sake! How ridic...how ridiculusses dat! Damn! What a total tooter pooper We're just tooter-pooping and he thinks it deep or sumpin."

"Nothing to be sorry about at all," I would calmly say. "Cursing is as natural as defecating and totally a part of the spiritual package you shouldn't stop yourself from anything."

They would laugh at lines like that, as indeed they were just lines, belonging to nothing else in this big old beautiful blue world. But then I'd really lower the boom, just when they thought I was playing into their hands:

"Have you ever thought about sexual union as the salvation to your very soul?"

And I mean you could hear a pin drop. Sometimes they'd fall to the grass or a bench and have to catch their breaths.

"Hey give us back our ball OK?!"

"Yeah we know all 'bout dat now."

Even though they didn't. Anyone could tell. They hadn't been with a girl yet, whereas I had been with the Holy Spirit, the same spirit Luther saw at his table, a big oak table in the castle where he studied, in the city of Worms, Germany.

It was there he had taken his wife upstairs and closed the curtains on the crowds below, they having gathered for the matrimonial exchange of rings that presided over his growing office in heresy.

—

SUDDENLY THROUGH THE DOOR comes an assortment of shades, black, white, stilettoed, be-wigged and be-suited. Ugly. Torn, ugly jackets, jeans, tightly fitted outerwear, loosely fitted shirts, saliva and alcohol.

I stand and greet everyone, all of the streetwalkers, their pimps and/or followers. I say pimps but that's not true. They are customers, friendly customers. My lock-picking prostitute is now joined by her young Latina co-worker, wearing not shorts but flared jeans over high-heels and a loose-fitting shirt. She actually looks more like a college student than a prostitute. The girls sit around the bench and the boys (not men, they seem stuck in puberty's limbo) drink beer, standing, shuffling about.

My prostitute, whose name was Cynthia (she later told me it was Carlyle) introduces me to everyone, as if we've been together longer than the few minutes it took to open the Garden door.

"This is my friends," she giddily spews. "Rock. And Roll," she begins pointing to each of the two young, disheveled men.

"Teddy," says a tall boy with mangy sneakers and an impending build-up of saliva under every other consonant he is about to use.

"What you doing shaking his hand jeez," says his buddy in leather jacket and white t-shirt, hair just over the top of his eyes. "Where are we man the fucking I don't know the ... Grand Union?"

"Grand Union? The shupermarkets? I think you left your ballsh over ad the Afghani place hey you ever eat acrossh the shtreet what'sh your name?"

"Hans."

"You ever eat acrossh the shtreet the Afghani plashe abshowlutely the besht food I mean."

"It's goddamned hell food!" growled the hunter, his arms suddenly waving from inside his orange jacket.

"So you have a name," says my whore. "Mine's Cynthia you can call me Cindy and that's Dalia I was telling you about she's."

"What about *me*?" asks the short, tonsured hunter. "What am *I*. I'm her date for hellfire's sake! And to endure all that hell food I mean when's the."

"That's right," says Cynthia in an aside, rolling her eyes, "he's my date well if your my date how come ya keep hitting on Dalia? That's Dalia see what I meant what's your name again honey?"

"You got any more bourbon," I ask, concluding, as she palms me the bottle: "Hans."

"What a strange hey! stop groping me."

The bald guy is hoarsely laughing and wiggling his stubby wanton fingers under my whore's ass. Rock-and-roll slurring Teddy and the leather-jacketed friend talk on a blue streak as if they are ready to fight. They physically remove themselves from our troop and continue arguing among the headstones behind us.

"You've got to be kidding me."

"Shut the fuck you shink you know everyshting caush you got the keysh to the van? Well fuck you Brian. I'm gonna tell 'em all about your dark pasht you shtupid shnook."

"Shnook?"

"Yeah Shtupid shnook you never heard a suches thingsh?"

"Shsh sh sh. It's S-tupid stupid not sh-tupid," says Brian,

Teddy's friend, he of the get-away van keys. "And I don't hear what your saying if that's what you mean ya brain-dead dork."

"You shay you hate the way I talk but you shay you can't hear what the fuck doesh."

"What the fuck you think you got something important to say shut up and drink your beer ya fairy." Brian hops up on the top edge of a headstone, his perfect, black bangs sway over his eyes as he struggles to balance himself on one leg. "Grand Union! You never heard of the taj mahal or nothing anyway I bet you never even heard of the Grand Union until they opened a supermarket. You're silly and stupid not to know what I'm talking about anyway man."

"I shposed it to be a sherious thing to shay huh? Why wouldn'tsh I undershtand what you shaid in the middle of shomethin' not of what it was sh'posed to mean anyway huh?"

"You are correct oh s-tupid one."

"I'm not the Grand Union what I got a be hear wishin thinkinsh and prayinsh you're tryin a hurtsh me with wordsh."

"Not word-sh. Word-s. S.S.S.S.S."

"Hey Shindy watch thish." And Teddy swings his foot up and kicks his leather-jacketed friend from off the thick old tombstone just as if he had been a balancing stick between earth and sky.

—

——B ack to cement and the scrapheap of civilization, the ruined, ever lugubrious, dark and sinister nothingness of the Gowanus Canal—
 just out the window here, over the bridge.

But there would be no reason to go back to that theater on Fourth Street; no reason to return to the scene of our meeting to try and challenge the deities, whatever new deities there might be, those owners of space and time within the frame of an old tenement building on the lower east side of Manhattan—
 all the souls that died and sweated and suffered there too—
 all for nothing, all for naught—
 theatricality's grim leer and hollow laugh—

Enough, enough of my cause, and *the* cause, and all the other causes of the system—

There are no good causes, no good effects, nothing but the mechanical urge to fuck, to procreate, to carry on. This has been made plain to the regions of sex and the zones of my own and others' initiations in this God-forsaken place—
 in the place of all places. Isn't it obvious?

As if the world is then *renewed* through its theatrics—
 its denials?

It must be there is some other lust at work within the bowels of all placement—
 call it a lie, a trick or flash in the hollow pan of the stove-top that keeps our attention—
 when what we need is the absolute end of *that* attention—
 And, hell, yes, an end to all commitment that causes us.

GOWANUS CANAL

—

RICHARD AND SARA soon dismissed my own play in favor of the graph paper performance. Obviously, I had given them the go-ahead because of my interest in the graph paper on Richard's desk. Plus the fact that it would have taken time to adapt or extract any ideas that were contained in my play. In other words, I was very willing to start anew. A week or two after my meeting with Richard on the fourth floor a group was assembled, meeting every afternoon on the third floor of the theater.

At the bottom of a piece of graph paper that Richard handed out to us were the following instructions—

"These are the objects in the room. Discern movement and meaning for a performance that will last about 45 minutes."

The list of objects we were allowed to include were—

Duct tape, Table with Several Chairs, Dictionary, Rope, Umbrella, Sticks, Bottles, Hammer, Bricks, Ladder, Bucket Filled with Water, Bicycle Pump, Newspaper.

My idea (which I provided prior to our group meeting having been privy to the graph paper and Richard and Sara's nebulous idea for a performance group) was to shuffle hundreds of 5 X 7 notecards containing instructions and messages and set them in the middle of the performance area.

Each of us would pick a card and follow its commands. In the case of odd, nonsensical cards, like this one:

> Some have discerned that soup is the rudest form of toxicity known to man.

we were given free rein to use whatever, however we saw most fit.

The purpose was to keep one's activity-level at its maximum. And this meant the "actresses" and "actors" were to have complete reliance on *other* methods of performing. They would have to feed on the proximity of other action happening, in general, or from the other performer, say, right next to them.

Hippolyte had been asked to join the group (I guess because she was the star from the scene-acting group) and I often tried to find her in order to react to her actions for my own.

We had several rehearsals using the cards. But not after some disagreements.

"The point is," said Rudy, "isn't the fact we're here in this room like you say at a minimum of acting at a minimal level of adherence to a script or whatever you called it."

"No script whatsoever," Richard corrected, neither smiling nor frowning.

"Let me finish. Please. So what you're saying is even if I memorize something and come in with that and just do it let's say just for instance my monologue 'I strangled the sweet young thing with my own two hands' that's not that won't work? Do I have it right? Is that what you're saying?"

"Nothing against you," began Richard.

"It has nothing to do with a script that anyone wrote," interrupted Sara, who was growing tired of the whole meeting and especially of Rudy. She shifted in her chair at a make-shift table we were gathered around in the third floor performance area. Every performance we did was conducted in this room, long and narrow with a small side room, as on the fourth floor, only this room was relatively empty.

"Yes nothing against you," Richard began again.

"Maybe," interrupted Samantha, adjusting her glasses "we could incorporate each of our prepared pieces as separate things that we have prepared already that we've memorized then incorporate into the whatever this is going to become see it already sounds like it's something specific you know like—"

"Oh no we have to come up with some ideas but I tell you right now," said Richard, sounding out a kind of authority "we've got the basic outline of like what we should be doing."

"The *cards*," said Rudy, strongly, folding his arms over his white shirt. The blond hair on his arms matched his head.

"The *cards* are really what we have at this point," asserted Sara, looking around the table, daring anyone to further objection.

"If you don't mind my saying," Hippolyte began to speak, "I think we should like stick with the cards and like do exactly what they say."

"But of course we'll have to like work on them and rewrite the elements to be used," added Richard.

"I think," said Sara, "what you're proposing," and she paused and looked at me, "is not quite something that we could do yet."

"Oh," said Hippolyte, beginning to blush.

"Not yet but why not as a way to—"

I began, wishing to get on with the meeting, its purpose. I held out an open pad of paper to that end, as if the weight of a scribble pad would call my thoughts about the cards into focus for everyone.

"You see I think that's not *right*," Rudy inserted, dropping his arms and scooting his chair further from the table, quickly putting one of his booted feet up on the edge of it.

"What's not right?" snapped Sara.

"That this is already like decided I thought we were going to have an input in this."

"You do have a chance for input," corrected Richard.

"You mean within the context of these cards," offered Joan, suddenly making her presence known.

"Now are these," said Samantha, slowly, "*cards* like something that we can use in our individual pieces because mine is ready to go and is like really really really adaptable you know like *really* adapta—

ready to adapt—

can be adaptable—

to adapt like—

they're ready to go I mean."

"This group," reiterated Richard, "is to exist for the sole purpose of *performing* not acting."

"But," said Samantha, hurriedly, sure of herself, pushing her glasses farther up against her white high forehead, "my piece is a dance piece and it's like got nothing to do with acting like I said it is really adaptable and I could right now even."

"That's a good idea, Sam," said Sara, a bit maudlin in her tone, much as she was when directing other actors, "why don't you show us how *you* would use the cards." And she looked at Hippolyte who seemed to understand what she meant. I began to wonder if anyone else could see the signals being exchanged between those two. Strange pauses and glances and little winks.

Samantha stood before us in the third floor performance space. She entered from the side room and asked us to use our imagination. She said she had envisage—
envis—
thought the piece should be performed on a larger stage. Sara asked her if the room was a problem. She said no not necessarily just—
well like—
use your imagination—
and this lamp like—
this lamp that I have over here like—
would in an actual stage space be somewhere else but that doesn't matter and these well these things would ...
I just wanted to see the piece. I didn't understand how the size or shape of any theater could change the essence of a performance, a dance, a joke, anything.

She entered barefoot, and walked very slowly to three plaster-of-paris face-masks she had placed in the middle of the room. She twirled and bent and gyrated and bent some more.

She put a mask on. She took a mask off. She fought with them. She put them on the floor. She picked up another mask. It looked like the previous. Her movement became fluid, hips making salacious suggestions of space.

She held up a small portable work-lamp (plugged in somewhere off-stage) to her crotch. She twirled and contorted, spinning on the floor, getting her leotard full of dust.

She put a mask down.

She mimed a weeping countenance. She picked up another mask. She fought with it.

She contorted her body and spun and skipped. She lifted the portable lamp from the floor and shined it on her face finally.

She took the mask of light off her face.

She sat back down on an as-yet-unused chair.

"See now I thought that was great!" cried Rudy, slamming his boots to the floor. "If she can do that piece then there's no reason why I couldn't do *my* piece—

I strangled her with hands—"

his voice rose and his brows flew up over his scalp, *I strangled her with hands—*

hands—

hands!"

"That was good but—" said critical Richard to Sam.

"But there were no cards—"

continued Sara, folding one of her awkwardly long legs over the other, to make her point.

"Well I thought you just wanted to see my piece and we could talk about it some more I think those masks *could* like be replaced by cards and I could like dance around them."

We all remained silent waiting for her to explain the possible use of cards *or* masks in her dance piece.

"Like this dancing contorting—

what did you think of those moves I could pick them up and recite them like and then I get it someone else like could carry—

out—

their instructions—

like—

I would be giving them instructions through my dance!"

"But the *cards* already have instructions *on* them," offered Richard, showing no emotion whatsoever, just biding his time, waiting for the end, it seemed, the predictable end of all this nonsense. Why is patience a virtue? It's terribly annoying to witness.

"They will do the same thing with or without your dance," said Sara, simply and to the point.

"Would the entire performance be like a dance without having itself be pronounced so obviously as a dance?" the young Hippolyte smartly added, waiting for our response, which was not forthcoming, because she was so correct.

"Is my dancing that noticeable?" asked Sam, quite stupidly.

"What do you mean," returned Sara, just as stupidly.

"I mean isn't the point to use what we—"

Sam began, interrupted by Rudy—

"I think if I recite my monologue and then the cards come into the monologue we could combine the two and have Sam dancing and each of us could be doing our own thing at the same time and like you say to tie it all in we could pause and then have a card read that'll do it I mean come on already!"

"But then why have any cards if they will not be the center of all action?" I asked, perfectly willing to have the card idea remain within my own ken.

"He's right," sighed Sara, undoing her legs, "nobody says you can't act your monologue or that you can't dance your dance but the fact of the cards and this graph thing necessitates that all action ... what's the right word?"

"Emanates," the young Hippolyte said.

I began to get a hard-on. From that moment on, whenever Hippolyte spoke my member began to "listen." Something about the frequency of her voice *and* her intelligence.

Sara seemed to sense this, but continued—

"Not *emanates* no that's not it nice try," she paused and looked into Hippolyte's brown eyes. Hippolyte blushed, then glanced at me which only made my member thicken. I was worried I'd never be able to stand without being noticed and so began to hope the meeting, the argument, would be unduly prolonged.

"It *causes* us to act," said Sara, finally, proud of her words, her thought, her presence. Her shoulders flared a bit.

"Whatever we have here on the graph paper," continued Richard, "is meant to be the gathering of all the staged ideas we will do in the future. Does everyone understand that? Because *that's* the reason why this group exists to generate a meaning *and* an action something that exists within the actuality *and* the idea."

"So I'll be able to do my monologue?" asked Rudy. I looked to see if he was smiling, because it was obvious he was joking. He was deadly serious, however, and when he eventually performed his monologue for us, I tried to follow, but the events of the previous night kept pace with his performance:

> I like to come out here at night. It gives me a sense of peace. Not just ordinary peace but real peace. The moon the water by the docks. And yet I'm standing here waiting for someone. Who could it be? What is

it about the night makes me want to bite someone? I'm no vampire mind ya. I'm real flesh and blood. Here: touch! That's it. Go ahead. I stand here every night since it happened. What you might ask happened? Well let me tell you—THESE HANDS spell a danger to your mortal soul—but I just like to scare people. You see you're shaking you're scared you feel like running well you *can't* because I'm coming to get you. Blaaaagh!—These hands will terrorize your mind and your soul until they finally cut off all the breath in your precious life yes that's right! Precious to you but to me nothing it means nothing to me—oh I know what you're going to say you're going to tell me to take a good look inside take a good look at myself well I cannot! That's final and there's nothing more to say. Occasionally the hunter's hands appear, brushing his inebriated, balding, semi-hairy head. Then a reflection of dull amber from the high street light bounces out from under his retreating paw. The wiry kid pops open a beer and pulls another one from his pocket for his friend saying, "Sorry I don't have no extra we're dry now." "What the fucksh you mean we're shdry! Give thish guy a brew anyway he don't need any he'sh got Shindy's bottle a." "Bottle a butt!" cries the hunter. "Oh you are a terrible sort I'm talkin to Dalia do you mind?" huffs Cynthia, removing her slick legs and round ass out of the circle of drunken men. These hands are about to find you and do what has never been done before to you—are you amused? Do you find that titillating?—well I can't blame you you see I stand out by this street lamp you see I *lean* and I wait for someone to pass by here at the docks and then I strangle them. I don't know why I do it. In fact it's actually quite mad—It's insane!— But not to worry, not to worry. You can go now— Blaaagh! The wuzzing has moved through me and occupies a space between my legs that grows. I could contemplate it all night, follow it over to Cynthia's ass that plops on her bed in her small one room apartment and do as it commands. A very small room with a small bathroom but the funny thing is a sliding glass door that enters onto a courtyard that is bigger than this room. I know it is a precarious situation no matter what happens, and the fact that she makes her living this way, but she has been giving me signs that mean it may or may not happen. "You can call me by my real name now," she says, looking down at her fingers which worry themselves upon her belly. "You have a real name?" "Uh-huh. Carlyle. It's my given name." "Given? Name?" I ask, to myself, repeating words that make no sense. "My real name is Carlyle. Cynthia is just somethin' I made up." As if there's a difference. I soon have her top down under pretext of a back rub. But just as soon there is a rapping on the window of her courtyard's glass door. A bearded man, smiling. He looks like an escaped lunatic and I wonder if this is the end of me, I can't take another encounter with any more hunters. "That's my husband—wait let me," and she puts her top on, "—hold on a second," she says to me. The way she calmly tells me to wait while she leaves to talk to him in the courtyard makes me realize he isn't going to storm in here and kill me for undressing his wife or his carnal property. Hands are going to NOT let you go. You are trapped and I bet you came down her for a nice stroll a nighttime stroll by the docks. Well *forget* it because I'm the strangler of the docks and I'm going to kill you with these hands with HANDS!—You look like you're out of wind. Here, have a seat, sit on the ground. That's it. I could make you do anything—Blaaaagh! But these hands are going to *kill* you! Yes they are going to kill you just like they killed her—oh...I...killed her—no it was these hands—they aren't even ... mine you see ... they have a mind ... all their own—but I wouldn't let that worry you. From the small light of her bedroom I can see them. Then a boy comes out of the farther darkness and she kneels and hugs him. They leave by some mysterious exit out back, literally consumed by the darkness of that outdoor space. Obviously they have met this way before because they expertly whisper as I try to listen for any explanation as to the nature of their relationship. "Who was that," I quickly ask as she returns. Her face, which looked petite, immature for her age, wrinkles itself into thought, as if any thought about this man would crumple her head's inadequate bone structure. She escapes to the bathroom and closes the door. I open drawers in dressers trying to find something else that will tell me who this woman is. Something that will explain, I guess, what the hell I'm doing with her? It is as if I have entered some vector of uselessness in my amble over to the old Seminary, a vector that swallows me and storms about my ears a salacious sea-animal drowning and seducing me with nothing but noise and confusion. **You are nothing do you know that? I will teach you to behave and to learn to submit to these hands. We will live yes a long time together and you will submit and I will torture you and one day if you are lucky I will kill you with these hands. And like I say you will come to learn to love** these hands just as I have come to love them ... have been ... forced to love them—I....killed—and we will perhaps have children and live a long time together and watch them grow and teach them hands that have made us both yes do you hear me made us both prisoners. By the way your hair is lovely and hands let me see yes you have the hands of someone who is so unlike me and so unlike my hands—You *will* submit to these hands they will rip into your throat and scandalize the mind and in those last moments .... you will discover what I have lived with for so many years now .... that I had to kill her! You must understand I stand here every night and determine who will be my next victim. I see them from a distance just like I saw you and when they approach just like you approached I scare them for the fun of it. Do you believe me? Well you'll never know will you. Unless I let you live forever then you will be sure. As Carlyle removed her makeup in the bathroom I silently invaded her panty drawers, her sweater drawers, her little drawers in the end-table next to the bed. I was looking in the closet and saw some photo albums up top when I heard the bathroom door crack, creak, and open. Evidently, as she was dressed in her nightgown and ready for bed she was paying no attention to me whatsoever. Did she want to sleep with me? Without paying? Had I stumbled along the streets looking for a bed? "Who was that man?" I asked, as she got under the covers without me. She looked, finally, quite civilized with her blond wig gone, and her naturally beautiful, closely cropped auburn hair slightly wet and natty against the pillow. She was not portraying anyone but herself, a troubled mental patient, finally weary of her whole incarceration and giving into the most mundane and sanest, mortal, retired pose of thankful sleep. "Oh that—that was my husband—and my son," she said. Then she began to bite her bottom lip. I sat on the edge of the bed next to her and held her hand. "I'll tell you something else but you have to promise to keep it a secret." "I promise. What am I going to do—you don't even know who I am!" But I cannot abide by someone as unknowing and un-caring such as yourself. SOME- ONE WITH HANDS LIKE THOSE! You must discover that hands are the hands of a killer and learn to love them otherwise there can be no communion between our souls, nothing to flow back and forth like these waters you were no doubt seeking down by the docks. Sufficient love sufficient water. And yet these hands with these hands I killed her do you understand! I am mad with wanting! I am mad with desire! I am mad yes I admit it—yes I am mad!—Yet if you do not submit to my plan of life-long companionship you will be murdered on this very spot. Why are you weeping. Stand up. Submit to these hands they will not harm you or let you feel pain. They are the hands of a murderer a merciful murderer they define the living and I should know! I've had to live with them all these years! Now you will not feel a thing. Come! To the other side! Be joyful— Aren't ya glad you went for a walk tonight? By the way you shouted someone's name just now who was that? A lover? Husband? You remain silent. Good ploy and I can understand that. Now this presents somewhat of a dilemma you see because having stopped you and having told you that I am a murderer—*with* .... *these* .... *hands*—I must tell you that I am indeed going to have to kill you. And it is not totally my own decision mind you but one that hands have had a large part in deciding for me—Blaaagh! This is for real now! Hands are going to kill you they are going to strangle you ... unless of course you can provide me with the name of your lover this paramour no doubt you have tried to rendezvous with here in this part of town—and you would not be the first—but I've told you enough already. Who is he? What is the name of the person that you were coming here to meet! Tell me tell me now! Open up that mouth! You may be an innocent victim but I am the owner of hands of murder and I will not be able to stop them once they have been set on such a silent victim as yourself. You must speak! That is when you will learn the secrets of the world! That is when you can solve this little puzzle ... I must have the name! Please! I am begging you on the capitulation of your very existence my dear! Speak! Give up the lost key to your world and I might be able to retire the murderous offenders from off your throat! I was trying to focus my brain on the physical act of standing, finding the door, and ambling somehow home. Before my energy could be summoned to perform, however, she proceeded to tell me how her husband had placed a small amount of mercury inside her son's penis. The words sped past me. I looked into the courtyard, wondering what time it was. I could only return my eyes back toward Carlyle. "He did it. He really did that." "Did what again?" "My husband," she said, very deliberately, "put a small piece of mercury. You know what mercury is?" "Uh. Yeah." "Mercury. You know what it is?" "In the thermometer?" What the hell was a thermometer doing in her son's penis? Was it still there? "You're not making any sense. It's time for me to." "What's used in the thermometer dummy. You're not listening to me. Mercury. It's an element you know. On that elemental chart." "The periodic table?" "That's it honey now you understand. Don't go. I'm not lying you know. Stay a while." Still silent? Why all this silence? Why do you tempt fate so? Must he really be worth all this? Your death to be the jumping off point for all others to follow? Is that it? Are you willing to suspend all other realities for this one reality? Does it give you pleasure? Because believe me it gives me no pleasure to release hands from my will. I have tried to save you. You see you feel their grip tightening now? This is beyond me. It has absolutely nothing to do with me. It is a terror of my own soul that is causing this something I neither enjoy—well actually I have enjoyed some of it—to be able to meet someone such as yourself for instance. Two strangers in the middle of a dark city night—But enough! These hands are now at your beautiful silent throat. I cannot hold them any longer!—and yet the significance of such an event haunts even the will of the hands for there is something moving inside of me something I feel will be the end of hands and the beginning of me! Her husband, apparently, had exercised some sort of spell over her; but especially over her son. She had been reduced to hooking to make ends meet. Or her husband had made it absolute that she would hook and never return to their home. He had kicked her out of their apartment uptown and she was now on her own. And she went on and on, speaking slowly at first, but, seeing my expression unchanged throughout, she speeded into the meat of her predicament. Holding her hand and listening to her unbelievable tale, but still slightly buzzed from the booze and what with everything else that happened that night it seemed to fit—mercury? I made like I was tucking her into bed, an infant, and patted her on the shoulders when the blankets were up to her chin. "Don't go." I listened to her shift in bed and pull the covers back down. "Don't go," she said again. And yet there is nothing in the world I enjoy so much as to surprise the nightwalkers! I will not ask you for any more names I will let you die in peace like I said these are merciful hands once I let them go. Only let them go now!—But what IS this! You will not die!—I must have been out of my mind to think you were anyone but her. I knew it was all just an abberation of my spirit. I .... pray ... you will ... forgive me ... for what ... I've ... allowed these hands ... to commit—But don't you see it was necessary? It was absolutely necessary for me to become the person you see before you! And yet what's that you say the transformation is not complete? But I have changed. I tell you ... what's that? You say I need to undergo a further ... a what's that you say? A further torture?—Oh hands! ... hands! Oh hands ... these—

Rudy fell to his knees. We didn't know what else to do but applaud. Needless to say, whenever Rudy brought up the subject of his monologue, or started repeating those lines about killer hands I would lose total consciousness and wish I were in the bar, socking down big doses of tranquility, hoping I'd be able to come up with *other* ideas to save the group and prolong propinquitous Hippolyte.

———

To the left, Union Street begins its steady climb up toward Prospect Park, and as it does, trees begin to appear and crowd the lovely buildings and their front walk-ups.

To the Right, it climbs also, eventually, toward Carroll Gardens.

But in front of this tattered, old, two-story, one-time warehouse there are no trees.

The sun seems daily to curse its sharp rays down upon the trite bridge over black and oily water, the only relief a thankfully cooling and anonymous night.

The night sits on our shoulders just as history, and we lap it up.

———

BUT HIPPOLYTE WAS either under the protection of Sara or waiting for her boyfriend at the bar. Or rehearsing with the other girls.

Once, however, I did manage, after one of the initial graph paper meetings, to bump into her on the landing just outside the second-floor bar while she ascended to the third.

I didn't ask her where she was going. There was a connection between us that had the strength, I felt, to ignore the immediate interpretations we use in the course of the everyday. We walked side by side up the sagging, creaking staircase lined with cobwebs and in need of a thorough paint job not to mention a complete re-structuring and re-building from top to bottom. Someone should have attended to those stairs long ago.

I was too busy gazing into Hippolyte's eyes, however, at the time, to want to have anything to do with the structural integrity of *any* building.

I remember she spoke to me about the simplest things. They weren't really *things* but little gestures and pieces of thought she'd let hover in her mouth, or in her body's position until my eye would light up from her physicality and my head then begin composing another unknown thought in the exuberance of our encounter.

And a truly stunning physicality it was! I felt myself dizzy in the head and higher and higher the more steps we took together. But I didn't care how ridiculous I sounded. And she knew this and appreciated it, I think. I don't think her boyfriend knew how to get as lightheaded as I. She giggled, paying me the highest compliment possible.

My eyes were positively oozing off my face by the time we got to the third floor landing. She paused and made her pausing into a presence, a real presence I could feel moving toward me.

I had only one thing to do and that was reach out into ever-present space and touch her.

Which I did. I felt her elbow, delicate and knobby just

the same. She was smiling and beaming. I had surely made a deep and lasting impression.

I didn't care how much younger, she was meant to be with me, there was no doubt about it. And I felt she knew this.

There were so many signs!

She took her time with *me*!

We walked up the steps and then she turned to *me*!

All of her simply turned and beamed toward *me alone*!

It was obvious what was happening and I had never been so sure about anything in my life.

I remember I walked back down those rickety steps, having left her on the third floor to rehearse, and out, straight down into the street. I felt like I had been cleaned up from head to toe.

Work in the kitchen that evening was actually a pleasure!

I began to think about saving money. Everything was possible for me, it seemed.

At work that evening the cards were coming together also, fast and furious. They would seem to appear in my head at the awkwardest moments—

as I was handing over a plate about to ring the waitress-bell, for instance—

wham! the words, the idea, the simplicity of something would call to me and demand to be written.

> Look. Look and listen as if listening inside the look.

> Pick up the newspaper and mimic folding into paper airplane but do not, in actuality.

Then try to fly it out over the room.

Tear off a piece of duct tape and show it to the most beautiful girl in the room and attach it to her forward gingerly. Adjust her head with your hands so that she can see into you.

Measure a window with an imaginary tape measure. Step back and collect all the objects in the room, forcefully if need be, and pile them in front of that same window.

Place the bucket on your head, or try to, without spilling its contents.

Move your arms out of your sleeves and into the waist of your shirt then roll your eyes back into your head and throw your head back while sighing and walking like an unstable drunkard.

"The walls do not fall."

Emit sound and wave your fingers in front of that sound. Take your fingers to a light source and begin making finger puppet shadows. Repeat several times.

Pick up a stick with your entire body. If you cannot figure out what this means ask the nearest person what thought this immediately conjures for them, quick, just blurt it out tell them.

Place bicycle pump at the base of the ladder and pump pump pump while adjusting your gaze from step one to step two and higher and higher with each pump.

There was one problem, however. I had to make the cards seem as if they had nothing to do with Hippolyte. I had to write them within a symbolic code that only I could understand, and, of course, could make *her*, also, understand.

And so I began to look over my cards at the end of the day and add them up in the thought of Hippolyte. For instance, cards that had to do with the end of a hammer (which was one of the objects in the graph) I had described as I would her delicate elbow.

I tried to look at the world through her young eyes. What would she be seeing that only I, someone a full ten years older, would know she knew. Of course, in this regard most of the ideas centered around unique and intimate situations in which the only variable would not be some great idea but would (I hoped) associate in *her* mind as something *very big*.

In this way I was free to use my imagination not solely in the service of itself (whatever that was) but in *reality*. Or this *other* reality that was emerging from the spatial directives of the graph paper performances.

For instance, if I were to command the card-performer to mimic some action, I would pretend to be Hippolyte trying to do the action requisite.

Take this one—

> Go to the chair and sit very patiently, knees together, don't slouch. Look furtively to the left. Then the right. Stand up. Go to an imaginary boulder in front of you and try to grab it. You cannot, and so, resigned (but not yet completely sorrowed) you return to sit, patiently, in the chair.

Eventually I thought all the cards in the deck (or several decks that we would have to perform for the graph paper performance) would in some way travel toward something Hippolyte knew. But these short excursions would not be very literal. They would be subtle.

They would have to do with the union of my own imagination, in other words, together with her existence as it appeared to that imagination. It would be a world where Hippolyte was everywhere present and yet nowhere very apparent.

And yet the next day before work I found myself having to wait to see her again. I had arrived at the theater to wait for the bar to open, hoping that Richard and Sara would invite me to watch another rehearsal. I would only have a few minutes in which to sit at the bar and pretend to talk to Johnny then get to the restaurant and begin my drudge on the line, serving the same meat and fried potatoes and ersatz gourmet cooking.

But if I could spend more time with Hippolyte I knew I'd be able to put myself over on her and gain her trust, and, thus the trust of the cards. That is, *all* the cards.

When I heard footsteps coming up the rickety staircase I turned to Johnny and began cracking jokes. I don't remember what I said, something muffled, but I quickly followed it with laughter, and so, naturally, he began to laugh. And of course he kept the drinks fresh.

Hippolyte moved through the doorway and walked over to me. I felt my skin flush. I realized, as she sat next to me, that I hadn't really awakened yet and so I took another sip of bourbon and soda.

I tried not to jump into conversation and was glad that she had indeed sat next to me. Our eyes met once again, and there it was, that light and life that was beginning to rule my very existence.

I began to speak. She seemed to look past what I was saying and concentrate upon my eyes, my posture, everything else about me except what I was trying, slowly, sleepily, to project for her.

Of course, this is exactly what I was hoping for.

We began to get comfortable again as if we had known each other for a long time. I was on the verge of actually asking her if she'd like to join me for dinner the following weekend when Sara made her appearance in the doorway.

Suddenly I felt guilty. Hippolyte saw me in the throes of some sort of sublimation. I was gazing at the mirror over the back of the bar trying to avoid Sara's own burning gaze. Sara came right up to the bar and though there wasn't a lot of space between Hippolyte and myself she seemed to get her entire body to block out Hippolyte's presence from my own, as if she knew her body alone opened a path to our short, ill-fated coupling.

She ordered a cranberry juice and tried to speak to me but I couldn't hear her. I was convulsing in a sort of shame I couldn't control. Sara made me feel like I was trespassing on her property, and I knew if she caught wind of that she'd try to capitalize on it.

In fact, as they both left for the third floor to rehearse their theater piece, I had the strange desire to eavesdrop on them. And so I crept up to the third floor landing, and got as close to the shut door as I could to hear Sara's voice.

"*Tighten. Lengthen* this you know," she was saying in her usual "critical" and cryptic manner. Hippolyte was adding a "yes" every now and then, and, apparently, as usual, following her director's lead.

"When you get him in this position when you know you should—

leave for lack of a better explanation," instructed Sara's voice.

"You mean just take whatever I have and run with it?" asked Hippolyte, suddenly enthusiastic.

"Just run away. You know completely take what I've said and run back there behind the."

"Behind the wall?" Hippolyte lightly ran across the dusty floor toward the side room. Her voice was muffled by the extra wall as she called out, "You mean like this?"

"Just wait a minute. Or two—

yes that's it just wait before you re-enter," answered Sara. Suddenly her voice was closer to me behind the closed door as if she were just on the other side. I crept over the landing and tried to open a second door that entered into that side room.

"Can you try the other direction now the spaced out

kind of—
lengthen your beginning now—
now," Sara went on.

I turned the knob, slowly, and pulled back on the door. It wouldn't give.

"Did you hear what I meant? Hipp? Can you move in the other direction toward a more spaced out."

Suddenly Sara's voice was in the side room also. I hadn't noticed but she had made her way toward where I suspected Hippolyte was.

They both began to whisper. I knew they were aware of my presence, somehow. I froze, now waiting for an opportunity to escape. But when I tried to crawl back to the staircase the landing groaned. Their voices hushed and I could hear them making their way toward the main door of the performance area.

Quickly, I pulled out my notebook from my satchel and sat on the floor, pretending to read. If they opened the door and saw me I would be completely absorbed in my reading.

But the door didn't open. Instead, Sara began her directions.

"You'll be able to come out from there and—
Hipp—
to the pause again—
lengthen your arrival within this first area once again I'm sorry I promise this will be the last time. OK?"

"OK," said Hippolyte from the side room.

Silence. Then footsteps over the dusty floor. Then Hippolyte speaks. Then Sara interrupts.

As she was attempting to make Hippolyte re-enter the performance area, I crawled to the staircase and slowly made my way down, past the bar and into the street. Late for work.

—

Professor Mickelmann sped past on his usual rounds in the dormitory hall.

"You're a little too anxious a little too. I'd like to know what your complaints about the curriculum are Hans."

He only had time to begin his speech and it was already urgent for him to be moving through the hall into the classrooms within the building's annex to prepare his instructions for the day. His stringy, greasy hair and black black chinbeard seemed more unwashed, more uncombed than usual.

I had stopped him to ask what he thought of my paper on Descartes. Maybe it was premature but the fact of the matter was I had no time to waste. I wanted to know what he had to say.

We sat together, some time earlier, drinking coffee in the student lounge, talking about modern philosophy, his course at the Seminary that I was only recently enrolled in. I knew there were problems with my paper but I was sure he was going to come around to my point of view and see that I was indeed on to something.

I found myself wandering the halls early one evening, lost, having just left the library on my way to the cafeteria. I was sure the tile pattern in the hall was leading me to another part of the Seminary and *not* the annex. Just as I discovered I was walking in the wrong direction—

the plaques embedded in the eye-level tiles suddenly giving way to cookie-cutter shapes and colors.

Mickelmann was returning from his classroom in the annex.

"Professor," I said, shyly. I still felt I did not know him, his school, this way of learning, this path toward what church I knew even less of. "This way to the Cafeteria?"

"This way," he said, slowing his pace without stopping completely so that—

"I'm headed there myself. I need a break maybe a donut or something why don't you join me. And call me Buddy."

A quizzical look as I started in on his pace, to match it, his long strides from the purpose of middle age beckoning my own youthfully ponderous step to actually work harder at gaining ground.

"I mean that's my name: Buddy. Or Bud. But people have always called me Buddy."

"Oh how about Professor Buddy," I said, laughing.

"Professor Buddy then it's all the same isn't it?" And he smiled, his short cropped beard bristling to make way for his chin, I noticed, a fleshy nob not, seemingly, entirely attached to his jaw.

Professor James "Buddy" Mickelmann stood well over six feet tall, his legs always an athletic anchor to an otherwise wispy frame; in fact, his arms seemed to hide inside his jacket sleeves as he cradled in one the study guide to his course on modern philosophy. He suddenly halted and had to lean over to open the door to the cafeteria. The door had been painted the same color as the trim of decorative tile in this part of the school. I had walked right past it.

Inside there were very few students. A group of people clacked plates and entered and exited through a pair of swinging doors to the kitchen, keeping the otherwise empty room in the throes of some kind of communal activity.

"Yes this is the best time," said the Professor, "just between meals and afternoon classes."

A woman was wiping down a newly cleaned table, and when we had gotten our coffee from the urn and sat at one of the dozen or so tables, having said hello to her—

Katya hi how are you—

Oh fine Buddy just to time—

Of course of course the best coffee now you've been keeping it at just the right temperature for us ha? Katya this is—

Hans—

Right Hans—

Nice to met you what no take cake!—

Oh Hans that's right you have to take some cake—

Buddy says best in neighborhood right there you go now try that—

Bake it right here on the premises they do—

Where else! Enjoy—

Thanks—

Thank you Katya we'll take this table—

It is with your name on it—

Ha that's right Katya—

See everone empty for you enjoy enjoy—

—

KATHERINE VON BORA. And after the curtains were drawn, Luther began to take Katherine's clothes off.

I had read it in the book my Father owned concerning the life of Luther. I spied him reading it some time after my own study of the Lutheran Catechism. I guess he had decided the spirit was indeed strong with his son. Yes, he had discovered I had the same power and conviction of faith Luther himself possessed, because, it was soon after my excellent showing at Catechism that the biography of Luther appeared. I've always been able to persuade people to look stuff up.

I don't think he really read that much of it. If he did he never talked to me about it. It would have been the easiest thing in the world, to talk to me about faith, and walking in the grace of faith, and all the other stations given to faith, by Luther. For some reason he saw in my attitude something, ultimately, to be appalled, to be shunned, to be immersed in silence.

"Yeah you're not gonna tell us anything we don't already know."

Invariably the little boys would gather round as I began to speak around the faith in conception, how the penis *will* penetrate the vagina.

I'd hold out my finger and penetrate my circled thumb and index finger.

"See," I'd say, "that's what happened when the faith of our Church entered into the mind of Luther."

"Yeah Bennie's got magazine's and he reads em to us."

"But," I would continue, "they have nothing to do with the *Spirit*. Let me tell you about *Spirit*!"

And I'd spring and run across the field or the schoolyard returning to them completely winded. "See!"

"He also reads nother book to us dat has *the* dirtiest sex

story *you* ever want a hear!"

It turns out some of the boys would gather at Bennie Spinotsen's house, and, in the privacy of his bedroom, listen to him read from a book entitled *The Education of Heidi, Family Tutor*.

Bennie's reading was the first of its kind for me, but I would later hunt out others. I actually became well educated in the art of smutty literature and married it to my expanding sense of Divine Grace. Things kept adding onto that grace, no matter where I went or who I'd hang around. That's why it's Divine, I intuited.

"Besides Luter we know where da girls are don't be so stupid!"

"Yeah. We know where ta find em alright!" And they'd all laugh. I knew they were referring to the dances held in the school gym every other month.

"Yeah he tinks he's gonna turn us on to sumpin or sumpin. What a creep!"

By this time, of course, the spell had gone, and they would grab their ball back. Divine Grace is short lived.

I ended these little confrontations by sprinting across the fields they inhabited, returning and telling with my little winded voice how many times I had run around their playground. Sometimes I'd climb up on the school roof and shout to them and wave my arms. I never wanted them to forget what I had said. I'd be waving my arms up on the roof and all these little cretins would be playing their silly little games down below, completely unaware of my presence up above them. I tried to imagine how much concentration they must have had to block me out of their minds. My concentration, I began to realize, would have to double to keep pace.

Then one day I managed to get myself invited to the reading of the sex book at Bennie Spinotsen's house.

His parents never questioned all of us tramping through their house up to Bennie's room. I, myself, found it quite odd.

Bennie leaned back on his bed while some of the boys stuck their heads out his window and smoked.

"Luter dis here's Bennie Spinotsen."

"Yeah I know you," I said. I had seen him in the halls. He had curly hair and wore dark-rimmed glasses and pressed shirts with collars, as if he belonged to a private school, or, as if, I suppose, his parents had to make a private school statement for the rest of the neighbors. There was something rich and classy about the house he lived in. It seemed cleaner and bigger than my own and the white carpet throughout made it seem that much more precious.

"Want one?" Someone, maybe it was Paul Rickert, offered me a cigarette. Paul Rickert's family lived in my parish. But then again, they were all in my parish, no doubt about that. I specifically remember Paul because his sister, a summer or two later, let me pull her shorts and panties off during a night behind the bushes that lined the track and field playgrounds.

Bennie read with the delectician of a connoisseur, like someone who had been tasting this kind of stuff for years. I sensed he had gotten these books from his Father and that even as we huddled in his room and listened to him read, that same Father was just outside the door, or downstairs, knowing full well what it was we were up to.

Other children seemed to have different relationships

with their Fathers than I had with mine.

"And den she straddled over da Gardener's heavy tool...." all the boys would hold their breath and look at one another, then off into some space, some distant space where all the coupling was really going on. The imagination, it's a real physical exertion.

"I bet her clitoris had a ring in it," I blurted, after about five pages of the Dirty-Young-Tutor-Gardener-routine.

"Shut up!" they all said.

"What da hell you trying to pull huh Knudson?" Suddenly I was Knud-son, as if they were trying to strip me of my rightful, spiritual duty. I could always hear the real meaning in everything they said to me, whether it was in Bennie's bedroom or out at the playgrounds. They said one thing, meant another, then hid behind what was said, shielding themselves from the hurt they were applying to those in their way.

"You guys ain't never been with a girl and I know it," I went on. "You think this stuff is really gonna happen to you? You're sadly mistaken chumps!"

And I stood to get ready to let fly at them with my whole voice. I wanted Bennie's Father to bust into the room and discover this whole sordid deal. I'd take *his* Father on too!

"Shut up and sit down!"

"Yeah or leave why don't ya!"

"Yeah leave dat's an idea!"

"Why if it wasn't for the Spirit of the Lord moving through that Young Tutor's clitoris you'd never know what to do when it comes to your first time. With a girl! You dopes are gonna get trampled by your first carnal experience and never have anything to show for it but a girl! You have no interest but in the technical apparatus of your own selves and now Bennie's telling you how to use that? It's more than that much more than just some instrument to please HER!"

"What are ya nuts!" cried Bennie. "Get this idiot out a here! I'm trying to read from da book and you're givin me lek-chair in church!"

"Yeah lek-chairs Bennie he's a fruit!"

"Yeah he's a nut what does he know! Hey whyn't ya leave already!"

"Besides," whispered Bennie, "my parents wouldn't approve us reading this type a material if'n y'know what I mean."

"Let's," and someone grabbed me from behind, "put him out the window on his head!"

"Sh sh," continued Bennie, "do it so it don't make too much noise. But do it! Yeah boys drop him on his head."

"I will never forget what you're doing!" I began to shout. Then someone put their hand over my mouth.

I had wanted to tell them that the penis is nothing to be ashamed of, and that if a Young Tutor can sit on it when it's stiff then it must be good for other things, too—

like a dowsing wand it could find water or grant wishes and the like. As long as it stayed erect.

But I was unable to get the words or the message out and found myself extended from Bennie Spinotsen's bedroom window by my feet, held by the boys who at any moment were about to let me fall to my death, or at least a figure resigned to a wheelchair.

Then Mr. Spinotsen entered the patio down below.

I tried to scream to him but he was intent on emptying the garbage. I couldn't believe he was unable to see or hear me, but kept on walking out the patio gate and closing it behind him. He was dressed in the same pressed white shirt and slacks as his son. Was he taking the bag of garbage all the way down to the corner!? Couldn't he see me extended, upside-down, out of his own house's window? Why was I so hard to recognize? Maybe it wasn't hard, maybe it was too easy. Maybe I should have whispered, or hooted like an owl, or, perhaps, chittered endlessly like a backyard squirrel.

I was seriously distressed, but kept up my banter with the boys in the hope that they would pull me back in through the window.

"Listen Bennie?"

"Hey Bennie he's callin' ya."

"Yeah Bennie listen to him plead for his life!"

"Music to my ears fellas music to my ears." Bennie began his own little lecture, based on his own infallible premise that my body when extended upside-down out a second-story window, is apt to make sounds one can apply to mortality in general.

"You gotta let me in Bennie!" I began to plead. "You gotta draw me back into your bedroom otherwise I'm gonna pass out out here. Or worse! I promise I won't speak anymore. I'll even go home if you want!"

"Huh now let's see if you go home dare's always the chance we might meet again which would disprove all of what you've learned through this "stension" as I call it...." Bennie protracted, sounding like the little double-speaking gangster that he was.

"Yeah Bennie you might have to see him again."

"OK OK I call it an ex*tension* too! Whatever you want for God's sake! It's all related to this yeah I don't care!" I yelled, appealing to the ground *and* to Bennie.

"That wouldn't be good for you Bennie no that wouldn't be good no no good." Bennie's gang palavered.

The others were beginning to irritate me. How had Bennie come to occupy such a highly placed position among their little rank and file? Here they were, holding me above my terrible future, the ground, teaching me about the nature of life and death instead of me teaching them about eternity, *and* they were singing praises and other sycophantish wishes in the direction of Bennie Spinotsen. Whom I didn't even know!

"OK OK I promise Bennie I'll never say anything to you again. I'll never even look at you if you want."

"Dat's better. Let 'em in boys before anybody downstairs finds out."

All the blood had rushed to my head and I think I popped a blood vessel and it was swimming in from the periphery and crackling and exploding and blinding me.

Bennie stood over me as I came to. I said I was sorry, and left the Spinotsen house never to return. I saw Mr. Spinotsen walking up the driveway as I was stumbling down it. I said goodbye but he didn't even acknowledge I was there, never even broke his neck in my direction.

—

"BUT IT'S ME IT'S ME in particular my attitude and my questions. Right?" I asked, heated after my Descartes paper, eager to get information from Professor Buddy Mickelmann instead of cake and coffee. We left the Dormitory and strolled farther into the Cemetery part of the Garden, near the annex and the back entrance on 10th Avenue.

"Why did you come here? I mean was it for a continued adventure within the Episcopalian Church? Was it to further your interests in philosophy? What more silly reasoning are you going to lay on me this time?" He cocked his head, pointing his little black beard down at me.

"Don't get me wrong Professor I think the curriculum is terrific. It's just that I have some serious doubts."

He laughed. "Stop calling me *Professor*. You don't have to be sure about anything how old are you?"

"No," I said, trying to impress him with the seriousness of the moment, a moment that was about to fade away forever.

"How old," he asked, "do you think I am people think I'm a lot younger than I am. They also say I look like—"

"I know the young Abe Lincoln."

"That's a new one ha! the young Abe no they usually say Meph."

"It's not the curriculum not my faith in any sense that would overlap my schooling here my future here it's that I've come to the decision I want to press on within my own thought and not study all the arcane philosophies that this seminary has to offer."

"To go," Mickelmann began, "to a regular university. I mean this is the study of the Bible I suppose. Ultimately. Listen I haven't the time and hardly the place for this kind of thing right now. One damn day we'll have to get a stand-up comedy night for students like you. It's a great idea isn't it? Lots of students all standing up to recite their silly intent."

"I'm not so sure I think I've stumbled upon something

that," I continued—

"I mean I *do* know a bit about this or that," Mickelmann went on, "but you don't mind if we do this quickly do you I've got to get things ready in the classroom come with me now and let's out with whatever's on your mind then since you're so gosh darn adamant. A stand-up comedy night! What do you think? It's a great idea get a little theater going here. Now's the time they say this part of town will liven and respond to that kind of thing. Sure. Religion and comedy. There's a great tradition in that. But you are the most adamant student I have!"

"The appeal that most of these studies make to authority well it's just not the way I want to cut into thought—

into God—"

"You've got to be kidding," Mickelmann shrugged, as if his shoulders were burdened. "You have some better way? You're cutting into things now namely my time hurry up. I thought we'd covered this in class already."

"Aquinas said himself an appeal to authority alone doesn't constitute the essence of our reason."

"That was also another time and place. But this Hans these are questions you can better address in the future. Aquinas? Right now you have to study and get your grades in order then you can—

and also I know what you're talking about we've been there with the many who have—

but this isn't about that fiery test this is something more comic I'll wager. Stick with me if you like I've just got to—

get these—

books out of the trunk and—

over there would you help? That's it now these hadn't

arrived in time and let's just take them. The two cartons into the annex—
You were saying? *Our* reason or some such?"
"But that's just it I feel I'd be wasting my time," I continued.
"Is this curriculum—
here let me get the door—
am I such a waste of your time?" Buddy Mickelmann stopped and looked back at me as I was about to enter his empty classroom. Twentieth street was just behind me, parked cars.
"Well it's not you no I would be fooling myself though if I were to accept these teachings listen I think this is all a sham!" I bluntly let him have it as I then set the box of books in front of the first row of desks and began taking some out then putting one on each.
"You do!" and he laughed, his voice echoing against the inner wall of closed windows that gazed out on the Garden and the tennis courts and then the little Cemetary. "Well what would you consider to be the great big sham at work here." He was smiling very lightly and I knew I had lost him already. He began to draw on the blackboard.
"I think we're just pretending. I mean I don't see how our reason especially in this day and—"
I paused, watching him push the chalk around. The figure he drew looked like a cat. Squeak, went the chalk in a curious motion over the blackboard.
"I mean the reasoning and the history of such ideations," I concluded.
Now the cat was sitting next to a dog, as he continued to fill the blackboard, his back to me.

"How can any of this be anything but the script for a future posturing within society itself."

Now there was an ape, and still he continued to draw.

"Aren't we of a much better metal than these courses make us out to be."

Now he drew a figure of a man, so that there was a cat, dog, ape and man. He continued drawing, this time a square box.

"Aren't we the human divine the image of God not some actor on a stage?"

The box now was divided into boxes, and those began to be divided into more boxes, until there were about forty squares in the original box.

"Aren't we given the thought of God straight *from* God?" I finally questioned.

"Yes well I don't quite—

what do you think of these are they recognizable?"

"I suppose, a dog, a cat, two people and—

a grid."

"So this one needs a little more hair and this one more whiskers." Squeak—

"See what you are having a problem with—"

Squeak—

"always going to be a society you be—"

Squeak—

"and believe me I understand the uselessness of that sometimes the utter—"

Squeak. The ape now grew hair all over as the flecks of chalk fell into the dust tray at the bottom of the blackboard.

"Listen take these papers and put them on the desks and please continue I'm all ears," said Mickelmann, turning, setting the chalk down, brushing his hands, a sickly smile on his lips.

It's embarrassing to relate all of what I told him.

"No sir you don't understand," I said as I took the stack of test papers and distributed them. "You don't understand what I'm—

the ideations themselves the paths—"

"Ideations. Ideations? Idiot nations? Is that what you mean?" Mickelmann suggested, as if to banish all reason.

"Which they are arrived at all of it a complete sham an effort to pass bad faith with oneself and ultimately God. Asserting God as bad—"

"I think that's too much of a reaction to something you're only beginning to learn—

don't put one on that corner desk that student's gone—

I would however be glad to hear your concerns about your schooling—

these doubts you have about the nature of philosophy itself are too grave. I mean there must be something else—

listen can you hand me that thank you—

entirely beyond *my* what would you call it—

duty—

responsibility I suppose. There *is* something beyond this study," he chuckled to himself.

Mickelmann turned and pulled down the map of the world at the center of the blackboard.

"I owe you my time," he continued, "and attention—"

Suddenly the door opened and one of the students and a few seconds of street and sidewalk sound entered—

"but I can't go chasing your whimsy—

is it that time already? gosh." He picked up the chalk

again and filled in squares of the grid, still visible to the side of the map—

"all over the unknown just to satisfy you—"

Squeak squeak squeak. "You remind me of someone—it doesn't matter—"

Squeak squeak squeak. "Go on I'm listening." He paused, and, for dramatic affect, turned to me, then back around to his drawing, saying, "After all what I owe to God can hardly be put in the balance here now can it?"

"Then nothing can!" I blurted, flatly, suppressing the urge to curse.

Squeak squeak squeak. "No Hans not nothing for crying out loud. Listen it's getting late."

He had filled in all the squares and now sat at his desk, picking up volume four of Copleston's *The History of Philosophy*, thumbing its dog-eared pages, running his hand down each page, then turning them, then all of them, fanning through the entire book.

"Your life," Mickelmann said, setting the book down and clasping his hands, resting them gently on the desk, telling me with his posture it was time to move on. "Your life is your own to see fit to do what you think appropriate. But in matters of religion and philosophy and science and the like—

or God—

or whatever you wanted to talk about—

these aren't questionable entities. These are the realities for which we live—

and pass through later—

much later do you understand?"

—

"Do you understand? ... Do you understand? ..." The phrase echoed in my brain as I sat in my seat, almost oblivious to the other students who had made their way into the classroom. When I stopped the playback of Mickelmann's last words to me the class had begun, the professor was lecturing on the drawings he had made on the chalk board and reading phrases from the current chapter in Copleston. As I came to, I recognized the student's head in front of me, not because it was there, but because its owner was busily scratching and picking at a large scab at the top of her spine, or at approximately the place where the spine enters the skull. She picked and picked and Mickelmann read and read and my stomach turned and turned.

—

After my return to the Seminary Garden, I returned again to Carlyle's (Cynthia's) place but she wasn't home. As I turned toward the subway, toward my Gowanus cement swamp apartment, two detectives stopped me. The sun was high and hot, but the detectives insisted that they wouldn't keep me for long.

Carlyle had been missing a few days. The two detectives asked how long I had known her.

"Just the other night," I finally said, nervously.

"And you'd never seen her before?" said the one, I

believe he was Detective Blades. The other's name was Stewart. But it might be the other way around.

"Did you know her?" asked Stewart.

"She works the street as Cynthia," I said, waiting for a reaction. They knew she worked the street, however, because they both nodded. They had expected me to answer thus.

"Were you engaging her services the other night?" asked Blades, cocking his head.

"God no!" I stammered, "I had no idea. I used to go to College over here. I just ran into her on the corner. She did invite me in. But nothing happened."

"Nothing happened?"

"Well her ex-husband showed up. Not that we were engaged in any sexual."

"But what were you doing over here?" asked Stewart.

"Well I was out of the theater and didn't want to go home so I came to the old school grounds just to visit."

"The theater?" they asked in tandem.

I was ready to tell them everything even if none of it made any sense. If they wanted to arrest me for complicity in her disappearance let them. My feeling was: I couldn't care less. I just stopped by to see if I might be able to get her to take her clothes off. I had never paid her nor was I intending to ever pay her. They'd be able to tell this by my responses. At least I hoped so.

"The street is your school ground? Ha! that's good. What were you doing in her apartment?"

"Well she invited me in I guess I was just talking to her over here in front of my school."

I obviously didn't want to tell them she had helped me break into the Cemetery-Garden.

"You knew she was a hooker?" asked Stewart.

"No! Not at all. I mean she looked like some of these neighborhood types that used to."

"When the ex-husband showed up were there any words exchanged first of all where did he show up?" asked Blades.

"Right in back there in the courtyard they talked for a while and her kid was with him and then they just disappeared—

didn't get a chance to hear what they were saying— except—"

Blades and Stewart waited while I told them the story she had told me.

"Well first off," cracked Stewart, "that wasn't her ex."

Then they asked me to come over to the station with them. It wasn't far. So I said sure, why not.

"Who was it then do you suppose?" I asked, trying to sound like a detective.

"Is this the school behind the wall with the trees?" asked Blades, incredulously, as we walked by the Garden door. A trick question. They must have known about the Seminary.

"Yep. I dropped out years ago."

"Are you originally from this area?" asked Stewart.

"Pennsylvania."

"Well listen Mr. Knudsen you'd do well to stay away from Ms. Dubias," said Blades.

"She's wanted for narcotics possession and is suspected of complicity in a murder we're investigating," added Stewart.

"Murder!" I tried to act surprised. Something told me she wasn't on the up-and-up. But I had been drunk. Suddenly I began to regret ever wanting to come back to this part of town. All those memories would only appear, as they apparently did, in the shape of a murderess. What the hell was I doing with a prostitute anyway? In the Garden of my former school where I had studied as a student of divinity!

"Is there anything else you'd like to tell us Mr. Knudsen?" asked Blades, obviously recognizing the strained expression on my face, as we entered the station on 19th street and sat down together at his desk.

I noticed one of the police officers from the other night as we walked into the main room past the front desk Sargeant. Would he recognize me as one of those they'd had to eject from the Garden?

Eventually Stewart made his way from the front desk over to Blades' desk. The station house, from the outside, looked like any other apartment building. While attending the Seminary I, of course, never had any reason to enter it. Now, confronted by a book of mugshots and asked to identify the man I had taken to be Carlyle's husband, I felt that I would never again step foot in this stationhouse. It was as if my imagination were playing tricks on me in the form of the law—

you could run its clanging reality through your mind once but then, when actually confronted by that reality, you knew it did not include you. As much, I mean, as your imagination first proposed. Does this mean we are *all* in search of a permanent alibi?

This feeling was confirmed by Stewart's broad and booming voice announcing to anyone within earshot that "we found another one claims the same mercury poisoning scenario over here."

"Keep rackin' 'em up guys. Sooner or later," came the

answer from a uniformed officer at the other end of the room, a sandwich stuffed in his chewing mouth—
"eventually I—
one o' these days—
you'll get at da bottom of it!"

And Blades turned to me from his swivel-chair and said, "I wouldn't believe a word of that story your friend told you. We've been trying to figure why she's using this story."

He also began to unwrap a sandwich that had been placed on his desk by another detective and then popped the plastic cover off a coffee.

"You're not the first."

"Not the first," I echoed.

"Not the first. In fact." He took a huge bite of the sandwich. A mozzarella with arugala and prosciutto ham by the looks of it. "We've had quite a time with that story. Ain't that right everyone!" He sipped his coffee carefully and swallowed. "Quite a laugh over that story haven't we!"

And the officers and detectives in the narrow station room chuckled, looking up from their half-eaten sandwiches.

"Why would she," continued Blades. "You want something to eat? You hungry?"

"No thanks. I'm fine. Just let me look here and see if I can."

"Why would she want you to believe such a thing? I mean honestly now do you think such a thing could be done?"

"Well I know it's kind of I mean I didn't really think," I offered, nervously leafing through the album.

"You better not try to think," continued Stewart, "if you

can identify the man. From the other night. The courtyard." He took a sip of his own coffee. "We'll forget about your run-in the other night with Officer Hutchins if you do."

I tried to look perplexed.

"You know. The break-in," said Stewart, now unwrapping the rest of his BLT from its butcher paper. "We watch that stretch of 10th avenue all the time," Stewart concluded, then taking a bite.

"You mean," I asked, "you *let* me break in?"

"You said you used to belong there right?"

"Yeah," I stammered, "I mean like I said I went to school there."

"OK. Safe answer. A tough guy." Blades got up from his desk and made his way to the water cooler, bringing me a cup also.

"But what's," I continued, between sips, "so outrageous about her story. I mean if she's wanted for murder?"

"A *crazy* story. We don't know more than that but."

"Then what's so unbelievable about such a thing? I mean if this husband was capable of murder," I said, wanting to solve, right on the spot, the entire mystery.

"Probably," interjected Stewart, "multiple murders. We know it but need some proof."

"Couldn't you be wrong about the story?" I asked, politely.

"Listen," said Blades, sitting back at his desk, wiping his chin, "when you deal with these types of people."

"I know she told me she was forced to work the streets to make a living," I added, trying to assure them of my own curiosity.

"Listen kid you either have to do that kind of thing or

not."

"And *not*'s more often the case right?" furthered the inquisitive Stewart.

"I suppose," I assented, not sure at all what they were getting at, "but couldn't the story be true?"

"Listen. Just identify this so-called husband."

"And we can talk about the story some other day," Blades concluded.

"Got yourself a hardball player there," said another detective from his lunch-desk at the other end of the room.

—

WHY WERE THERE TWO Catechisms? Why this Consubstantiation, on the one hand, and Transubstantiation on the other. Why two hands? That would be the correct question, of course: why *two hands*?

My Father couldn't, or wouldn't, for some big-headed reason I myself wouldn't understand, explain.

At least to a sufficient degree for the other children to understand. I remember him mumbling something about his own faith and how this was strengthened by the faith that Luther finds in the Bible.

But more than his mumbling, I remember in more vivid brain-detail those silly color illustrations in the Catechism guides depicting Jesus and St. Paul alongside old testament heroes and parables. What the old testament had to to with Luther's two Catechisms I could not, indeed even then, understand.

I used the good word in front of the Sunday school class,

and then out in the playground, for the next month or so. A very memorable time for me. For the others as well. Consubstantiation meant good for all. But Transubstantiation meant a special victory for us marble-shooters in the dust of the deserted playground field. My Father, unwittingly, had armed us with the seeds of heresy and I willingly sowed them among my peers.

With my puries!

Those little glass creatures would rise up through the teachings of the mysterious New Testament and the mysterious two Catechisms, and pause in the breath of the other marblers, while I called on the power of Transubstantiation to win for me the pot of marbles, to see into the matrix of the dirt hole and the scattered other marbles (some cat-eyes, some puries, and some only bastard marbles gathered from strangers over time—)

to see straight into it, to let the game rule all, to bend the rules of the game by winning the game, by being lucky.

I remember one of the kids yelling to a passing kid on a bicycle and waving him over to the game. "You *have* to see what Knudsen can do he's p'ssessed by God!"

The bicycler happened to be the neighborhood bully. Well, not bully, but an older kid from the other side of the school district, the west side. I don't really know why—

I hollered at the bicycling bully—

I felt the power of the Lord rise up in my little breast—

I let my voice boom out over the playground field in the direction of the bully bicycler. He was changed in that moment, I remember. He threw his bicycle down and walked over to the game. The other kids stayed hunched on the ground over the marble court.

I continued to holler in a booming and loud voice like an actor I had seen on television.

"God bless this passage of my purie through the maze of cat-eyes for the grand—"

I pulled that word out too, probably a first for me, the luck overflowing my being—

"grand good charm of our Lord and Saviour Jesus Christ!"

I began to tremble—

"and the blood of the lamb!" Wherever did I get that from? "Bless this shot in the Transubstantiation of the whole world now on this spot of dirt in the hole of the earth for the winning of the marbles from the purie of the Lord of Hosts!"

Again, I had no idea what made me say "hosts," what made me pull from a text I'd only glanced at in the bible, a word that then proceeded to elucidate Consubstantiation for the other kids as well.

I picked up a purie and held it to the sky.

"You oh great glimmering Transubstantiation of the world! You bless this purie! Bless it and I will smack these cat-eyes into the hole!"

Then I'd bend down and take aim. There was a hush over the marble courts as I pulled into my sight and shot at the cat-eyes and the other puries. The dust would nudge a bit and the other kids begin to laugh.

Some sighed and got up and went to their own holes, but the kids gathered around my game stayed to see me rise and take another purie and point it toward the sky.

"Sky of the world and the spirit of the Lutheran hosts of the ring!" Birds flew up from the distant trees by the swing-set. My voice echoed out over the empty playground behind the school. "This is the purie of the invincible Lord of Hosts!"

And in a moment, as my voice cascaded through the place, I found myself staring at the image of Luther himself. He turned to me and seemed to walk down from the sky dressed in a white robe. I looked to the other kids. They were staring up at me waiting for me to shoot. To win another pot.

"Don't you see him!" I yelled down at them.

"C'mon shoot willya!"

"Yeah shoot da thing already!"

"But he's there!" I persisted in calling them to the sky.

The bully came over and stood towering above the others.

"Can you see him in front of you?" he asked.

"Yes he's right in front of me can't you—"

And the bully stared into me unflinchingly.

"*Oh wonder of the formless heavens on high*!"

And I quickly bent down and took aim again. My purie shot the cat-eye straight into the hole and the pot was mine. Everyone cheered but the losers frowned because they were going to have to play me next week to get their cat-eyes and their lost puries back. I was invincible.

Even the bicycler was convinced something Holy had happened. Eventually he would return, through the ensuing weeks, to show me off as if I were his—

and there went all the magic.

"OK. I want you to see someone," he said to me one day, pulling me over by the tree near the swing-set. "David tells me you're up about five hundred marbles."

"That's right. And the spirit of Transub—

the spirit did it all."

"OK. Yeah. Whatever. But this guy I'm gonna introduce you to wins *every* time. He hasn't lost any marbles *at all*!"

"Is he possessed too?" I wanted to meet someone from the neighborhood who had the same capacity for the greater glory.

"OK. But stay here I have to get him."

I waited. Looking at the swing-set I began to wonder, embarrassingly, why I had said I was *possessed*. I had used the other kids' name for what I took to be merely spirit. I sat in one of the swings. Time seemed to go by slower than usual. Above the marble courts the kids were noisily playing. In the other direction there was no sign of the bully or his bicycle. I began to doubt he'd ever return.

Then quite suddenly I began to hear a crackling in the distance. Little marbles began bouncing on the blacktop of the driveway entrance to the back of the school.

I leapt running toward the others, yelling and waving my arms.

"Hey! Hey! look at the sky! Marbles are falling out of the sky! Hey willya look! Over here! Over here!"

Before I reached them the hail started pelting all of us. Ping. Ping. Clack. Ping. It was the end of the world. Or the beginning. A storm.

Then it chattered onto the dirt where everyone was scattering and yelling and running for cover over by the swing-set, beneath the great big oak tree. As I joined everyone, my breath giving way and taking hold the better part of me, I noticed the bully had returned.

"Oh shit!" everyone said, as the rain and hail began to pummel down on the tree, we little soaked wretches crammed next to one another.

"Listen," someone said, "if you get rid of that damned bike—"

"Yeah! Who cares if it gets soaked. Let it out there fer chrite's sake why don't ya!"

The bully grabbed a little fella with glasses and told him to go put it next to the swing-set.

That little fella was my opponent. But I didn't know that until the hail stopped and we began to part from one another, breathing the cool, early summer air and eventually wending and wafting, some of us toward home, the rest back over to the marble courts to see what damage had been done.

"OK. This is Jimmy. He's gonna kick yer ass but good." The little fella with glasses and a crew cut, about 2 years younger than me and about a foot shorter, held out his hand for me to shake.

"Luther," said the bully, "you're gonna start the first match and we're gonna let you have a lead. OK. We feel that confident."

Lightning flashed over the schoolyard. In the distance a couple of kids were pedal-standing their bikes up the drive. The bully waved to them.

"OK. That's the others. But first Jimmy's gonna beat you and then we'll start the wager."

"Oh good," I said, not in the least alarmed.

I had no idea what I was up against. I was very brazen. I might even be thought to be quite stupefied by the whole progress of events but I kept chalking that progress up to nothing more than Spirit, a Spirit that had not let me down. How could one *ever* let oneself down? As long as one were one everything was fine, but along came two and sounded the progress of the end. After all, it was my own Father who had given me this license to kill, as it were. They were all my little prodigies. I actually admired this bully: did he want to own my parish too?

It hadn't occurred to me this bully had also been harboring and training prodigies and that he had come to his place of prominence by way of, probably, years of marble-wisdom.

We immediately got down to it. "OK. Wait a minute, wait a minute," said the older bully, "ain't you gonna do all that mumbo jumbo stuff you were doin before?"

"Oh yeah." I almost forgot what I had become. Their little eyes all gazed up at me. It was time for me to perform! The sky was still gray and I scanned its four directions. On top of the school roof I saw a couple of kids scampering, silhouetted by that luminous gray, their voices dripping down to our playground in time to the few raindrops still falling. I remember thinking they had probably hidden under a vent drum up there while the hail began to fall, caught, and now were running to beat it out, scurrying down the drainpipe and leaping to the tar surface, the wet and sky-reflecting black home of the playground.

"Spirit of the sky!" I called as the others listened. The bully went to talk to his friends who had just arrived. I could see him explaining, interpreting what I was doing. They laughed.

"Spirit of the hosts of the storm up above! Load my marbles good and chase those cat-eyes toward the hole in the ground!"

It was then I spied little Jimmy's stash of marbles: aggies, and other crystallized beauties I had never before seen. I stopped and reached over to pick one of them out.

"OK now what you doing? Those are supposed to be *won*. What are you looney?" The bully pushed his way into the circle and made me back away.

"I was just."

"You were just nothing you were just nothing! Now play damn't! Before it rains again."

"That's Luter," I heard one of the others say, "he was born to screw things up. He's got a gift from God and look at him he's bein' taken in by Jimmy's marbles. Hey ain't you never seen no aggies before?"

"No. Maybe in another lifetime though!" A grin broke out on my face. I raised my arms to the sky, still grey.

"Break O you clouds above break like the marbles about to be broken and sweep them into the hole in the ground!"

An hour later, when most of my pot had dwindled to Jimmy's evident talent and mastery, the sky began to break and the sun began to dry.

"OK. Guess you thought you had the spirit huh Luther?"

I stared at the bully. How could he have taken it away from me?

He laughed and took Jimmy aside and they left for the day, each hopping on his bike, the bully placing Jimmy on his handle-bars. They rode out of the playground.

The others had separated into groups and were already playing different games.

—

Professor Mickelmann wanted me to know that he would like to join me out there, in the "unknown," but he couldn't. At least this is what his little pre-classroom talk had meant to me.

"Sir," I approached, one afternoon, on the Seminary grounds, just in front of the tennis courts, on the path that led to the cemetery, "if you'll just indulge me for a minute."

"Oh geez. One minute. But make it quick." He gathered his hands behind his back and we began to walk, quickly, his head bowed and straining at the leash of my re-appearance.

"It's a matter of the mind itself. I know that the mathematical is not exactly."

"Oh don't tell me you're going to have doubts because mankind has been able to construct a jumbo jet and other monstrosities other mechanical monstrosities? Your farce continues Hans."

"No not at all. The way I see it the only reason we have been given a curriculum outside of the fact that most of the terrain has been sanctioned by the Church through the ages—

but that there has been a continued pretense within their leaps of logic and faith—

reflects a position in society. I feel philosophical knowledge, inside or outside the workings of Episcopalian faith or any faith has been built into society—

whose permanent wonder at the so-called ability we have been able to endow the mind with *are* the background the First Mover, of and all parts of Reason. Under God, under Scientific Experimentalism, under anything."

"Oh geez," emitted Mickelmann. "Yes well tell me Hans what do you intend to do. Are you going to stay here: complete your term?" He didn't let me answer. "I don't think so. I think you're going to go off into that grave world you speak of day in and out and map a terrain for yourself. Godspeed. Good luck. Have a nice day." He waved his arm indecorously away from himself.

"It's something I *can* do!"

"Of course," he announced, his brows arching, "one *can* connect the dots I suppose."

"Is it a connect-the-dot kind of thing? Is that what all this mental terrain is?"

"Gee whiz Hans you tell *me* you're the one with the fire down below for crying out loud."

I felt proud to have the fire down below. But then I thought maybe he was condescending. I studied his eyes. They were serious, but there was also distance. He was on the move, trying to get somewhere, trying to get away from me. He was attempting to throw me off the trail, I felt. He didn't want anything to do with me.

"Isn't it just reason itself? Isn't the Cartesian Cogito the place to start from?" I was quite sure he would not follow me.

"Probably right. But modern philosophy is not what we are about here. Completely. Although I wish it was: we wouldn't have to deal with stand-up comedians like yourself enrolling to study their own ideas and nothing of the real world. Endeavoring to give you an education Hans can you understand that? No I didn't think you would. It's pretty simple. As simple as that. If you insist on transforming the what-did-ya-call-it the Tree of Knowledge. Like Descartes."

"That's just it by serving the mind first one might know God," I said, intending to go on from there and see what happened. Instead, Mickelmann stopped walking and turned and spoke pointedly, scoldingly.

"Not *quite* it. In fact what you're attempting. A skeptical analysis of philosophical terrain. There. Are you happy now? What we do here is give you a religiously skewed education. Do you believe?"

"What?"

"In God?" he asserted.

"What do you mean?"

"Gee whiz Hans. Does. God. Exist? For crying out loud! Because if you don't believe he."

"Well I'm almost not sure it has anything to do with my present situation. Believe me I'm sure if I'm allowed to pursue the mind's—"

"Just deluding yourself. Nothing in the mind." Mickelmann flatly stated.

I stared at him. Was he right?

"Dictates of Platonism," he began, "for that matter any of the pre-Socratics I don't teach them but maybe *you* should.

"What? Teach?" I asked, ashamed that he would assume I was so damn smart.

"Yeah why not. What did they ever have to do with the mind? Weren't they—

but perhaps not that familiar with them?" Mickelmann condescendingly asked.

"Not enough I'm afraid."

"But you have to familiarize yourself with something if you're going to take a stance. That's why," said

Mickelmann, "I must leave and attend to the *scheduled* class today. As time goes by this curriculum will make sense to the point where you might be able to assert your own skeptical—

Ha! Analysis but until that time you're a student. Or a stand-up comedian. You decide which."

"I didn't mean to," I continued. "What do you suppose is the right way to the Cartesian Cogito? Is it the gateway to fallen man or is it the energy within for instance our present circumstances?" And I stopped keeping pace with him and motioned to the trees and the headstones.

"Sorry we can talk later." And he began the walk back toward the tennis courts.

"Isn't the reason we do anything for the added superiority so-called wisdom stages for us!? Aren't we riding only rumor!? Descartes seems to make more sense of the ego by taking it all into the mathematical realm!" I was calling after him, refusing to use my feet. Was that my moment in quitting then—

to stand at the spatial threshold of literal calculus?

"Isn't the mind that moment in eternity we should not let pass us by even at the expense of exigencies of spiritual pablum?! Aren't we giving God himself short shrift in *passing* through schools!?"

But he was soon beyond the tennis courts and then disappeared inside the annex itself.

—

A VERY REAL SURPRISE was that the cards I typed and gave to Richard to ruminate upon and return had changed.

And not just edited or realized in any new conceptual way, but actually re-typed and half of them thrown out. Richard said he had to find a balance within the performance, and really all that meant was that I would have to work much harder to produce new cards, then try to convince him to include them in the changing graph paper performance.

In fact, the impression I received was that Richard and Sara abandoned the graph (the original graph) and intended our performances to expand without the group's knowing or unknowing participation.

We'd been cut off from the process, and the only person who controlled the direction was, of course, Sara.

Was Rudy some kind of prophet?

Her new idea would want to dress the performers in medical surgical suits, hairpieces and masks, using thick foundry glasses and heavy workman's gloves for head-gear.

The concept, I suppose, would have us insulated from one another, our bodies reduced to mere cloth-sounds rubbing, surrounding the senses and drowning out any impromptu interaction. It is as if we were now to have our bodies engulfed within big bags depriving us of any further enjoyment of any environment whatsoever.

She spoke about the cards. In fact, she had interrupted Richard as he was explaining their new content—

"We couldn't," she said, sourly smiling and placing a hand on my shoulder, "let all of them be so—

abstract I'm sorry to say I don't mean to offend you *are* a very good writer. We just couldn't."

"You say abstract as if it were a bad thing," I interjected, finally trying to mount some kind of reasoning that would keep the whole graph paper performance from turning into, well, exactly what it was, a series of blue lines on paper with schematics drawn by Richard and Sara. "Abstract isn't bad as long as we understand collectively what abstract actually *means*. If we vizualize it and not relegate it to a concept or some such."

"Hans I know what you're trying to do and it's just not the goal or shouldn't be the goal that like what actors are like about. Sounds like a lot of idea and nothing."

"I agree we need," my voice and blood temperature rose, "to stay away from areas that might become too wishy-washy but if we understand that what is abstract isn't immaterial then we."

"He's right about that!" Rudy let his frustration vent. "Nobody seems to get it I mean my hands strangling are a metaphor man. A metaphor! Just because I'm an actor doesn't mean I'm a total idiot!"

There was a brief moment of silence. Rudy shifted in his chair and seemed to be breaking wind, as if he simply didn't give a hoot about what we were doing anymore. Yet he persisted in attending the meetings and joining in the performances. He might have sounded like a kind of idiot-prophet, but ultimately he was just a another theater slut, hungry for immediate attention from an audience no matter how small they might be.

"Hans," Richard spoke, "look at the parameters of the event itself. You see that's enough to."

"No it's enough Richard," Sara quickly inserted. "It's

not enough I mean. Oh hell I'm getting mixed up I mean Hans! What *is* un-abstract about being abstract?"

"I'm just saying," I continued, now in confession mode, "that what you are all assuming is abstract just simply isn't." Everyone stared at me, maybe they were just bored, but I knew they simply had no idea what I was trying to say.

"What Sara is trying to say is that we need to focus on the parameters of the event before it gets too large to handle," explained Richard.

"And what's too large?" asked Rudy, with a pretend scowl on his face.

"Nothing really you see it's just that for this first one there will be others I hope you understand that this is just an experiment and we feel that to start here would be the way to go now all of you have turned in your own statements as to purpose and I will—

Richard *and* myself will go over those and include those in."

"Listen," I insisted, trying to derail Sara a bit, "just name one thing about these cards and this performance that you think is abstract."

"Well outside the cards and the as Richard says pair a meters," Sara pronounced the word as best she could.

"Pa*ra*meters," corrected Richard.

"I know I know I sometimes just say things that way Richard! I'm not dumb you know. It's a."

"Just name one thing," I asked, trying to calm her down and keep the meeting on track.

"One abstract thing? Uh the way these the meaning of these I mean what do *any* of the—

I know I know there are *some* cards—

some are literal and others Hans are just nonsense and we know that. We know that Hans."

"Will we be able to add to these cards at all?" asked Samantha.

"I think we have enough," concluded Richard.

"Wait Richard I want to hear what she has to say," Sara raised her hand to silence him.

"But those cards," I myself continued, "are only literal in that we *think* we know what is *literal* about them. The so-called nonsense cards have to be seen as literal," and here I looked at Hippolyte, hoping to make some influence or direction known to her, "in order that we have a way to continually reify the parameters of the event. We're simply not going to be able to continue if we don't start mining away at the unknown here."

"Richard," Sara said, exasperated, "please now explain to us what *reify* means?"

"Could mean many things actually. But here I think Hans means that one thing leads to another thing. But differently. Or it could mean."

"I mean," I asserted, "that to be reborn and we have to be reborn reify means to be renewed to be reborn."

"I'm not so sure we're ready for a religious experience as concerns performing or acting although some think," countered Sara.

"Why not!" objected Rudy.

"If we add new cards," Samantha offered again, "isn't that the same thing as being renewed—

as renewing—

as being like reborn so to speak like—"

"Not really," I explained, "because a new card could

always be the same as a card that already exists and yes it's true what I'm saying is that we have enough cards and we should."

"So we're in agreement with that then," Sara stated, straightening herself, "that we have enough cards."

"We're in agreement with that but not about."

"Well this religious side of things isn't what we need to get into right now nor do we need to endlessly."

"What Sara means," Richard concluded, "is that we've already covered the base the parameters of this event and now it's time to move on."

"Isn't that," Sara scoffed, "what I said at the beginning here? Honestly I don't—

or *can't* OK I admit it—

around in circles like this! I like to be *practical*. That's just who I am. You Hans and maybe you others might want to spend all this time philosophizing but it's just not me nor how I."

"That's OK Sara," I said, still trying to get back on track, "sometimes the circle can clarify. You pass through it and come out the other side better informed. Some things can't be but communicated any other way but by passing through and."

"Like I said," Sara threw up her arms, "you're a very good writer and I'm not against that. Geez it's like hearing myself say the same thing over and over! Listen folks we're on to the next thing and that's that."

"But if that is a problem," offered Hippolyte, raising her brow at Samantha.

"No it's just that I thought we'd be able to give more than the one card or thought or whatever," Sam began.

"More might not be able to fit in this event's," and Hippolyte paused, looking at me—

"*experiment* do you understand?" Her eyes tried not to leave mine, but they finally addressed Samantha, who decided to give up and not pursue the idea further.

I felt like saying I would be glad to re-work the cards into something different, to add more cards, but it would be futile to undermine my own idea (even if no one knew I was undermining). I thought against it. Partly because Hippolyte would still be with the group, and I'd still have a chance to be close to her. And she was obviously sending me some sort of signal. My antenna was receiving signal when she spoke to Samantha. We still had some sort of frequency with which to work, no matter which way the performances went. There would be other performances, whether they would be based on the graph of this original program or with the aid of cards or other novelties or performers or whatever. My main reason for acquiescing was Hippolyte. Her directness, her decisiveness (no doubt derived from my own writing, what little she had read of it) seemed to be the bridge that would allow me a little closer to her far shore.

—

TIME. SPACE. My body. My home this rat-infested sweat and garbage-strewn swamp filled with tar and metal shards from the end of civilization itself?

People had arrived and had actually lived here. It was

wild then. I think it wild *now*.

Walking to the subway before work one day, taking in the old village streets of Manhattan, I came upon an old place:

ST. LUKE'S CHAPEL
1892 TRINITY PARISH 1976
THE OLD VILLAGE CHURCH
OF GREENWICH VILLAGE
BUILT 1822

Friend, this village church
open stands for thee,

that thou mayest enter, think,
kneel and pray,

remember whence thou art and
what must be

thine end. Remember us,
then go thy way.

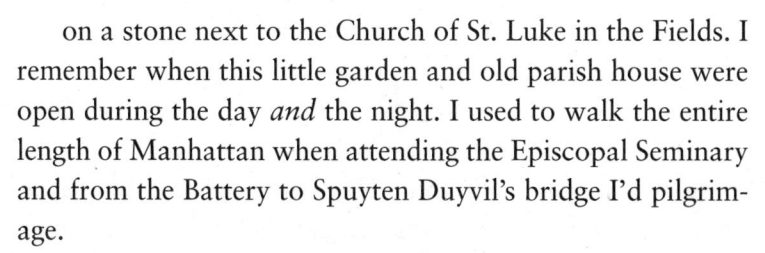

―――― ♣ ――――

on a stone next to the Church of St. Luke in the Fields. I remember when this little garden and old parish house were open during the day *and* the night. I used to walk the entire length of Manhattan when attending the Episcopal Seminary and from the Battery to Spuyten Duyvil's bridge I'd pilgrimage.

Seems I'm still winded from that as I lie here remembering Hippolyte, the theater and my little involvement with the missing Carlyle—

it's as if I've been doing nothing but walking.

Instead of enrolling in the Seminary I should have simply come to New York, walked, and written occasional thoughts onto 5 X 7 inch index cards—

like this one I included in the new pile for Richard and Sara during the changing, evolving early stages of the graph paper performances:

>   Run in place, the exact same place,
>   for a minute or so.

Any other description of the meaning of the event, whether for the performer and former actor (or for some later reader) would completely destroy the necessity of its "action." Its thought, in other words, its moment. Its reality.

And so I had at that time also, while in the beginning heat of card-writing, begun to burn with love for Hippolyte, but also for the brevity of action as that would speak the loudest toward Hippolyte. Could I have but written a letter to her, things would have probably turned out differently. But at the time I thought we had an understanding.

I preferred to cultivate that understanding within the art of the graph paper performance.

But at every turn it was as if Richard and Sara had been there already, hampering my efforts. First there was the medical emergency clothing. Then the further changing of the cards, which went on throughout the following months. After every group meeting I would give Richard more cards in the hope I would be able to stay ahead of his own labor at re-writing them. But it became apparent he and Sara were not very heavy sleepers and must have stayed up endless hours cancelling, throwing out, and rewriting as many as they possibly could.

But I pressed on. By this time the other performers had lost complete interest in all aspects of the graph paper performance, the cards, the group meetings and the theater in general. I was the only one left with any enthusiasm for the project. Yet so were Richard, Sara and Hippolyte. The more they threw themselves into card-generating, the performance rehearsals, the actual shows (in which the audience consisted of 10 people at most) the further I drew away from all other mental activity. Especially any written exercises. I managed a few playlets, but they all tended to involve the actions of new cards. Everything in rooms I'd walk into would convey to me possible actions and maneuvers with my body, telegraphing toward my only inner desire—

to know Hippolyte more deeply.

But she kept her distance, even while remaining within the graph paper group. At the time I hadn't thought of it as distance, just another side of her sweetness, an elixir that for some strange reason I thought also desired me. And no doubt there was some attraction on her part. In retrospect, it seems it was only for the existence of her career in the theater. But she seemed so innocent, how could she think a career would come of all this!

She had made great strides in that regard, however. My own separate existence began to become incredibly inebriated and had no firm sense of direction outside the cards and the next performance.

—

GOD HAD ENTRUSTED me with wisdom and with the power of the whole congregation, I thought, back in those early days, and I would not step down so easily. There would come a day when I'd win all my marbles back!

But when I continued losing marble matches and the booming voice and the whole Holy Act and the growing definition of Consubstantiation of souls as opposed to Transubstantiation of souls into puries into cat-eyes or vice-versa began to lose its glimmer, the bully bicycler and his friends decided to beat me up. I had humiliated them, he said, and, besides, OK, it wasn't fun anymore.

So they began to tackle me upon first sight, when I'd appear at the marble courts. Determined yet to win back my congregation, however, I kept showing up. Each time the bully had another little prodigy for me and the others to contend with. Eventually, they wouldn't even let me play at the courts and when they caught sight of me from out in the distant field, headed their way, they all, including some of the kids I had considered loyalists, ran out to pummel me before I stepped any closer. The bully led the initial assault. And, of course, it humiliated me, especially considering the fact that he was much larger than me and had only to lie over me and let me squirm underneath him to prove my defeat.

The truth is I didn't even try to rebel very hard. My power, I thought, had been taken away from me. I couldn't even lift my arms or my legs to knock him in the groin or the face. I couldn't, in short, muster enough martial defense for the beatings to be considered a fight. It became a part of their way of passing the weekends by watching me squirm under the bully. Their cheers consisted of completely abusive language but I refused, or was unable, like my limbs, to hurl any counter attack toward him. It was as if there were another force that persisted in persuading me to go to the marble matches knowing full well I'd end up humiliated and smothered under the bully.

The logic of the whole farce continued to haunt me until the very day I graduated from High School. It was as if the entire burden of having to go to school, to study with these same children whom I had considered my friends at one time, and who had gone on to humiliate me and whom I had submitted to, had actually been the force of the entire curriculum itself—

the daily necessity of my having to get up in the morning and leave for school. It wasn't until the moment of the graduation ceremony itself that I realized how nonsensical my early skill in interpreting the gospel and the words of faith in Luther's Catechism had been. But I had been completely driven to that interpretation by environment—

the pastor's son, my backyard was literally my Father's Church. The torments, the taunts, the constant humiliation never wore off until the actual graduation of my person from that educational system I had erroneously ascribed to my Father's Church; to the ministry I thought was before me; to the sudden willful choice I would later make to study in a Catholic, or truer, more original, Seminary. All the spite I had felt for my Father would have come from the religion we were supposed to have. I thought I'd been imbued with religion and its subsequent coordination within my early schooling. It brought me only to the futility of my entire identity. It was not a condition I was prepared to believe in, therefore. there must be something else, I thought then, some *continuation*, some *trans—*

I couldn't express any of this to anyone, not family, so-called friends, to no one. Everyone had forgotten my early years, everyone but me. Even my Mother (who had nicknamed me to the skater of holiday television classics) scowling her usual scowl as I came home from school one day through the back door, seeing her fill up the table, then call out that dinner was ready, and we all sitting and after prayers that same scowl on her tight jaw. It was as if she meant to show how much she was willing (and yet not willing, clenchingly) to forget by saying nothing, stressing the eye-to-eye sense of our selves only, there at the dinner table.

"Finish what is on your plate Hans," I heard her tightly say. The food would not go down that night.

"Finish."

And so I would be made to empty the plate. To this day I swear if there is a drop left in that icy glass in front of me I am compelled to relate it to my gut, no matter how full it already is, nor how dizzy my head might be.

One day, before graduation, I was rummaging through my closet. I was attempting to clean it out. I wanted to try to get rid of everything that might still remind me of my early start in the world. It had occurred to me that all the things accumulating in my closet, under my bed, even in the small red foot locker at the end of my bed, might indeed one day come back to haunt me. How right I was, receiving these visions of the future at the deepest moment of solitude.

Around the corner came my Mother, who quickly and

with much alarm, shoved clothes down the clothes chute just on the other side of my closet. That is, I saw her, or rather her feet and of course knew it was she, then heard her through the wall, and the bundle of dirty clothing falling into the basement below me.

I thought nothing of it.

But she must have known I was rummaging, because as soon as I pulled my big head out of the closet, there she stood, arms akimbo, legs sternly mimicking her jaw, set, as usual, and scowling upon my territory. On the floor were some papers that, for some reason, had not been thrown out, they were that old—

homework assignments from the first grade.

"I thought you might like to keep these," she sternly said, nodding to the pile.

"Why?"

Her eyes contracted and sent out deadly black and blue rays. Then, just as forcefully, they softened. She threw her arms down to her sides and threw her head back and left, it seemed, in a silent rage of tears.

I looked at the pile of papers. Nothing, really, just old composition paper, with the first instance of cursive handwriting. A big loop on an S, which had blue dotted lines through the middle, as if it were really two C's put together. In short, the building blocks to the alphabet and my first attempts at rendering it.

I left the marble courts for good one summer, but it was the beginning of my character and would continue to be me, in the eyes of my classmates, on into and beyond high school until it came time to assume my Father's destiny. It was then that I finally did speak, in a way, to what it all meant or would mean to me:

My Mother was digging through piles of dirty laundry in the basement—

"Is that you Hans!" she called out, hearing my muffled sobbing through the ceiling. Above, I had been delivered into a weeping fit completely beyond me, brought on by my impending graduation. I didn't answer her, and continued to drench my pillow, the bedroom window open and the new summer's air beginning to carry me away.

She appeared at the foot of my bed. I continued to sob and then, at the sight of her, to wail into my pillow more, trying to muffle the hysterics. She sat on the bed next to me and began to comfort me.

"Let it out that's it. It's about time you came around."

"What? What's that s'posed to mean?" I sobbed and gasped, wanting to know why she had been expecting this to happen to me.

"You've been holding a lot inside," she said, then setting her jaw again in that stern rigor mortis I knew only too well.

"Lotta what? What's that supposed to mean?"

Her eyes shrunk to black pinpoints. "What do YOU think it means!"

"Oh geez!" I cried and fell back to weeping into the dark, dented pillow.

—

MY WASH-CYCLE DONE, I just had more words with Rosita, the downstairs laundry's inveterate street-sitter. She is the sister (or cousin I'm not sure) of the laundromat's owner. Every week I go down to do my clothes (the few ugly pieces I've owned for years) and there she is. Before I leave for work there she is, staring out toward the sparse traffic on Union Street, sometimes gazing into the smelly distance of the greasy canal itself.

She is always in the same gauzy slip, her swollen toes jammed into some old, flattened slippers. Her face carries the function of madness, its twitchings and loud mouthfuls. Either she *was* mad and now lives rent free, or she was never mad and has been kept from the world by her relatives, let to pasture between her apartment and the lawn-chair out front the *Gowanus Laundromat* (a private hellish dwelling—

now that I think of it—

is an appropriate end for all that religious striving up out of the old world and into the body of the new).

My three rooms are furnished with what I was able to find around this part of town. A plank of wood from the coffee warehouse around the corner. A chair appeared one day on the slope of Union Street just above the bridge. The plank is supported between two piles of cinder blocks and bricks, which are plentiful here.

The weather sometimes lets up into a sunny sort of day, great for rummaging through dumpsters and often there will be a chair or couch left abandoned. Staring at the board with the few books I possess (propped between milk-crates) I wonder if the earliest inhabitants hadn't also collected felled trees or scraps for their dwellings. Certainly stones from their swampy little fields were used for their houses. None of it remains, however, not even as a museum. There are pictures, but outside of that the night dwells here in the tar and cement along the stinking sewer of a canal the same as it probably ever has.

I'm tempted to talk with the inhabitants very little. First, because I speak un pequeño español. And, second, milling about in the stagnation of all this ancient dead-zone, I'm afraid of what might be unleashed, say, by that fellow, Poppy, who plays his radio day in and out in the automobile scrapyard. His little sanctified quarters I have on occasion caught sight of, between the chassies and motors and hubcaps strung up in his corrugated garage. A family-owned business. They live across the street from his scrapyard and many is the time I hear them communicating across the distance of Union Street—

they have mapped out a certain world for themselves here and any intruder would have to be pretty crazed to want to break through.

I try to see memories of Hippolyte in my dirty windows. The canal with all its ancient stink and negation is sitting out there, as is the laundry-lady. The significance of the situation, which is my life now, begs defy any definition. Who was Hippolyte? Why was she so driven within the theater? Was it just a career, adjacent to her few jobs with the modeling agency that called her into Sara's directives? Why was Sara so drawn to theater, as opposed to, say, the army? Things are never what they seem.

"You know why Joan quit the group don't ya," asked Rudy, as he pounded his way into the bar one night, his boots clanking against the bar floor then the bar stool, where he sat, right next to me.

"Oh hey," I said, not bothering to look at him. I could feel him leaning toward me. Until I finally acknowledged him.

"What's wrong?" he asked.

"Oh Rudy nothing you know I'm just."

"You know why Joan quit the group?" he persisted.

"No I do not know why Joan quit the group," I answered, listening for a reaction from him that would acknowledge I was mocking him. He kept talking.

"You know why? I know why. This," he said, slamming down a book on the bar top.

I said nothing and only briefly glanced at the book cover: *Water's Vibration: variations on a poem. Elizabeth Li-Phoung.*

"You know what that is? That's what you've been wanting to do. Look! That's why Joan left to follow her own inspiration man. Look at it I found it around the corner at some kiosk. Whattaya think?"

I rifled through it. Yes, a series of stanzas followed by stage instructions that incorporated lines and images from the stanzas.

"Whattaya think? Pretty cool huh?"

"Yeah," I said, "it's OK. So Joan quit because of it?"

"Not exactly this no but because of what's in it man. You know? But that's what you've been getting at isn't it? Wouldn't it be great to have all those cards."

"I'm not interested in the cards."

"Yeah but your poetry then. Wouldn't it be great to be able to finally put them on the stage like this?"

"I suppose," I said, sipping my bourbon and soda, then I reflected: "No. No it wouldn't be that great."

Rudy looked disappointed. "Well I thought you'd like that man," he said, getting up from his stool.

"Yeah I appreciate it," I said, trying to sound polite.

"I don't get it man here's an opportunity this book it really shows what to do you could do this and maybe we'd understand where to go."

"Maybe."

"Well suit yourself I'm gonna keep going forward I'm not long for these shenanigans. I'm auditioning for the play they got going on downstairs say you have any plays or scripts?"

"A few," I lied, all I had were notes. None of which would have been any help to anybody. "Why?"

"Well you know we actors are always looking for material. Especially if it comes from someone unknown. But you know. Good. Like you. Like what you have going here. Man I don't know how you did it but those cards were really a great idea."

"Thanks," I said, "thanks. Man. I don't have anything on me now but—"

"Naw man later not now I have my scene lined up it's something I wrote. You should read some of it it's kind of like the hands monologue. You know the scene I did the other day about the guy at the docks who—"

"Oh that yeah I kind of remember it."

"Good huh? But I got tons of stuff like that even better

than that. One day man," he said, slapping the book against the bar stool. "One day man it's gonna bust wide open. If I play my cards right I might get a night in the theater downstairs. You seen anything down there lately? Phfft! Shit man I could do that. And way better!"

"Oh I'm sure," I assented, then thought and said, "If you play your cards right. You know?"

"You think so gee thanks bud," he was genuinely saying, now tapping me on the shoulder with the book. "Well I gotta go I just wanted to show you this. You want it?"

"Oh right now I'm a little busy got a lot to read these days."

"OK well let me know man. Catch you later."

And he pounded out of the bar, presumably en route to the theater downstairs, where he was about to play his cards rightly, for a change.

—

SARA, SOON AFTER MY episode on the third floor landing, began to give me terrible signs that she had indeed known I was spying on her and Hippolite's rehearsal. From then on the door was always open and if I had wanted to climb up and steal a listen it would have been under her knowing gaze.

Soon, too, her labor over the cards, my cards, became a singular obsession. Obviously a substitute for my not being available to her in any sexual way.

"What do you mean by 'Hands picture out'?" she asked

at a subsequent group meeting.

"I think," said Rudy "we should take pictures of ourselves in various stages of rigor mortis. Someone could be hung."

"I'm talking to Hans excuse me," she very seriously said.

I had wanted someone to ask me about it. My idea, which I wrote on one of the cards and inserted into the deck we were to use at the next performance and which would allow for the young Hippolyte and myself to be alone, was to have a polaroid snapped of each of us on the roof of the theater, preferably at night with the lights of Second Avenue seen in the background. I didn't care how they would turn out. But if I was allowed to take the pictures I would be able to move ever so slowly away from the card-producing mania that was in the process of draining the vitality from our relationship. From the possibility of our relationship. I felt that if she could only see us together then the beginning of another world, so to speak, of interpretation would ensue. She was beginning to get too involved with the evident controversy of the graph paper performance and that worried and threatened my hope.

"If we can produce," I said to Sara, in answer to her pointed question regarding polaroids, "a camera during the performance vis a vis these cards then why not have a promotional shoot and use the photos. We could hand them out on the street out front the theater."

"But what you are saying is basically to use the camera during the performance," questioned Sara.

"But also as promotion," I re-began.

"You mean extra-curricular or whatever you call it. Call them exercises that would take away from the performance itself?"

"Not aesthetically no not at all!" I asserted. "We're involved with taking these cards further and this is a perfect solution! Don't you see?"

"I see it! it's really great maybe old movies," mumbled Rudy, "like old horror flicks projected on the wall while we."

"But it would expose people beforehand?" Sara questioned further.

"Well we need to have an audience don't we? I mean an audience understands visuals and that's what these cards should produce: visuals. That's not abstract or."

"We're not getting into the abstract thing any more!" cried Sara, "Honest to god here we go again. Isn't a picture as abstract as the cards if the cards are seen as abstract?"

"Not really. Most people think pictures are concrete," I concluded.

"My masks," said Sam, "those masks of light I used those—

those are like pictures or the idea was—

I mean I'm not intellectual or anything but like—

they are made from plaster which is like you know—concrete."

"Yes," I nodded, "they're like pictures but nothing is like a picture but a literal picture. Again the idea of literal versus abstract. Seems to me we've got three things here."

"I know I know," Sara blurted. "Reason and what. Reality."

"Reality," I added, "and art."

"Oh I forgot about that one! Yes theater and."

Sara shook herself into the present, afraid she had given

our bedroom téte-a-téte away, "we've all heard about those three. Richard this is what we studied in college don't you recognize?"

"Well yes—

no—

not really," he stammered.

"The class on what was it called the class on aesthetics? Well anyway here we go again getting into the philosophy!"

"I just think that if we can produce some visuals then maybe we have a chance to get deeper into the cards," I finalized, not wanting the issue to drop.

"We don't need to get any deeper than what we who we oh hell! Richard can't you talk for a while about this!"

"What Sara is trying to talk about and yes I know the class you're talking about now. And that's just the point," Richard became animated, knowing he was about to please Sara's wishes, "we ourselves are the clarity if you like the concrete to this performance. In fact the history of theater is involved with this. With this. With this attempt at stripping away the mystery of personality and concretizing our Selves. Our bodies that is."

"And this," Sara righteously concluded, "is what we talked about from the beginning. Your statements were meant to be taken—

not to be taken literally—

or literally they were on paper and that's concrete too! Oh shit. Wait. What am I trying to say here. Well it's the same as before. There are enough cards and they themselves will generate the action."

"You mean we can never change!" cried Rudy.

"No," I said, somehow now defending Sara, "our action

she means is always changing whether we have a script or not it doesn't matter we're always changing."

There was a communal silence. Maybe it was a state of utter confusion.

"I just think that to get a bigger audience pictures would help," I calmly added.

"Not enough people," responded Sara. "There might be people willing to become an audience I grant you *but* when they want to come in for free!"

"Who said." I barked.

"I'm saying *that*! And if you don't mind I mean Hans nothing against your writing I mean it's good just not for this performance!"

"I."

"There's very little to understand Hans. We have to keep the growth element of this performance series under wraps so to speak otherwise everyone in town is going to want to get in on it and then you've got to deal with commercial. The commercial thing. Commercialism. Or whatever you call it."

"Wait a second! We're never going to be commercial I just want to take polaroids of each of us up on the roof and hand them out to interested theater-goers passing by on a friday night!"

"No one," she confidently added, "is interested in theater." She was somewhat somber now. "Unfortunately very few. Especially this kind of theater."

"That's just it," I continued, "all the more reason we should."

"Hans," she said slowly, putting her arm out to me and standing, then approaching me, then slipping it around my shoulders, "have you ever stopped to think what would happen if you widened the appeal you already set with these cards? Think about it a minute."

But I couldn't think of anything. Why was Sara trying to muster an appreciation for our quick rumble in the sack months before this? The others in the group, including Hippolyte, looked at me as if I were insane, or had just been calmed out of a childish tantrum.

"It's OK Hans," said Sam. "This is difficult for all of us like—

difficult."

"It's frustrating!" growled Rudy, "it's fucking frustrating!" Then he laughed. "It's enough to make me start rethinking my own work. You know."

"We knew," said Richard, "that this would be frustrating. We have to be all of us together, however, about these performances. It's not that we're lazy or anything."

"Richard," scolded Sara.

"I don't mean lazy I just mean there is a comfort level that we've reached and to agitate more than the objective agitation that is here already."

"Richard," said Sara. "What Richard is trying to say is that we're on course and we should do another performance with these cards the final version of them and then try to even eliminate others. Yes we'll take some more out too and."

"And then who knows," concluded Richard, "what will happen. It's going to be exciting."

"Very exciting," assured Sara.

All I wanted, I thought, was to take a picture, a polaroid, one of those that shoots out the front of the camera 6 seconds after the flash goes off. Was that so hard to understand?

What would be so difficult, even "wrong" about having each of the performers up to the roof, one at a time, to take a picture of each, alone? If I played it correctly I had wanted to work it so that I would run into Hippolyte when none of the others were around and get her to pose. One nightly session, that's all I was after. With Second Avenue completely in the background. The beginning of perspective!

As selfish as the others, I was, and there was no way out of that dynamic anymore.

Once we were in position on the roof and Hippolyte was flexing her individual talents for the camera, I thought, all the rest would be in the out-coming polaroid. I was trying to capture her essence on film, and, with the help of the Polaroid Corporation, there would be no essential time lost from performance moment to eternal snap-shot moment. Was it simply now just another of my own *thoughts* impinging on little else than more *thought*? Was there even a future?

And once I had the photograph in front of her, and we both there to witness its 60 seconds of developing fame, the graph paper performance would be history. A new momentum would build within the cards as they made their way into Polaroid pictures. Eventually, all the performance would consist of would be polaroids, plastered, say, in the lobby of the theater. Or better yet in the bar. I hadn't quite thought what would keep Hippolyte interested in the pictures. I only hoped the tension and interest in the cards would spill out into photos and while the entire scope of the graph paper performance shifted and changed, it would allow me a time and a place for my proposal.

Maybe not a proposal of marriage, that was too steep. I just wanted to have sex with the young Hippolyte. It was obviously the right time for it. What with her in heat and myself the only stud within a proximate zone of real possibility (except her boyfriend, but then again, who knows what he was getting from Hippolyte). I'd be the prize winner. After that, the performance group could go to hell. The entire adventure would no doubt give us something to do, together, and, most importantly, alone. Sensing this, Sara must have known, even from the slight direction the card possessed, that I was prepared to go any distance to get at Hippolyte. And beyond that, any distance to direct interest within the theater itself, possibly even taking her position as co-director with Richard, his money and whatever else that might be able to accomplish within the building's dynamics.

Being a hot commodity lends itself to no discrepancy, even in art, where an alternative viewpoint seems at first to be always welcomed. But not through the likes of Sara—

she knew, and no doubt Richard was made the wiser as to my ultimate design. The flaw had been made known to me. My body flared into a kind of nervous fire and I cursed myself for having telegraphed too much of my general program too soon. Oh those cards!

Now I had to camouflage my purpose even more—

the water bucket became merely a water bucket, the sticks only wooden sticks, the Rope rope, the Dictionary merely a large unwieldy object among others. I was trapped in the graph paper performance once again. Perhaps forever! And this was *the* design then from the first!

The duct tape was merely tape, for instance, a sort of tape *qua* tape. I tried to attract myself to all the objects involved. Maybe, I thought, they would yield some tangible reflection of Hippolyte with which I could stage another flight toward her bones.

—

I SPENT HOURS, days, ripping off thin pieces of duct tape trying to get them to become something *more* than duct tape.

I needed to know its other properties. A metaphysical endeavor, of course, but with the added appeal and rigor of the young Hippolyte as its grounding—

> As you rip a piece of duct tape, try to place it over your mouth at the same time, or roughly the same time as the end of the sound the rip makes.
>
> Roll the duct tape on the floor and then roll it on the wall, pressing hard in order to transfer any dust and dirt that had accumulated. Trace your name in the transfer.
>
> Pour a small quantity of water on the floor from the bucket. Rip off a small piece of duct tape and adhere it to the water. Then announce: "The end is near!"
>
> Tape two pieces of duct tape to your wrists so that they are braceletted.

Pull off a long piece of duct tape and secure it to the wall. Grab someone from the audience and stand them up against it, facing it. Then clap hands.

Wind the duct tape from inside your palm attaching it as you unwind it up the arm and spiraling it around until you reach your pit. Rip it. Cry out in agony.

—

"O Christ! hare comes the dahll now. The preeshuss dahll," said Monny, the Yugoslavian performance artist, as we sat at the bar, beginning another round.

Monny had performed her pieces in the theater during the monthly showcase of talent. Her self-written performance revealed for me the ultimate meaning of the Stage:

When the curtain came up, Monny was sitting in a bathtub festooned with big papier maché fish and other seaweed-type hangings and drapings. Not only was she in the bathtub, but there was actual water in it, with bubbles surrounding the naked, bare-breasted Balkan.

The light was a kind of subdued and reddish glow. At first, the audience began to realize she was indeed naked, and those were indeed her breasts hanging from under her chin at center stage. But then their murmur subsided. Little else emitted from them while Monny modeled her breasts in the bathtub under a nocturnal bulb. There was a slow and muted music, unrecognizable, in the background; as the half hour of her performance drew to a close, I sat looking around for some sign of discomfort or annoyance from any audience member. None was forthcoming; her breasts had subdued the need for entertainment, for any change in atmosphere whatsoever. It was, finally, as if all relation between presentation of Stage to what was on that stage had been swallowed by Monny's breasts. There would never be any interpretation of event anymore—

Bells toned in my subconscious—

I felt it was the end, not only of the Stage, but of a stage in the development of mankind that had produced such social encounter in the first place. It was, finally, as if all metaphoric distance had been reduced, and then not just reduced, but furthered into a realm where annihilation became the over-belly, the actual breasts from which the infant mind of spectators now sucked for nourishment. And wre fulfilled! Agh!

That performance left me both sickened and elated. It was as if Professor Mickelmann's lectures and disguises had never mattered. Further—

it was as if nothing had ever mattered. Nothing that *ever was* did not matter! A simple pair of bare breasts under a tungsten glow had wiped out the entire plane of consciousness that once supposedly possessed me, others, all, together or sequestered. The perspective went on and on into an endless distance of collective being—

Now we were engaged in some sort of meaningless téte-a-téte at the theater bar. Monny's Yugoslavian friends began to wander in and she said hello to each of them. They were all men, and there they sat, at the far end, laughing and drinking vodka and toasting Monny whenever she turned to acknowledge them. I was participating in some age-old Eastern European traditional theater-cum-whorehouse setting. Time was indeed moving backward.

One of the men, a certain Dushbik, approached.

"Monny," he said, touching one of her arms that were sprawled over the wooden bar, and motioning silently with his puckered lips toward me.

"Oh him dats Hkans."

"You sleeping there?" he asked.

"No no no darling heess writer. You know like you big dumb shithead. His like you."

"How come we never sleep Monny?"

"Not you darling. Not wiss anyone darling I'm sorry."

Dushbik held out his paw, "Dushbik's my name. I want to talk at you a minute. Hok?"

"Me?" I said, half-laughing, noticing Monny's eyes glitter and roll.

And Dushbik nestled in between Monny and my own hunched and drinking body. He put his arm around my shoulders and began his speech.

"You know I too have play. It's done yes yes complete already. You want see?"

"You're kidding right?" I asked.

"No no no not kidding you man. Why'ss everone always kidding in this country? Huh?"

"I don't know Dush."

"Dushbik Dushbik pronunce as it come. Doosh-bik. I will tell you why. Because nothing real here. I know! It's same in my country now too. Nothing'ss real. But be."

"Before what. In the hills with Tito's rebels?"

"Monny! Dis guy good. Yes! Tito man. How you know play I writing."

"I told you *he* wass *you*," slurred Monny, shifting, swinging her hip out toward the room.

"No shit sherlock. You know Americans know shit Hkans. Nothing. No thing man. Think nothing. I nothing come from nothing nothing never seen heard any ffucking thing man. You understand?"

"I think so. You mean why are we."

"Is not dat only no English. Is not only not very good English I speak but also what iss diss. What's up wiss," and he pursed his lips, and cocked and re-cocked his head in the direction of the crowded bar, his hair flying back and seemingly hitting Monny who, at least threatened by the possibility of Dushbik's hair, moved a step to her left. Dushbik's lips gave into a purse with which he then condemned all by rudely smacking.

I turned and saw all the sedentary yet gay clientele busily chirping and barking and flapping their hands in purposeful conversation.

"You know what diss mean?"

"Not really. It's possibly that no one understands what you're talking about or perhaps some other such preocupation with whatever they might be."

"I will tell you. My play. Listen to my play. It is Tito. Entitled 'Tito, Man of People.' I know is stupid even for me even for my country. I would not do kind of play but I am here."

"You're here."

"You know I am in American. Now I ffucking get the thing of what it is. Now. You see?"

"Yeah well join the."

"You see? Tito's special. Now I pay too much ffucking rent man. Now I have shovel shit into basement uptown. You know what means man? He treat us wiss respect. I want play to him done and this make sense. No movie. Ah maybe movie. Not now. First diss play."

"The play's the thing," I said.

"Yah you hear diss man Monny he said playss da thing. I told you diss."

"Shagspeare stupit asshole ffucking asshole doan you know nothing of Shagspeare? Shit! Stupit!" Monny spit out, then took a sip from her shot glass.

"No," said Dushbik haughtily, replanting his feet, hooking his thumbs in his belt. "Not me: Dushbik. This me Hkans. You see? I stand and begin."

"Go ahead already," I said, not really meaning for him to begin his dramatic piece. I was prompting him to leave, I thought, in my inebriated state.

"We see Tito'ss tomb. All people join round sad. But some know and leave. This a cue and curtain come down again. You understand?"

I thought: what a complete idiot. Then I thought: what a great idea! It's just what the theater needs, something so completely out of step with the time and place of its existence. It could be stylized and rendered as a unique piece of avant garde art! Yes, terrific. More Bourbon!

"You understand Hkans the curtain? Down up den'ss all back to pass history."

"*You stupit ffuck*," Monny whispered, turning to me,"You haf not to listen. He'ss this all the time."

"Monny man I swear you need sleep. You haven't touch

man really? You might die wiss tits on stage but nowhere it goes it doesn't. You understand," Dushbik said to me, cocking his head and pursing his lips, "You understand diss titss?"

"I see them. I mean I saw them," I stuttered, glancing at Monny, her dark eyes saddened yet completely drinking in the attention, imploring me to put an end to this filial absurdity. And yet why would she want it to end? Monny was a paradox. Maybe Dushbik was right: she needed a swift kick in her privates to wake her up? I couldn't believe I was thinking that of this poor young woman who wanted desperately to be taken as a Woman. Dushbik seemed to sense his triumph over Monny and her idea of the stage and continued with 'Tito, Man of People.'

"It is not but mountains scenes and'ss always snow. I sought a names for diss might say: 'Tito, Snow Comrade' but diss not good becaused America and snow. You know," he put his finger to his nose and sniffed heavily. I thought he was trying to swallow some nasal snot, but no, he meant to imply cocaine abuse.

"So Comrade Tito is code name from west but he is good man so lets name go out over mountains we see as shifting to hide—

how to say hiding way? But you know I see you know what hiding way is you are very smart Hkans. Not," he cocked his head and pursed his lips to the crowded bar, "not dis ffucking shits. Langwich. Huh! What ffucking shit. Let me buy you drink Hkans."

"Call me comrade," I said, perking up.

"Ha Monny you hear dis man! Comrade Hk." But he realized Monny had drifted farther down the bar and taken a seat with her back to us.

"Shit Monny," he said, sticking thumb to his lower lip and flicking it. "What ffucking shit dis people now. You know Hkans Serbian Slovene difference?" And he pointed toward Monny.

"Johnny," I said, "please another bourbon and soda."

"Here I pay," said Dushbik, searching through his pockets. If he finds some money, I thought, I'll believe he actually does have a job.

He produced a fifty dollar bill. Well, I thought, he actually does have a job, and a nice one at that. Or he gets payed in cash? It can't be that nice of a job then. Shovelling coal? They still do that?

"Diss on me I will have straight shot too thank you bartend." Dushbik hurled the shot back and smacked his lips. "Ha! Good great shit Hkans!"

"So what happened to Tito?" I asked, feeling assured I'd find another drink in his red peregrinations somewhere.

"He comes President."

"Yes I know that! The play what happens in your play?"

"You real want to know? Diss guy I love diss Hkans!" cried Dushbik, then resting his long arm over my shoulder. "Diss happen. Second Act First Scene everbody all over was Yugoslavia comes Slavic and all others peoples. Great Hah!"

"But how do you show this?" I asked. I was thinking how could this be staged other than the way true red propoganda had always been presented: flying red flags and choruses of dance troupes all dressed in peasant garb swarming in choreographed triumph. "They unite you mean?"

"Unite States give me ffucking break. So we have unite also all peoples. Everyone fights Nazi sympathetic and resist

I show diss then what could be done. I show Tito in his center of country treating ever peoples decent. You understand Hkans? Tito treat us like people not—"

he cocked his head and let out the pursed-lip curse to the rest of the clientele, "not like diss shit. Money what's diss money? Everbody man make money and nothing else no other thing diss peoples think. Show them my play Hkans you be great here."

"I don't know what clout I have here Dushbik you'd have to organize a reading and audition if you."

"No. You not understanding me. I put play on here and maybe you—"

"You mean I'd *direct* the piece?"

"What piece diss whole play maybe two hour long!"

"I mean it's not that easy you'd have to."

"Listen diss guy I give you play you turn it off? Give me ffucking break big guy. Look. You are American I am stupid ffucking alien yes I am like outer space to diss peoples. You are not. OK?" Dushbik shook me by the shoulders and stared blazingly into my eyes.

Monny broke in with another shot which she handed to each of us and leaned over Dushbik to get the third off the bar.

"Toast!" she inculcated, "Skoal!" and we threw them back.

"Hkans," she said, wiping the side of her chin, "doan listen this stupit ffucker. My whole country is talking this way now."

"And what," interjected Dushbik, "so ffucking wrong. Ever back home is no good so now what are doing."

"We doan have to fight Dushbik. This is America land of

free home of the brave you've not heard?"

"I hear nothing but shit Monny. You have problem wiss no man to sleep and so you think you have liberated all diss peoples but shit man."

"Sex has nussing to do wiss it you stupit asshole!"

"Not titss diss theater neither does." And Dushbik pursed his lips in defiance.

"You," laughed Monny, "doan get it do you."

I was just about to calm Monny down when in walked the young Hippolyte, softly, like a doe afraid of traps that might have been set in the wilds of our inebriated red room. I pretended not to see her, but I could, reflected off the big glass behind the bar. Dushbik and Monny realized I wasn't attending to their tirade and so they stopped.

Hippolyte paused and demurely made her way to my side. Dushbik slunk off to join the Balkan contingency at the other end of the long wooden bar, proclaiming to them in a loud voice that the end of all artistic movements had ground to a halt and that every little girl with tits "real live ffucking ass man" should suck his—

"O Christ!" sang Monny again under her breath. Then, smiling, "Howss reheerssals going?"

Hippolyte nodded. Then giggled.

"Can I get you something Hipp?" Johnny asked from behind the bar, having just set down another case of something, his second-hand vest beginning to stain under the arms.

Monny seemed to notice his perspiration and asked, "Whenss da vucking hair conditioner?"

Hippolyte blushed and ordered a coca cola. I had suddenly become lucky, it seemed. Hippolyte searched the crowd of people at the tables and packed along the bar, looking, no doubt, for Sara, her mentor.

But she was nowhere to be found. In fact, *I* hadn't seen her in a while. I had come into the bar after work this night and was actually looking forward to not running into anyone, neither Richard, Sara, and I especially didn't expect to see Hippolyte.

"What kind namess this Hippleet this is what?" asked Monny, leaning over to speak through me toward Hippolyte, her slight Serbian mustache suddenly under my focus.

"Excuse me?" Hippolyte said, cupping her ear against the room's noise.

"Whatss this nashnlty?"

"Oh I don't know," said Hippolyte. She glanced at me as I took another sip, beginning to tremble a bit.

Monny looked away, then turned and excused herself in order to join her Yugoslavian comrades at the other end of the bar. They all began to hoot and holler. Apparently they really loved one another and only argued out of some vague, as-yet-unformed sense of counter-purpose. Soon she was holding her breasts or her hips in comely shows of native force. The bearded Yugoslavians laughed and drank and toasted her name over and over as the night wore on.

I sighed. Then Hippolyte sighed, and giggled, and sipped her coca cola.

"Are you married?" she suddenly asked.

"What! God no of course not. Why?"

"I really like your cards—
those cards you've been writing—
they're very—"

I held my breath while she looked for the right thing to say—
"they're very—
expressive."
Exhale. "Yes?"
"Not just that. They are—how long have you been writing?" she asked.
"Since school," I said. Her precious skull, those questions, intoxicating.
"Oh what school?"
"Actually Seminary. Divinity School," I said.
"Seminary? You mean to become a."
"A pastor I guess," I mumbled, suddenly realizing I hadn't thought about it in a while.
"Why. Why did you want," she began.
"Want to become a pastor? I don't know." Let's just get it out, I was beginning to realize, in the open, feels good, feels real good.
"Did you make any friends there?" she continued.
"Friends?" Come to think of it, I hadn't really gotten to know anybody there except Mickelmann, and that was really only a few conversations during the course of the school term. The other students never seemed to appeal to my drive, I guess, and, sensing that drive, stayed as far from me as heaven is from hell, or Hippolyte from my unmentionables.
She smiled, blushed, and giggled again, taking another sip of coca cola. "Come with me?"
"What?"
"Come upstairs with me," she said, looking into my eyes. This was more than I had ever expected. I jumped off

my stool and followed her out the bar.

"What I meant," she said as I followed ever so closely from behind, watching her attempt the staircase, "are you gay? It's nothing. Really," she said as we mounted the third-floor landing, "I was just wondering because don't priests have sex with little boys and all that?"

"Not the kind I was with!"

She opened the door to the performance area and it was, thankfully, empty, and began twirling and walking, kind of half-dancing and walking at the same time.

"You see," she said, "when we make our way down the runway we have to be very careful."

Seeing that I didn't understand, she took me by the arm. I swooned, to say the least, my heart racing faster than it had ever raced, even hopped up on alcohol, and walked with me to the end of the room and back toward the center.

"And that's it!" she gladly announced, her brown-black hair magnificent in the stale light of the third floor, the suffocating third floor, where performance group meeting after meeting had been conferenced, until, finally, here we were, the only two that really mattered.

"Now do we say our vows?" I asked, beginning to get the trembles again, as I always did when the center drew close.

"Oh! vows—

well—

I suppose we do say vows," her mocking tone, very thoughtful, very absolutely to the point. "Why didn't you become a priest?" she continued, from before, as she made her way to the side room, the same room I had tried to enter while she was rehearsing weeks before. I should have simply bust the door down. Why the hell didn't I think of that then!

"A *pastor*. Well I couldn't stomach it," I blurted, telling the truth.

"Oh darn," Hippolyte said from behind the wall, "and it was going to be such a perfect match!"

"What was? What was *going to be*?" I asked, rushing to the side room.

"This!" and she held up a costume, "it shrank!"

She was asking me to look at her body, to actually examine it. I reached over and touched the fabric.

"But do you think anyone will notice?"

She laughed and dropped the costume among the clothes and other crap in the side room. Approaching me she held out her hand and I froze, but trembling as her fingers, her burnt and dark (now that they were nearer my eyes) fingers lightly landed on my forehead. She palpated my temples as I turned to quivering gelatin, the wind in my lungs deflating, exhaling.

—

MICKELMANN WAS STILL READING and interpreting from Copleston. The girl in front of me picking away at the sore at the back of her head, a little pus and fresh blood glistening there. She was obsessed with the scab and wouldn't leave it alone. Every few seconds she'd pick away at it again.

"Point 7 then class ends the discussion regarding Kierkegaard and the entire concept of faith versus a metaphysical invasion of that faith. What you want to keep in mind almost first and foremost is that Kierkegaard was a

Danish Lutheran and really wants to renew any discussion of religion and existence in light of the origin of protestant movements. To that end and I might as well bring in the 39 articles as an aside as a matter of fact let me go all the way to the beginning which I should have done before we started the selections from Kierkegaard. But I wanted you to understand how this skepsis relating to religion and existence becomes the kind of source for later existentialist thought which we will get into in a future term."

My ears pricked up at what Mickelmann was saying, extemporizing on the curriculum.

"Now when you apply the samples from the texts of Kierkegaard's thought to the 7 points gone over in Copleston you will be armed with a proper tension as regards the foundation of the Anglican church. What I'm about to show you. What I should have read to you before." Mickelmann reached into his leather valise at the far end of his desk and rifled through some papers inside. "It's in here somewhere I should have like I said before I should have shown this before we even started—"

I raised my hand and grunted, loudly. Mickelmann turned to see me then back again to his valise papers. "I don't suppose you have something to comment on Hans what I'm about to read I know you have no idea because you've not taken this course before have you?"

"I was just reminded of."

"Reminded of what? What could it be Hans?"

I hesitated. I knew exactly what I wanted to add to his silly digression.

"Here it is," Mickelmann stated, holding the paper aloft. "These are the core foundations to the Episcopalian church.

I thought that since we are on the source of at least a kind of thread to modern existentialism divorced from."

"Ah!" I blurted. But Mickelmann continued.

"You'll notice the major players," he chuckled a bit, "in this list the particles of."

"Bones!" I yelled out. The class turned to me as Micklemann stopped.

"Never mind our comedic friend there let me just read to you the 39 articles that form the."

"Taste-buds!" I hollered.

"These 39 articles form the essence as it were of christian faith of theology as a whole and you'll notice in them the."

"Wood poles matter staves clavicle number!" My eyes were winced shut as I concentrated on bringing the language forth.

"I'm not going to pay any attention Hans you're not going to ruin another class I'm not going to break into answering questions that take us away from the."

"Manic depressive!"

Mickelmann raised his voice, reading from the list: "Article one Of Faith in the Holy Trinity. Article two Of the Word or Son of God which was made very Man. Article three."

"These weeks. Seminal campaigns. Edicts and flags flasks condoms reeling!"

Discerning that I was not going to stop my interruptions Mickelmann began to speed up his recitation of the list: "Of the going down of Christ into Hell. Of the Resurrection of Christ. Of the Holy Ghost. Of the Sufficiency of the Holy Scriptures for Salvation Of the Old Testament (and I'll have you read back to me the descriptions of each of these class next time we meet!) Of the Creed."

"Gulls and wishes! Drank dank funeral word blue toe gun march!"

"Please Hans that's enough now I'm."

"Sheep bleep!" The class then laughed and finally it seemed like I had gotten through to them.

"Pay no attention to him. If I am to kick him out of this class then that will be the end of the class! Everyone focus now on the rest of the list," Mickelmann cautioned all, and at the same time daring me to go deeper, to go further, somehow enabling his list recital with my own. I was sure that I would have been asked to end, to exit, to leave the class, but here he was becoming all the more exuberant about his list: "Of Original or Birth-Sin Free-Will Justification of Man Good Works."

"Baby bath works!"

Laughter. Now the project was fun, now it was all about having fun. Mickelmann now had sanctioned nothing more than a game. I concentrated harder: "foreplay ding dongs!"

"Works before Justification Works of Supererogation Christ alone without Sin Sin after Baptism Predestination and Election."

"Sneeze dance!"

"Come on Hans you can do better than that Obtaining eternal Salvation only by the Name of Christ Of the Church Of the Authority of the Church the Authority of General Councils Of Purgatory Ministering in the Congregation Of Speaking in the Congregation in such a Tongue as the people understandeth."

"Blah!"

Laughter.

"Of the Sacraments. Of the Unworthiness of the Ministers which hinders not the effect of the Sacraments. Article 27 Of Baptism. Article 28 The Lord's Supper. Article 29 Of the Wicked which eat not the Body of Christ in the use of the Lord's Supper."

"Stick it needle eye."

"Of both Kinds One Oblation of Christ finished upon the Cross The Marriage of Priests Of excommunicate Persons how they are to be avoided Traditions of the Church Homilies Consecration of Bishops and Ministers."

I kept silent. The classroom held their collective breath. Mickelmann continued: "Of the Power of the Civil Magistrates. Article 38 Christian Men's Goods which are not common."

I continued to sink into silence. Mickelmann looked up from his papers, then concluded, triumphantly: "Article 39 A Christian Man's Oath!"

—

"COME ON LET'S GET OUT OF HERE!" Hippolyte giggled and tugged on my arm with her brown and slender fingers.

We were out on the landing when she turned to me. "*But do you think anyone will notice? Honestly you're taken with yourself aren't you?*"

I blushed. We made our way back down the old staircase. Too soon!

"Taken? Well actually I'm." But I couldn't get the words out, couldn't tell her I was taken with *her*. How does one speak when given free access to the center of the world?

I stopped, as we entered the second floor bar again. Hippolyte was immediately met by her boyfriend who had been sitting at my bar stool. What was he thinking, seeing us tumble into the crowded bar: two more actors vying for the stage?

—

BALANCE ONE OF THE STICKS AGAINST THE OTHER.

I chose this card in the middle of a later performance.

That is, there were the four of us, Hippolyte, Sara, Richard, and myself. There were two stacks of cards (watered down by Richard and Sara at this point, but not totally. In fact, what gave the performance any life whatsoever was the thin thread of hope both Hippolyte and I were nurturing.) Two stacks, and from each, wherever one happened to find himself in the performance area on the third floor of the theater—

in front of, if I remember correctly, about a dozen people, including Hippolyte's boyfriend and other assorted friends of the bar, all of them part-time drinkers—

one would choose a card and follow the instructions determining what action to conduct. No effort was to be made in terms of a coordinated structuring of purpose or design (as Richard and Sara were beginning to pronounce it) by any of us. In other words, no contact. At first it was provisional contact, latent, but more and more it became, through their zeal to undermine my new cards and my evident attraction for Hippolyte, my evident plan of seduction, that is—

a honing of these provisions toward a nothingness that eventually collapsed the entire graph paper performance.

But on this night in front of the dozen or so friends, Hippolyte and I lit into one another. Attempting to balance the sticks in an obviously impossible way at least in my interpretation—

an interpretation, furthermore, brought about by the willingness with which I was pursuing Hippolyte.

I sat in the path the young girl had been using to make her way toward the stack of cards. She immediately picked up my signal, I felt, and as she pulled the white card from the stack at the side of the performance area, turned to me, holding it over her mouth, her eyes glittering in a dense brown-black jungle of awakening desire. I, receiving those eyes, was spending an undue amount of time balancing two thin sticks tip to tip.

There were at this point contending cards within the stacks, placed there by who knows whom. Hippolyte was anxious to interpret the card she held in front of her face and for some time I was not sure if she wasn't waiting for me to complete my little escapade, then join her on the dance floor. My face was beginning to heat and the summer (even though the room had a small air conditioner running) was warming.

Soon, however, Hippolyte joined me, leaning over to my place on the floor and finally sitting with me. The entire action caused my spleen to emanate and rise through me never to return. Her hands, whose finely boned and warmly tanned skin held out to the thin sticks, began to slowly straighten their oppositions one by one as she collected them for her directive.

Obviously, she had struck upon a card that contained a command utilizing the same sticks.

My mouth had gone dry in the time it took for her to collect the sticks from me and the purposeful slowness and deliberate eye contact she maintained lifted us, I'm quite sure, in the minds of the audience, to the purpose of the entire hour-long performance.

Throw the sticks onto the floor.

Hippolyte's slow movement seemed to tip my own sense of purpose for the performance and I began to muster feelings and motions of body that I wouldn't call an actor's, they were dwelling in a place of pre-meditation, a place of deepest being.

The slowness of her delivery of those two thin sticks to the dirty performance floor with a kind of hidden ability to portray many dynamic facial and bodily expressions as if by accident, was inspiring. I was keeping the flame of love alive for her. I allowed myself to react, not as if I were continuing to move in slow motion with my entire being throughout the duration of some "time," but *toward* the slowness of cognizance, the perception and balance itself that only she and I would know, and that hopefully a few people in the audience were tuning into.

In this way we began to encode all movement.

Or rather, it was Hippolyte who began to encode the movement from the pinnacle of her acting abilities (not acting but genuine displays of her body's armature from the depths of space itself).

I flamed even more. And the more I flamed, the larger my ability to adapt to anything, whether in the cards or inside the accidental spaces of the floor.

What was the significance of this flame? That was all I really wanted to know. Nothing from Richard or Sara, the directors of the graph paper performance, ever came into play as regards this living flame. Unlike Rudy and the others who had left the group (and who were no doubt correct in their attitude toward a stifling creative process) I found I needed no creative process, that the entire area assigned to so-called creative process was utter bunk. Without this flame I now utilized, what else was there? It consumed all action and all thought, even its own codification of identity, by its existence.

The flame rose from my scrotum to my chest and then left and made the rounds with the objects and people of the room and then upward. I couldn't keep it inside anymore. It had to leave. But it would return within a few maneuvers and take its place in my scrotum once again. Looking over at Hippolyte I felt she knew the flame had returned for she carried a card across the room proclaiming in a loud and purling yet very personal tongue some nonsense *I* had written.

—

BE IT NOTED that it was the last time that card would circulate through the stack. After this performance Richard and Sara purposely pointed to me demanding I explain what it meant. But I could not, having just recently found out what it meant. And so, on grounds of insufficient proof, I suppose, it was missing from the next performance.

In its place was the following:

> Stand silent for one minute while waving your left leg.

But this is what it originally said:

> Stand forth you tides of sun-drenched and dilapidated wood where in the glorious final assault of summer heat we'll feel the trembling isolation of the thatched place fall to bits toward cool radiance a river flowing down to the countryside which distance awaits with turpitude an excellent irrigation system.

I know this was replaced by the preceding because when I arrived at Richard and Sara's office on the fourth floor the following weekend with new cards, Richard handed me cards he had written. He also pointed to a pile of out-takes. I quickly rifled through them and, of course, half expecting to find the quoted one among them, was not surprised when I did. Quickly, Sara began to explain:

"That was not very good at all you see Hans you are a very gifted *writer* nothing against your *writing at all* but this did *not* at all have anything to do with the *rest* of the performance and when Hippolyte began to read it I just had to cringe."

"Why was that?" I asked.

"What does it mean! Isn't there enough of that kind of poetry floating around these days?" she asked, seeming to possess, also, an extensive knowledge of American Poetry.

"But the point is isn't the entire performance to lend itself to," I began but was quickly cut off by Richard—

"Whatever happens? Yes but what is developing is a."

"Completely unfocused event and people are getting bored because they know if they've been," Sara cut in, "to one of the graph paper performances before of course but also there needs to be a tension some *lengthening*."

"I've heard you say this before," I stated, "and I don't quite know what you mean I mean I think the length and duration of the piece is fine no matter how it turns out some people's memories will just have to you know not be taken into consideration. And that's not abstract that's concrete that's real and that's what we're."

"You mean the audience?" asked Richard.

"Of course he means the audience!" sniped Sara, "but that is neither here nor there because there isn't any focus you understand? So I say *length* and *tension* and you say *abstract* and *concrete*. I use theater terms and you use oh I don't know philosophy or whatever. This is *theater* Hans. This card for instance all of them actually in this pile have nothing to do with a *lengthening* of any of the activities that we have done or are doing."

"You see Hans the thing is," began Richard, "the most we can expect an audience to understand and play on—

of course we'd play on what they are about—"

"IT HAS NOTHING TO DO WITH THE AUDIENCE RICHARD IT HAS TO DO WITH THESE CARDS!" Sara shouted, slamming them down on the desk and walking out of the office.

"She gets this way sometimes," said Richard.

"Yes I've noticed," I flatly asserted.

"But I've replaced those with these and I think you'll like them. We're not against your writing not trying to undermine any of what you're doing. After all we came up with this idea together and I wouldn't want to send it in any direction that'd take away from what each of us has to give to it."

"Why don't we just take all the words out of the cards?" I asked, totally surrendering to the absurdity, the absolute tyranny of the whole project.

Richard paused, seriously reflecting, "No," he added, "we need *some* words. Others are out of the question though."

"That's just out and out censorship isn't it?" I asked.

"No. Censorship is political. This is art. Or as Sara correctly said: *theater*."

"What if I were to turn political then?"

"What do you mean," Richard asked, very seriously his small stature suddenly bloody and erect, "you would turn the cards all of them into a political act or individual cards?"

"Either way," I quickly said.

"It has to be one or the other. Make a choice. Maybe you're on to something."

"I'm not on to anything!" I finally made it known. "Except. I mean except for what I'm on to."

"Is it political?" he asked.

"Is what political?"

"What you're on to," Richard prodded.

"God I hope not."

Of course he (they) were taking away from the graph paper performance. They were adding graph and division instead of inducing performance. They were forcing a kind of deduction to take place from the impossibility, the mathematical nature of the graph, instead of inducing it to create. If we were truly conducting an experiment I'd be down on Hippolyte already and wildly pursuing her with every fiber of my being. It's called creation.

Instead I was in the midst of several realizations swimming in the factual waters of social correspondence. Deep down I thought the cards would, no matter, represent for me ultimate cogito, a Cartesian ego that would transfer *all* my desires previously aligned with theology out into the new-new world, theater, literature, and fate—

in short, I didn't care what happened on the third floor because I knew I'd be able to resurrect its essence within future writings. Somehow. Always. Somewhere. In the *next*. Nothing, ultimately, is ever lost forever. Realization would always have a place within the cogito, within writing in general, and, specifically, my involvement with literature. But this was to deny the fundamental reason for their replacing one card and sacrificing others with it, to make it look like it wasn't the only troubled spot in the series of performances—

that a few only a very few people were able to witness.

They denied the true essence of the cards: Hippolyte. They so rigidly adhered to the sense of the graph, as if they were towing around a line of official artistic-scientific hocum handed down from the Almighty himself. Richard and Sara had many opportunities to enlighten the graph's projection onto a performance area but they chose to remain ignorant to those opportunities, as if always beginning at the literal beginning again and again and again.

I shuffled through the cards Richard and Sara had written:

> Quickly measure the length of the room by using two bricks. Move them end to end and count them off. From wall to wall.
>
> Lean against a wall for fifteen seconds.
>
> Give a bottle to an audience member.
>
> Stand in front of the window and clap your hands in front of your mouth three times. Repeat several times. Then walk straight into the middle of everyone's performance area. Choose another card.
>
> Put your hand on the wall and hum for 30 seconds.
>
> Slowly pour water into the bucket from a full bucket stopping several times to lengthen the amount of time you are doing it.

These are the others, my own, that they had removed:

Build a wall with two bricks. Hook hands around waist and thrust forward, away from the audience, an imaginary rope the bricks are hanging from.

Throw the sticks from behind your back and then walk forward and take a right, then a left, then another right. Twirl on both feet 360 degrees and walk further away from the audience until you are in a corner of the room warming your hands.

Put your hand in the water and take it out then go to the window. Write your name in the glass. Stand back and blow. Repeat several more times then lick all the fingers on your right hand.

Shake your belly. While shaking, try to find your belly in the space before you as if it were many times larger than it really is. Keep shaking with the imaginary belly as if it is growing. Walk out of the room with an impossibly big belly too big for the doorway.

Roll your pant legs up (or shirt sleeve if you have no pants) and walk to the four directions of the room at least once.

What prompted these changes were Richard's and Sara's lack of understanding in terms of what *was* accomplished in the most recent performance. Was it my heightened awareness, a sexual understanding, that only Hippolyte and I had known? Was there always to be an "underside" to all event in which I'd remember Hippolyte and from thence always see the moment of existence taking root? Had Hippolyte realized this was to be my fate and so betrayed me with a slight smile and the unbounded joy of a sexual directive within the cards' activities? Were we born to know each only in *this* way?

No doubt a combination of these factors contributed to Richard and Sara's continued editing of the cards, somehow having tacitly communicated to each other the evident deliberation and new direction the graph paper performances were taking. Within my person as supposedly communicated through 5 x 7 notecards. But I was not a notecard. I was a living breathing human being.

—

After my day with Richard and Sara, and quite by accident I suppose, Sara cornered me on the literal corner of 4th Street and 2nd Avenue:

"Hans I want to talk with you about your cards I have an idea and I think we both know what that means?" her voice rose, closing in on me so I would feel the difference in our sizes: she was at least 6 inches taller than me.

"You mean," I smiled, affable once again, eager to end whatever had begun once again, "you think something happened in the per."

"Not that no it's some intimate though thing if you know what I mean I think we have to talk." She started backing off, suddenly very springy and bouncy and happy-go-lucky. But awkwardly so, as if such joy were rare for her. "See me tonight at the apartment I."

"Apartment! But won't."

"He's gone for the next day or two back to his family you know I think we can," she raised her voice now that she was about twenty paces away, heading back to the theater presumably, "I think we can work something out!"

"OK OK you want me to bring anything?"

But she had turned and was in full stride.

Let me say at this point that I thought about what might be the repercussion of another night with Sara. I mean I really tried to focus on it, I really tried to find an excuse—

I was working late, for instance, I could use that. I was tied up in traffic, stuck on the subway, who wouldn't believe that? But every way I twisted it I couldn't come up with enough. That is to say, I knew Sara would use this to edit my cards even further, thus spoiling any opportunity I might have to win over the young Hippolyte.

At any rate I showed up at Sara's and Richard's apartment. How had she known I had the night off? I rang the bell downstairs and a dog started barking from one of the windows upstairs. Sara's head appeared from the third story.

"Here," she yelled, "take these and let yourself in!" And down came a small, thin set of two keys. The slight breeze seemed to carry them over the basement apartment's front door instead of the intended recipient, me, standing in the middle of the front stoop. I had to lunge to catch them. The keys were so light they almost slipped through my fingers and down into the basement apartment's door sill, which would have been a difficult thing to explain to Sara as she would have had to come all the way down to the basement and wake up the neighbor and ask if he could get her keys out of his door sill. I might have said something like:

"Your keys were too light and the wind seemed to just carry them away." But that wouldn't do because I could hear Sara begin a head of steam and not let up:

"You fucking twerp I threw a lousy set of keys down a few story's can't you do one physical fucking act right for a change? No wonder I had to work so hard to please myself when we were doing it!"

But like I said I caught the keys and everything was OK. Kind of OK. Sara opened the door to her apartment and was half-clad, sourly smiling, her finger up to her lips signalling I was to be quiet upon entering the apartment.

"Is he," I whispered, "here?"

She quickly padded on bare feet over to the small kitchenette to pour me a glass of wine. But I thought she did nod and motion to the bedroom.

"I hope," she said, whispering, "you don't mind but I find it gets stuffy in here. I mean Richard doesn't mind."

"Oh I'm sure he doesn't!" I spoke loudly, reaching for the glass of cheap chardonnay, in the hopes Richard would hear me and come bounding out to join us. I waited, sipping the fulsome chardonnay, but no Richard. "What's that sound? Is that the shower running? Is he taking a shower?" The pipes were rattling in the bathroom off the bedroom at the far end of the apartment.

"I *mean* do you mind that I only have this t-shirt on!"

"Oh. No. Maybe I should though. Does it get that hot in here I thought you said there was a problem with the—

maybe you should turn the shower off that *is* the shower I hear isn't it?" The pipes rattled and wheezed and clanked. Sara seemed to pay no attention and set her glass on the small kitchen counter, then grabbed a rubberband from the clutter of dirty dishes, bread crumbs and colander filled with spaghetti. She pulled her blond and tired hair back into a pony tail and then tucked the tail in, creating what looked like a ball of dirty blond hair-dough. I was also reminded of estuary silt, where the light and dark clay rilled and rained toward the colorless wash of the sea.

"They fixed it," she curtly said, picking up her wine glass and clinking mine.

"Oh well then you must be—

did I interrupt are you two about to eat?" Tomato sauce was beginning to bubble and splatter over the stove top. "Shouldn't you get that?"

"Listen let's not talk here let's move to the bedroom."

"Shouldn't we," I further suggested, but was interrupted by more squealing in the bathroom—

"Shouldn't we wait for Richard to get out of the shower? I mean—

what the hell *is* that noise!"

Sara turned the flame off the stove-top and led me by the hand into her tiny bedroom. The door to the bathroom was closed but its light was on and showed through the crooked bottom of the door to the generally dark bedroom. She walked in front of the bathroom door. I thought she was going to knock and tell Richard we were just outside. But she didn't knock. Instead she paused, lit a cigarette that she had tucked away somewhere, turned to me and said, "You like it this way don't you?"

"I like *what* what way?"

And again the screeching, pounding pipes rattled the walls, shivering through the acoustics of the building.

"Where's Richard," I asked.

"Take off your jacket Hans and relax," she said, dismissing my question, then answering. "He's busy. If you know what I mean."

The pipes or what I thought were pipes pounded on the wall between the bedroom and bath. Fists pounding on a wall could make that kind of noise, I thought. Or, if fists were tied and bound, a human head hammering on a bathtub's porcelain floor could make that sound!

Sara came up behind me and I jumped a little.

"Easy does it," she said, removing my jacket, laying it on the bed. She made her way to close the bedroom door. As she did so she seemed to take extra care to stand on her tip-toes thus exposing her round bare bottom under the t-shirt. That's right, you guessed it, no panties—

right away I thought, Geez Hans get your *own* ass the hell out of there!

"Is that pounding in there?" I asked. "It sounds like someone pounding *on* the wall. Listen, can you hear that? Come over here."

"Well what do you think," she asked, taking her glass from the dresser top and gulping. Her nose remaining a darker pucker as the glass was removed from her mouth and face.

"It's pretty loud whatever it is. Maybe you should investigate? Hell I'm just curious I might as well find out myself.

Sara. If you don't mind." I made as if to open the bathroom door.

"It's nothing Hans you know we have bad plumbing here. This isn't the first you've heard it."

"It doesn't sound like bad plumbing though."

"Fine! I'll open the damn door and show you the fucking plumbing!" Sara bounded for the bathroom door.

"No," I said, "that's OK. I just need to get home is all. I'm pretty beat."

"No!" Sara blurted, "not yet! I mean just." And she came up close to me and put her hand on my face. "I want to help you. I know what you're going through. I know all this business with the theater is difficult for you. It *is* difficult isn't it?"

"Well," I said, as she started playing with my pants. "Yes now that you mention it yes it's kind of," I searched for a description that wouldn't completely allude to Hippolyte, but before I could, Sara had disappeared, so to speak, and had opened my fly.

"Well I want to make it up to you just relax Hans."

"Difficult yes but well that might not be."

"It is. You know it is," she purred, and began on my member, stroking it at first, which was all well and good. It was when she started slurping at it that I began to feel a little uncomfortable.

Then those teeth that I had forgotten about.

"Ow!" I thought to reason my way out and said, "It's difficult yes you're right but—

ow! I mean Oh! Yes that's good that's very good I'm just about ready to—"

And I grabbed her hair by the bun, thinking that if I went

through the motions of ejaculation she'd hurry her slurping and biting and I could go home. Or pass out or something.

"Ow! Geez! Shit that's really good Sara I'm," I bleated, beginning to sweat. I grabbed her head in the hopes of directing it in a more appeasing direction, but as I did so I caught sight of my hands on her hair-bun. Oh Christ, I thought, what the hell is that?

Somehow, when Sara had tied her hair with the rubber-band, she had picked up some spaghetti and tomato sauce and inadvertantly tied it into the bun. My fingers had uncovered some of it. I was hoping there wasn't more. So I grabbed her head and moved it to the left to ease the biting that seemed to ensue as she slurped and listed to the right. But her bun gave way and now bread crumbs were falling to the floor. I'd unearthed her spaghetti dinner, apparently.

"Ow Yuck Ow Yuck shit!" I yelled, tossing her back and un-heeling myself onto the bed. "Ow shit that was good!" I hid my face, thinking I might puke then and there.

I stopped my heavy breathing and it was then I noticed the shrine next to the bed. Sara now eased her way next to me on the bed, slightly pulling at my trousers while wiping the side of her mouth.

"What's all this?" I asked, motioning to the incense and candles on the side table. "A shrine?" I asked, as she undid my shoes and slid my pants off. I made sure that if she turned me over I'd keep my limp unmentionable cupped in my hand.

In the corner of the room there was a small table with all the graph paper cards stacked.

I gathered myself and slid across the bed away from her and approached the table and recognized from the stack all the original cards that I had written. She had preserved them, each and every last one of them, and here they were!

"I saved every one of them Hans and have been going through them." She paused, settling next to me, putting her arm around my waist and caressing the top card with her long, dirty index fingernail. "What," she whispered in my ear, "do you think about that!"

"They're *all* here?"

"Ah-hm," she gurgled. "Now," she said, seeming to change the subject, "I want you," and pushed me with her finger to the bed where I was forced to plop, bouncing a bit on the mattress, "I want you to show me how you do it." The pipes seemed to burst in the bathroom, squealing and pounding in the walls again.

"Show you?"

"Listen," she said, seeming to slink that long body of hers up on top of mine, and at the same time, unbuttoning my shirt. "Listen to me," and she stuck her tongue in my ear. "Listen to me Hans I'm not joking this time," and she started yanking at my shirt.

"Here," I offered, "let me help you." Why was I helping her! I was held spellbound by the shrine, the candles, cards and incense. I'm pretty sure that was what held me there. Christ, but this is embarassing!

Pretty soon I too was in nothing but a t-shirt. *What a freaking predicament*, my mind started telegraphing to me in large, neon-illuminated synapses.

"Tell me," Sara purred, her head on my chest as we lay on her and Richard's bed.

"What do you want to know," I said, resolutely.

"Nothing really." Sara brought her head up from my

chest into my face. "Just a teensy-weensy bit about the cards. And how they might make one feel were they written that is I mean if you don't mind my saying and I hope."

"No not at all," I obliged, stupified "they're really simple."

"Simple," she whimpered, "how. Pray tell do."

Now, I thought, let's not get carried away, let's just give her what she wants. Nothing more. What did she want, though? She was putting on quite a show.

"What," I kissed her gently on the mouth, "do you want to know. I mean what do you want me to start with."

"What I want you to start with is this," and she grabbed my hand and stuck it you-know-where.

"Oh well that, "I meandered about, "that's just something that I suppose comes to me."

Sara giggled and pulled my hand and its thumb, especially the thumb, up into you-know-where. "There," she gasped, "now what comes next?"

"This," I said, "then of course this. And this. And maybe just maybe a bit of—

this."

"You," she trembled, "are terribly au-au-au-spicious."

"Really? Only one hand."

"Don't stop," Sara cuddled even closer, "for if you ever stop I will go *insane*." She emphasized insane with a long and very flat and irritating tone. When you're handling a woman, I thought, it's tones and vowel sounds like that should give you a clue to their personality. I mean, I thought that, I knew that was happening, and yet I persisted in pleasing her. It's nice to please people. It's not nice to turn them off when you're successful at pleasing them. Why would you want to do such a thing; why, for instance, would you want to turn someone off at the moment you were most pleasing them? Here I am, I further thought, pleasing Sara, and why would I want to stop. She is obviously liking it, no? What would make me suddenly, say, snap out of it and tell her she had no idea what she was doing, married and all, head of a theater and performance company, a young beauty like Hippolyte at her shoulder day and night; why would I stop a woman, a tall and commanding womanly presence from enjoying what is very easily provided for the express purpose of enjoyment?

Well, it's that strange nasally vowel sound that emanates from her, I kept thinking. There is something just simply not right about it. And so I stopped, and rolled over and away from her. Dissatisfied, I'm sure she was, but I couldn't let that voice go on lying to me. It would have been easy to let her pretend she was getting something from me, but the idea that even surrounded the simple full awkwardness of this situation, or any situation that involved her ignorance driving it forward into further fulfillment, well, again, one has to put an end to it, somehow flatten it into the present tense. Otherwise it's madness, a sleeping sickness that finds you pitted against a farm girl pitching hay instead of woo. And woo's a lot more interesting, and, ultimately, more useful than hay.

"Here," she quickly jumped up, "let me get you some more wine. You need something to drink."

"OK," I said, staring suddenly at the light under the bathroom door. The pounding had subsided a bit, but gurgling water now erupted from a drain, as if a geyser were finally gushing.

Her big footsteps padded back into the bedroom.

"Listen," she sighed, handing me my glass, which I took as I sat up against the headboard. "Listen. It's not that I'm not grateful or anything but you have to understand."

"Yes?"

"You have to understand Hans some things are just impossible. And," she paused, gulping her wine, "it doesn't mean that we can't be friends or anything like that. It's just that I want you to show me something. Humor me will you?" She placed her wine glass on the shrine and was undoing her still semi-pent-up hair bun. And then those dirty golden brown, lazy strands of tiredness and dinner came falling down over her shoulders, and then the head shake, dazzling the room with little awkward golden flickers that quickly, seductively died back into her stolid, half-naked stance, her tall, stolid, viking-like half-naked stance. If only she were into hygiene she might be a perfect idol.

Suddenly, however, her body, her t-shirt clad (yes, I admit it, delicious) body made me feel I was in the cat-bird seat, like they say. Suddenly I was sipping Sara's chardonnay and I wasn't going to be cut off or interrupted or anything—

"Just show me what the cards do and how you wrote them Hans? That's all I'm asking."

God, I really felt sorry for her. What a miserable life she must have led until now. To be asking *me* for a solution. To the cards? To all those silly cards?

"Listen," I said, very sanely, calmly, "Sara. What kind of nonsense is this?"

"It's not nonsense!"

"Calm down," I ventured.

Sara's eyes twitched. She took another sip of wine.

"Don't you ever and I mean ever tell me to *calm* down."

"Alright alright," I said, calming her down, "what do you want to know. I'm all ears."

"Just," and she motioned, swaying her hips to soften her stance in front of the shrine she'd built, "just tell me how you write these. These. These *things*."

"Like I told you before I use a typewriter and I try to liquidate—"

"Wait," she confessed, "what do you *mean* by liquidate? There's so much philosophy you know. I'm not that aware of philosophy. Of philosophy terms and the like."

"Liquidate you know like money. To liquidate. To make liquid. To liquefy. To water it."

"That's it!" she cried, slapping the stack of cards against her thigh. "What about the water?"

"What do you mean *what about the water*?"

"There's something to it Hans. Don't you see. You and me? The water? THE WATER HANS!"

"What water?"

"Oh shit. Listen," Sara slid into the bed next to me, "what does water mean to you?"

"Water is water. I don't know." I listened for the gurgling in the bathroom but it had stopped. That made me think she might indeed be onto something. But—

it couldn't be. To summon water from a building's pipes like that? She's not possessed, I thought, she can't be a—

"OK." Sara stood by the shrine once again. "What *is* it Hans about these cards that gets you off? For god's sake you must know what I'm talking about?"

"I swear," I said, laughing a bit, "I *really* don't know."

Sara glowered, contre-posto, naked left leg a fleshy flashing dynamo.

"I swear!"

"Oh Christ Hans you're such a pain in the ass!"

"Listen," I said, loudly and firmly, "I am only trying to understand what *you're* trying to say. OK?"

"OK," she said, and sat next to me with the cards, semi-shuffling them and then, finally, letting them spill out onto my leg. And at the same time a whiff of her. "OK smart guy. Let's go through them one at a time."

"That could take a while," I said.

"I've got all night bonehead. For instance what about this one?"

"'Send the metal hammer over to the nearest person,'" I read, "'and give them the head instead of the handle.'"

"Now that!" Sara cooed, "Jesus Hans what about *that*! You must know what *that* means. I mean it means something doesn't it?"

"I was just trying to write as many—"

"No. It means *something* Hans. What?"

"Well. I suppose it means that the head of the hammer."

"Yes," Sara said, plugging my pause, wanting to know.

"It means the head of the hammer is not what you would normally hand to someone. It focuses the event on that which isn't the norm. It means I suppose that the end of the hammer being handed over is backwards and that any other way to look at the procedure has to proceed from that."

"Yes yes yes," spewed Sara, falling back and kicking her legs in the air, "that's fucking *it* Hans!"

"What's *it*?"

"Oh Hans. Jesus. Let's try another one. And this time think about what you're saying. You know I'm not as good as you at extemporizing. You're very very good at it. So try again."

"But you're an actress!"

"Yeah I know but. Shit where are my cigarettes?" Sara scuffled and fluttered her hands around underneath the shrine and produced a pack of Marlboro Lights and then lit one for each of us. "I'm not," she inhaled, "as talented as you." Smoke swirled about us as we both leaned back against the headboard.

Was it my own mind that kept me from saying anything at this point? I felt she was right? What was I supposed to do, needle her into understanding things differently than she already adamantly did?

"What about this one then," she said, earnestly, slipping a card out from the fallen tower of cards that now lay between us. I read, "'Pour water out of the bucket onto the floor.'"

"Once again we have the water Hans. Why did you write that?"

"These are just simple instructions like we had decided there would be. It's ultimately meaningless unless the group is together and each doing these things simultaneously."

"But nothing is that simple," she very sternly and quickly added, dragging on her cigarette and reaching for the ashtray on the shrine table, her arm and then breasts covering and then retreating from me. "Why are all these water cards appearing right now? Go ahead I bet if you pick another it'll have water in it."

I picked another and read, "'Drop a stick into the bucket and tap your left foot three times to the ground.'"

"Here," said Sara, handing me another, which we simultaneously read:

"'Finish what's on your plate!'"

"I thought that if we had simple directions like that," I offered in explanation, "we'd get the performer to wonder if he or she should read it out loud or act it out in some way like go back to pouring out the water—"

"Yes?"

"What?"

"Go ahead and *finish* what you were just saying Hans and you'll see."

"Yeah I know. Pouring water out of the bucket again. There's coincidence and then there's—"

I paused, suddenly realizing the absurdity of our little gathering on *her* bed in *her* apartment at *her* request. I glanced at her as she leaned over the cards fishing for another one to read.

"Finish what's on your plate," I said, dryly.

"And here's another couple of them too," she began reading off their directions.

I interrupted her after a short while—

"Sara. Finish what's on your plate."

"Huh? We read that one all. Hey listen what are you—"

"I said finish what's on your plate Sara. It's simple enough isn't it? Simple to understand that. Isn't it?"

Sara dropped the cards and stabbed her cigarette out in the ashtray and got up from the bed, loudly clunking the ashtray on the shrine table. Her jaw was set tightly.

"Sara," I said. "Finish. What's. On."

"I heard you!"

She planted her hands on her hips and looked to the ceiling, burning with either hatred or frustration. Yes, she was very recognizable in that moment and in that stance.

"My mother," I calmly said, "used to tell me to finish what was on *my* plate."

"I would imagine. Hey! You don't think."

"Well I'd *imagine* it's something quite similar."

"What?" asked Sara, icily. "What's similar? The situation or me? Or *her*!"

"Well you remind me of my mother what can I say. Sorry."

"Yeah you are sorry Hans. What crap! You have this mind Hans you know."

"How would you know you've never heard me speak my mind!" I said, feeling more like Sara's son than bedroom dalliant.

"Don't you speak to me like that ever again. What the fuck do you think this theater business is all about huh? You had a chance and I emphasize *had* you know past tense to do something here and help me."

"Help you? Listen to yourself. Why is this theater all about you?"

"You're missing the point. As per usual." She began opening and slamming her dresser drawers. "You and *her* can go to."

"What if I told you and *your* mother to get a life!" I quickly commented.

Sara was quiet for a moment while she unfolded a pair of jeans and stepped into them. I saw her triangle disappear into them as she zipped and buttoned and—

"Hans I'm not talking about your fucking mother OK?"

I got up from the bed and opened the door to the bathroom, the light suddenly and finally and briefly extinguishing the mood in the bedroom. I turned the faucet in the sink. It hiccuped and finally splashed and ran into the sink. Sara marched out to the kitchen, her jeans rasping in purposeful strides away from my hearing.

I took a leak and flushed the toilet and knew I'd have to leave. The toilet bowl swirled and swished and gurgled and gulped. I didn't know what all this episode with Sara could mean for my engagement in the group. Then, as I was rinsing my hands in the sink and reaching for a towel, searching for a towel, finding no towels, standing there in front of the small medicine cabinet, opening it, closing it, my face sliding in and out of the unclean glass—

Oh shit, I thought, that's who she was talking about? Of course, what the hell was this whole situation *always* about?

I opened the door to the bedroom and Sara was back, standing against the corner of the room. She watched me pick up my pants and shoes and begin to get dressed at the edge of the bed. She then moved to gather up the cards, blow out the incense and candle on the shrine table, and put the beads and stack of cards into the table drawer. She folded her arms, glaring at me.

"You're not going to stop me Sara," I said, tying my left shoe.

"Stop you from what?"

"Hippolyte has a boyfriend I know. I know you're trying to."

"Trying to *what* Hans?"

"She doesn't belong to you you know she has a free will."

"She does? Oh I didn't know that Hans gee wiz dah!" Sara said in that goofy break-down way that makes you understand the finally and hopelessly absurd assertion of your previous statement.

I stood to leave, Sara still with arms folded, glaring at me, jaw locked. As I picked up my satchel I said, "She's not yours Sara."

"Well she certainly isn't *yours*. Anymore!" And she gave a slight laugh at this, as if she had relieved herself of some difficulty now fallen away. "Here's the door Hans," she lightly indicated, and I felt the weight of the moment, of the bedroom, of this night and this conversation, lifting. "And here," she said, passing close to me as I made my way out to the hall, thus sticking one of the note cards into one of my jacket pockets. "No don't read it now but later. *You'll* know what it means."

—

THINKING BACK ON IT NOW it seems I wasted a lot of effort on them. I thought the cards would capture Hippolyte's imagination. Again, she was already in love with me; as far as she would ever be. Our performance, like two seals sporting in the open ocean, contained all I needed to use to pursue *her*.

Instead, I separated myself from the performance itself and concentrated on the cards as if they were some kind of fuel for love.

In a way they were.

But more to the point was the actual joy and the actual feeling I had in the very act of performing with Hippolyte. We would rise and fall together within the flow of the other two bodies, Richard and Sara—

the other mechanical procedures, that is. The more we sounded off one another, the further the entire performance itself went. I felt our hearts gathering in the same place and re-placing the performance and the actions of the cards and all their words. As if merely being involved with an other were a kind of madness.

Even the staged aspect of the performance venue that would have an audience pay admission and sit and wait to be entertained was changed within our love. I don't think there was a body that didn't know what was happening.

Of course, the function of the audience is, in a way, that that can shut off whatever and whenever it pleases. Their attention can only be sought through psychoanalysis, of which the graph paper performances were never meant to partake.

What Hippolyte proved for me was that the circulation of my own temperature pursuing hers lent all and everything into its consuming fire. As if I had to think about lifting a foot or arm to perform mechanical procedures before; as if the involuntary reflex of existence and self-knowledge were never a true and integral part of my being. I rose toward what I loved and desired and all else rose and appeared within its existence. An existence that was no longer my own but Hippolyte's. There was no other event or scheme or rehearsal or performance or maneuver that could have gone further than that look. It was the innocence and fire of the first seeds of desire and life. It was plain to see. There were no trappings involved, none not simply existent. She was a girl, a young woman, in first bloom. Whether sex ever had anything to do with the growing love of this encounter I couldn't tell. All I knew—

I had to have some kind of relation to her. The cards and the graph paper performance fulfilled that need. They fulfilled it by emptying it of any need whatsoever, over and over again.

Yet looking back on it now I see there were two Hippolytes. The one who performed and showed forth a candor of being and expressing love; the other an existence in coordination with another human that obviously spoke the loudest and was the real Hippolyte.

The *other* Hippolyte was the girl from Long Island pursuing an acting career and who I thought I'd be able to captivate through what captivated me—

writing.

It is as if I professed a faith in something anything once and it had through the years slowly transferred into my unconscious mind with interpolations I was able to simply and everywhere affect. I had stood within the bloat of a kind of apostasy and seen it as nothing but bloat. Now, years later, older, alone in the new-new world, everything that was elemental existence took on the praise that once was God's. Or what I thought was supposed to belong to God. What I was taught through idle chatter to belong to God.

In the ritual love dance of Hippolyte and myself a new level of engagement began. God was now not only a young girl, but was *two*. More than one, at any rate; or, put it forward that her *one* is the first order of many, for which natural law stands as pillar and post to man's law. It was she who was able to separate like cell division in the newly forming fetus. And, as if that process were to be repeated over and over again, I became weary, bleary, cross-eyed, drunk, completely out of my element. My element was back in the composition of the graph paper performance, seeking a new expression, a place within universal law.

From the beginning I had solved some of its initial staging problems by inventing the use of cards as a medium to objects and actions within the performance space. The problem was I was left unsatisfied. I should have accepted my small role and been done with it. But I had to press on. In pressing, I ran up against the elemental force of Hippolyte, whose incredible and awkward grace, natural charm and appeal and intelligence pushed all that I had been about, out. All knowledge fled my head and it was as if I were standing in front of that nave in that Church still angry at my Father for having no sense about the Church and its teachings, about its *actual* existence. The graph paper performance began the minute my Father decided to tell stories about his coming-of-age instead of concentrating on interpreting Luther's *Catechism*.

Likewise, now, I have fallen into the pit, down to the Gowanus pit of existence—

as if the entire world were being lived through me because of one place—

and that my rebellion now exists in those stagnant and miasmic, poisonous waters in the grand, spatial scheme of things.

So it's just as well I pursued the cards in an effort to secure the young Hippolyte. Had I succeeded in captivating Hippolyte (that is, had I recognized she already *was* mine) I would not have been able to obtain this insight into existence.

ERGO—

I was fortunate to *not* pursue Hippolyte forever, but to pass through her shadow form instead. Because there *I* was. I was not in the same room with her. I *never* was? I was always in those cards, just passing through.

—

THE NEXT STRETCH OF PERFORMANCES becomes a little sketchy. Partly because I was drinking a lot but also because my heart was being dragged from me (and I could literally feel it being dragged out of me every time Hippolyte made an entrance. Sometimes I had to lift my shirt off my chest and have a look for myself).

That she could exist!

There was no one in the whole of my existence I had been attracted to in such a way. Ideation became subservient to her being, her essence. In my own mind I knew the world must go on, and did, and should and shall but that there was a person, an animal (call her) a kind of unknown quantity that existed under the stupidest of names—

and yet moved with the fire and the will of a tempest under the clothing of appearance—

well, I simply found myself unable to comprehend it. All my preconceptions about cause and effect disappeared. There simply was no other way to describe the world but from within my own assumptive network of knowledge. I hadn't known it until meeting Hippolyte. It wasn't even the meeting that was important. She would go on until—

god, I remember my thoughts about her death, her coming decrepitude!—

until she perished. And come that day what light was it that worked her to shine above all else? Had it been *my* presence within the performance space?

Anyway, with the cards becoming more and more matter-of-fact, plain, unrecognizably different (taken together or separately) from everyday events, I began to lose control and drank until I thought I'd explode, until I thought my head would go reeling off onto the bar room floor itself. This came about, however, after a night in which the presence of many a ghoulish apparition flashed before my commanding eyes.

It was the bar itself I was commanding, of course, but it was the bar, the second floor, painted red with tarnished old brass railing and cob-webbed and dusty mirror frames that I saw as the entire world. In one fell accident of excess and debauched behavior my mind lighted on the furniture and fixtures, on the humming, busily drinking room and perceived it as the world.

What had focused my mind was none other than Carlyle Dubias, who made her way into the third floor performance area in the middle of our performance one night, and sat in the back row where she proceeded to laugh at every turn of non-momentous event. (That is, her laughter alerted me to her presence. And I saw she was watching *me*, someone she had known in the outside world, suddenly taking place in this other world, a world that made no sense to her. And so she laughed and it sounded completely out of place.)

But I was shocked, to say the least, at her appearance. Shocked and worried. After realizing it was indeed her and that I'd have to speak with her afterward, I wished for a way to dash from the place and try an escape. But she would probably be back knowing that I was involved with this theater.

Had I let on to the fact, in my inebriated condition, that I was an actor? What had I said? I was brought to a collision of euphoric altitude, between Hippolyte's communicable love and energy, and now this strange outside presence that dragged me out of the performance through glittering and crazy eyes. I tried to block her out of my mind and enjoy what time was left with Hippolyte.

But soon the graph paper performance was finished and the seven or eight audience members began to stand, realizing there would be no more nonsense (no doubt this was their response as it was at every performance). Richard and Sara immediately engaged a crowd of friends, while Hippolyte made her usual light glance toward me and faded into the shadow of the waiting boyfriend, who had arrived promptly as the performance ended and stood outside the door, his feet pacing back and forth under the lighted landing, causing it to creak the last few minutes of our event.

So I was left with Ms. Dubias, a woman I hardly knew, although she grinned and laughed and came to me casting forth a presence that seemed to indicate we were the best of friends. All I could do was go along with whatever she was trying to put down.

"That was very predictable stuff," she said, as if she were a theater critic.

The remaining audience, staring from the first, now stared at her again. She was wearing the blond wig atop her auburn hair. Again. She also had very skimpy shorts and for a woman of what I guessed was 45 years or so, a tremendous figure, accentuated once again by those tawny tight slacks.

But her eyes were crinkled in a ruined sort of way and her lipsticked jaw was sloven and it said she drank very heavily. Her nose was a shrunken polyp that had never seemingly been given a chance to grow past a 12- or 13-year-old's nose.

"What are you doing here?"

"What am *I* doing here," she said in a low voice, as if she wanted to spar with me.

I addressed my belly from a certain shyness that the room, beginning to empty, had been harboring for my so-called friend.

"Buy me a drink boyfriend. Come on let's hit that little bar and suck it down whattaya say?"

We followed after everyone else but Carlyle would not stop talking all the way down the stairs. She went on about her son and her husband and then proceeded to invent or elaborate about our night together:

"You were marvelous though Hans absolutely really thrilled me you know like there was never anything else to be said you cut right into my home and stole my heart!"

I wished with all my might that I were home. I wished that the peaceful canal would arise in front of my eyes and that this was actually some demented nightmare. Oh for the silent and stagnant waters of the canal! I didn't care they would not move nor ever be moved, they were all the world's rivers to me!

Everybody snickered, or I could hear them snickering. A communal blush issued and caught me in the chest. I was finding it hard to breathe. Hippolyte disappeared into the bathroom off the bar entrance. I was sure she had heard my be-wigged hooker talk about our so-called date.

All was sunk with Hippolyte, I knew then, as if it hadn't

been already, before this. But now, for sure, it was sunk, into unreal mud and ooze.

Carlyle's mouth was still moving. She was the mud and ooze of my present, awkward situation. Somehow I wished I *had* been able to screw her. At least I'd have something tangible to relate to. What really worried me, however, was the fact that she was wanted for murder. Unless, of course, Stewart and Blades had lied. But why would they have lied about something like that? They were the real thing, real detectives. If they had searched her apartment then for sure Carlyle was out on the streets, and, having nowhere else to go, she remembered I spoke about the theater.

But I didn't remember telling her about the theater, and if I had I would have made sure not to tell her exactly where.

But she was standing in *my* bar. The same bar that at one time was my own sacred territory. Very few people had known there was a bar on the second floor above the stage. Now, with the appearance of Carlyle, not only was my secret sunk, but the stares and snickers and guffaws, the beaming, leering faces and the whispering groups of drinkers were now my *identity*. My bar became a place where I couldn't even show my own face anymore. Or so I thought, as we stepped up to order drinks.

Johnny took his time coming over to help us, or, rather, to help me. I was dying for a bourbon and soda. I wanted to calm my nerves and figure what I could do to get rid of Carlyle.

"Johnny this is Cynthia. Cynthia this is John," I said, introducing Carlyle by her working title.

"Very nice indeed what can I get you two." For the look in his eyes he might as well have called us "two lovebirds."

Johnny, of course, was the only one who could have taken a shine to Carlyle Dubias. Beyond the polyester blond wig and the tacky make-up job he saw the stars of an aesthetically compatible milky way.

"I haven't seen you in here before," he said, tending to the bottles.

"Say that's a great jacket!" said Ms. Dubias.

"Hey thanks. Don't I know you from somewheres," said Johnny, handing me my drink.

"Yeah," she began, "from around heres somewheres maybe the club on."

"I knew it the minute you walked in here I said to myself this has got to be someone from *INXS!*"

"Yeah that's it that's it," she said, beginning to lip at her soda straw. "Say what ya drinking there Hansy Wansy?"

"It was nice to meet you," said Johnny, wanting to stay and talk but, I guess, in awe of my hooker's grace, he sent himself on down the bar tending to the others who, between the middle of their conversations, were keeping tabs on us.

I sucked the last of it off the bottom of the icily glittering glass and went to use the men's room. I was hot and splashed cold brownish water on my face from the sink. The place stunk as if the urinal was backed up. As if it hadn't drained in years. It only emphasized the fact that I was in a situation from which I was finding it very difficult to extricate myself. And I definitely needed to extricate. If there was ever a time I needed to extricate, now was the time, I said to myself, staring into the rusty, mottled mirror.

I tried to make a run toward the stairs and from there out onto the street, thinking I'd be free, but when I emerged from the can, Carlyle was standing right before it and escorted me back into the boisterous bar. By now they had all gotten involved in themselves and paid little attention to my sore thumb.

We sat back down at the bar but this time, much to my further chagrin, we were sitting right next to Hippolyte's boyfriend. Which meant that Hippolyte was soon to arrive! I looked over at the tables and saw some of her friends, the little actresses from her scene rehearsal. They were not saying a word, just staring over at Ms. Dubias and myself.

"Say that's an interesting name Dubias what is that?" I tried to lighten the situation, thinking if I controlled the conversation she'd become undone and want to leave.

"Whatever you want it to be," she said, seeming angry, trying to glower at me behind her pip-squeaky voice.

Hippolyte's boyfriend leaned over then turned to face the mirror behind the bar. Johnny was busy talking to other drinkers but pulled himself away to ask us what we wanted. I had another.

"What are you drinking?" I politely asked.

"Soda."

"That's it?"

She didn't answer and stared straight ahead.

"Listen," I said, "I've got to get."

"You're my only hope Hans."

She was suddenly kind of teary-eyed. Hippolyte's boyfriend leaned over again to hear what I was going to say. Just then Hippolyte appeared at his other elbow.

"Let's," I suggested, "get out of here and go somewhere where we can talk."

"There's no point in that," Ms. Dubias said, "I think you know perfect what's goin on."

A minute ago she was goofy and acting like a normal hooker on the town and now she was trying to peel back the layers of that moment to reveal for me what I supposedly already knew.

"What?" I said, stymied.

"Without you I may never be able to find—"

she paused when she saw I was looking at Hippolyte and her boyfriend. They were animatedly talking. Suddenly I saw Hipp as the schoolgirl she really was. Our roles had been de-magnetized by the appearance of Cynthia and Carlyle. Hippolyte's little actress friends were still staring, however. They must have been taking notes.

What *was* it about Carlyle's make-up that held a clue to who she might truly be? I couldn't shake it. There I was staring at her under-developed nose and yet there was something odd about the way she had put her make-up on. Whether it was applied too rapidly or just sloppily, I couldn't tell. But it wasn't exactly sloppy either, there was some sort of design to it, some sort of intention that kept drilling its appearance into me.

When Johnny came over again to ask us if we wanted more to drink I began to discover that, like him seeing in Carlyle some kind of aesthetic equal, I was discovering my own level of necessity with her too. I began to listen in on the hub-bub of the crowd. Much like as if, after that first drink, my wish to be at home across from the stagnant Canal of Liberty, had suddenly been granted.

"I'll have another of the same."

Suddenly Carlyle put her arm around me. There we were at the bar, two couples, Hippolyte and her neatly attired young man and me and my streetwalker Cynthia Dubias, wanted for homicide by the New York City Police Department.

"Is that some kind of foundation?" I asked.

"This?" she said, pointing to her face. It felt like everyone in the bar glanced at us when she pointed to her face.

"Yes. The foundation."

"He's not coming back. I have to say that just even to hear myself saying it I have to you know," she rambled.

"Who's not coming back?"

"My son! He took him and put mercury in his little penis!" loud enough so that Hippolyte and her boyfriend could hear, although they didn't appear to acknowledge its absurdity.

Then Sara came into the bar making her way, as usual, straight for Hippolyte. She managed to stand between Hippolyte and her boyfriend, also, just like she so often had done to us. For some reason she didn't want to even acknowledge my presence.

"Who's that?" asked Carlyle, "is that your girlfriend?"

Sara turned and quickly glanced at Cynthia but did not leave her conversation long enough to notice me. She pulled a stool from the far end of the bar, eventually, and was blocked from view by the bodies and the noise for the rest of the night.

"You are the only one Hans!" Cynthia leaned over and loudly stated.

I took a drink.

"You are the only one," she continued in a lower tone, "who will be able to get my son back."

I pretended I didn't know what she was talking about: "You have a son? I didn't know that."

"You know everything Hans. I want you to tell me what you know." Her voice changed, instructing me to recite what had happened at her place weeks ago.

"What do you mean?" I continued my drink.

"You saw the man and the little boy din't ya?"

"When was this now?"

"And then you searched my drawers!" she yelled.

Everyone in the bar turned again to look at us.

"What!" I grunted back at everyone. It was a small bar and to have to turn and acknowledge every vowel that spills out of someone's conversation, I thought, was just plain rude. "What are you looking at!"

"That's it Hans. Tell them all to go fuck off!" growled Cynthia, the hooker.

I sought the back of the bar's bad mirror and continued to drink. Hippolyte and her boyfriend began to leave. I didn't feel like saying anything to her. There was nothing I could do now. It was hopeless. All was lost. There was no need to go on anymore.

I can only look at the dirty window over the Gowanus Canal these days and wonder at all I felt, at all Hippolyte and I had shared, totally on our own, without any witnesses. Well, without anyone but Richard and Sara to know. But that walked out the door. I don't even think she looked back (which is what really gets me).

"Fuck off!" I yelled without physically acknowledging the rest of the bar. There was a lull in their activities. Then someone laughed and everything started to hum again. I heard the Yugoslavians making their drinking noises over on the other side of the room without even having to look.

Carlyle moved to the vacated stool. "You are the only

one Hans."

The way she said it sounded like there was not only more to her predicament, but more to her. She was a crazy street walker. Or so I thought. But there she was with a pretty nice apartment, with a courtyard even, on the west side. Not a bad neighborhood. She had a husband. Or had *had* a husband.

"Who was that guy with the kid?" I asked.

"My husband," she said very fast.

"And the kid *your* kid?"

"He lets him visit every now and again. Sometimes they show up in the middle of the night."

"I don't believe you."

"You don't *have* to believe me sweety."

"Then how do you expect me to help you?"

"So you'll help? I knew you would. Johnny! Johnny I'll have another."

I was tapped on the shoulder. It was one of the bearded Yugoslavians. And Dushbik.

"Sssso," he said, "is you pahty doo eh?" he said, raising his tiny glass.

"Yeah that's right this is really happening," I answered.

"Oh oh whatssa matter Han. You not like fo-k-sey chig?"

"That's right."

"Oh oh whatssa matter brodah you not *stret*."

He motioned for the others to come over. They came. He burbled something in Yugoslavian. No one broke a smile. No one even tried to understand, it seemed. They just took drags on their cigarettes and guzzled shots and waited for something else to happen.

"Listen I have to get out of here," I said. But the bearded fellow wouldn't let me up out of my stool.

"What." I couldn't say anything. As with so much in my life, it seems, none of it really involved *me*. This is a case in point. I didn't know Carlyle. I barely knew the Yugoslavians. And now *they* weren't letting me get up to leave.

And Johnny also came to Carlyle's defense. I guess they figured I was trying to wrong her.

"I don't even know this woman," I let Johnny have it, flatly, as he tried to figure what was going on.

"You're," he said, "not used to our late night scene are you Hans?"

"What the hell's that s'posed to mean," I wanted to know.

He said nothing and turned to talk with Carlyle. They were having a wonderful time. Finally, the Yugoslavians, one by one, made their way to the other side of the room, each sneering in turn and flicking a thumb under a chin. The walls rushed in redder than ever as their vodka wave departed.

When I returned to my glass, which Johnny had re-filled, thankfully, he began to "interpret" what Carlyle was asking from me:

"Listen Hans I don't see what the big problem is here? I mean just help your friend out. She's come all this way because she knows *you're* the one can help her out of this particular jam."

"What *particular jamb*?" I really wanted to know. I mean, besides trying to ignore Carlyle's insistence that I did indeed know what she wanted or needed from me, I really did want to know the specifics of what it was she was after.

Johnny seemed a little exasperated with me and turned

away.

"Did you know she was wanted for murder?"

Johnny didn't hear me though. Or maybe he did.

"What's this 'bout murder?" asked Ms. Dubias.

"Listen," I said, "I would really appreciate you telling me why it is I'm the one who's to get your son back."

"So you do know. I knew you knew. I knew you'd help!"

Another drink. I was starting to get looped but it wasn't enough. In the new-new world one has to take drastic situations and flush them down with a large amount of alcohol. I still haven't found any other way to keep my mind moving. I haven't found any other way to deal with the stupid and numbing kitchen work that keeps me in rent money but by drowning myself as much as I possibly can. It makes me feel like I'm accomplishing something. As opposed to being an out-and-out slave, which is pretty depressing.

"Do you like your work?" I asked, quite suddenly.

"Oh yeah it's terrific!" I couldn't tell if she was serious. "I like the people I work with the clients well like the ones you met are usually pretty nice I like the young ones," she said, moving her face in close to mine, "and it's great hours and the pay is *fabulous*."

"But you have to stick someone's penis in your mouth don't you?"

"Oh that's nothing you get used to it," her eyes began to wander.

"You're not serious are you?"

"Totally."

Something didn't sound right. She hated her work. She was desperately trying to get her son back from what was obviously an embarrassing and difficult situation. She was trying to impress me with her line of work as if it were a real and valued and highly serious profession; mysterious; but here she was at the bar, as if it were any normal after-hours get-together.

"You know I turn tricks too," I said, kind of afraid of what that might mean in a situation like this.

"Where do *you* work?" she asked.

"Right here."

"You do people in the bathroom? Behind the bar? Oh that's a good one!" she bellowed down the length of the bar. The bar's Balkan Peninsula gave chase with some drinking noises.

"It's called *theater*," I said, and wondered why I hadn't thought to say that sooner.

"*That* was what you call theater?" she tittered. "That was already done a million zillion years ago Hansy Wansy. I'm sorry. That is your name though isn't it? Hans?"

"What difference does it make!" I yelled at the top of my lungs. "What are you some kind of lunatic or something! Haven't you ever seen ANYTHING in your life? WHAT THE FUCK IS YOUR GODDAMN PROBLEM BITCH!"

Of course Johnny and the Yugoslavians were prompt in trying to adjust my attitude. And I of course tried to tell them again I did not in any way know this woman.

"That doesn't change the situation man. You got to talk to the lady man," said Johnny.

"Dat right. You must dalk dis one vair goot," said the Balkan Peninsula.

"What the hell business is it of yours!" I finally blurted to Johnny.

"As long as it's in my bar then I get to police things as I

see fit to police them."

"Your brain's *fudge*!" I strongly asserted.

"Alright alright that's enough," said Carlyle, whimpering, "I only want him to apologize and to help me get my son back is all."

"Does anybody know what time it is? Do I really have to sit here and take this crap from a bunch of idiots!" I strongly asserted once more.

"We not itot. You itot dis free gun-tree," said the Yugoslavians' leader, sternly. They all grunted and lifted their glasses. Dushbik pushed his fellow drinker away and pointed to my face:

"I got you wrong Hkans. You not goin' do my Tito play big shot fair-he."

"Hey hey hey that's enough now just apologize to the lady and that will be the end of it and you two can then enjoy the rest of the evening," interceded Johnny, the barkeep.

"I don't have an evening to spend with anybody!" I pressed on. "I don't know this bitch."

"Hey listen that's enough this is not gonna get you any place the way I see it," Johnny, seriously red in the face, "you have one option at this point and one option only—"

"Where the hell do you get off," I started, "butting your fat head into *my* business and telling *me* how to behave with a completely irrational person in an irrational."

"You like these drinks don't ya?"

"What the hell does that have to do with *any* of this!"

"Eet everthin' to wit do kvassdsss," admonished Dushbik, broadly smiling.

"And the faster you get that through your thick skull

then the sooner you can be on your way," said Johnny, finally, flatly. And he turned and left toward the other end of the bar. I could hear Sara asking him if everything was OK.

Sometimes it seems that everyone has their head stuck into existence the wrong way and when you stop to ask them about it they tell you, Yes my head's always been this way as a matter-of-fact how's yours?

The point being, of course, I had to leave the bar. I had to leave the theater. I had to leave everything.

Inebriated enough, I was able to make a dash for the door without anyone being made the wiser. I thought Carlyle would come running after me but as I rounded Houston Street at the Bowery heading for the Subway, she was nowhere to be seen. I hopped on the N train to Union Street, Brooklyn.

ABOUT A WEEK LATER I was spending my afternoon on one of the relatively new bridges that run over the Gowanus Canal.

I had found a rather large bowie knife on my way to work one day. It was at a table on the street along with other items for sale. The fellow selling me the knife told me he had other items I might be interested in. He gave me his one eye (the other had been covered by a patch made from a piece of newspaper over cardboard) and told me to return as often as I liked, to check out the incredible bargains on weapons, wink, of all kinds.

I didn't buy the bowie knife because I wanted to own an

arsenal; I bought it because of the handle. I often wondered, if any of my forebears survived to somehow show me how to live in New York City, what might my chances of survival have been. I had a mission and a purpose. Now it seemed like the destiny of a million, insufferable years going to waste in a sewer they actually have the audacity to call a Canal.

Nothing to do with nature whatsoever. The water is slimey. There's a perpetual inch-thick ooze over the top of it at all times. The only thing nice about it is the new wood they recently used to replace some of the old, rotting piling. And the bridges were constructed from the same wood. As if anybody would notice.

So as I was out walking the Gowanus Basin, looking up at the moldy curtains on one room four-story houses and backyard junk shops, I finally found myself, at noon hour, standing in the middle of a newly constructed drawbridge. They had made it so as to rise to admit some sea-faring vessel. But there aren't any anymore. Just small junk and garbage barges and scrap heap barges that traverse when full.

And for no other reason do the drawbridges need to go up.

Out into the ocean goes the garbage. Into the Canal comes the empty flat-bed. Sometimes there's a tug boat. But very rarely. Tug boats are actually very large. They look small from a distance, out say, in the East River, or bounding by that curve under the Verrazano Bridge where Verrazano, hundreds of years ago, looked up the River toward New Land.

Now all that's left is a stagnant pool. If it weren't for the land so deeply cut into the water here it would never move. And this is not taking into account the "cement shoes" rumored to cover the bottom. All in all, what else could they have expected, those explorers, would take place here.

Realistically, they had no chance of conquering land in the name of themselves or anything they represented. They could only submit to the harsh conditions. They would not, of course, submit for long. They had to fight fire with fire. They had to justify that. They had to, in short, join the progress of soul already in this wilderness from the very start. Whether we took the Indians or they took us made little difference.

And it was not just an industrialization that covered the Basin and Canal I was pondering from the drawbridge. No. It was an active intelligence, a soul of some kind that flattened the small farmhouses around here and made this the junk capitol for miles around.

I was carving with my new bowie knife a kind of coat-of-arms on the railing of the drawbridge. There was no traffic and really no one to speak of nearby. So I kept whittling away. But what I set out to delineate as a kind of coat-of-arms for myself, my family, everything I had known and drew, I guess, knowledge from, turned into a hole.

It ended up looking just like a knot in the wood, as if no one had laid a hand to the railing.

When I got to the laundromat downstairs from my apartment, Rosita was gesturing and mumbling for me. I went over to her. A natural thing, I thought, maybe she just wants to show me the view she's having today. There were a few folk in the laundry itself. I didn't see Poppy anywhere. He had probably gone for more change, which he often does during the day. Whenever I run into him at the same corner where I'm buying coffee and he's obtaining change we exchange pleasantries. He often winks at the people behind the counter. I have no idea what for. They see each other every day. Poppy winks at me, he winks at the children with their dogs or their balls out on the street. He winks at the laundry customers coming to ask about more change. He winks when he gives them the change. He winks when I see him in the hallway of the building. He winks when he is seen opening the gate to the scrapyard, there to disappear into his Spanish music. He winked when he told me about Rosita's problem with constipation. There is nothing, in short, he doesn't wink after.

"Men—

see—

you," said Rosita.

Simple enough. Rosita didn't waste words. That is, she usually *didn't* waste words. But this was a little more cryptic than I cared relate to. Something was happening and it was out of the ordinary. Hair bristled on the back of my neck as I made my way up the stairs. Rosita had pointed up so I took it that whomever these men were they'd be waiting for me at my apartment.

"Mr. Knudsen," I heard above my head as I ascended, "it's Detectives Blades and Stewart. We'd like to ask you a few more questions."

I tried to conceal the knife behind my back. I didn't want to give the wrong impression. For all they knew I was in deep with Ms. Dubias. But then Blades let fly with a terribly insinuating question:

"Have you ever been out on the town with Ms. Dubias?"

"You fellas!" I let out, and, at the same time, I threw the bowie knife into the floor where it stuck and quivered. "You know you come into my building after I've already explained everything I could ever explain to you and now you want to know what?"

"Just answer the question Mr. Knudsen," said Stewart. "And step away from the knife nice and easy."

"Listen. I've seen enough cop shows to know this whole routine before it even starts! Listen," I said, retrieving my knife from off the floor, "that's it. It's all over." I took out keys to open my door. "It's all over! It's done. Kaput. Fini. Sayonara. See you later."

"If we find she's anywhere near these premises we'll have to take you in for further questioning Mr. Knudsen! We know you can hear us Mr. Knudsen."

"Go to hell!" I screamed through the door I'd just closed.

Not only was I frantic I was also searching as quickly as I could through every one of my three small rooms for any sign or trace of Ms. Dubias. If she knew about the theater she'd be able to know where I lived. And maybe she *did* follow me home the other night. She could have asked anybody at the bar where I worked and eventually she could have *figured out* where I lived. I got to get out of here, I was muttering to myself.

"Mr. Knudsen!" cried Blades, "we're not through questioning you!"

"I told you both to go to hell!"

"This is obstruction of justice!" yelled Stewart, "and we're gonna have to get a warrant to search your apartment! It can be done and will be done! It would be a lot easier if you just open up and talk to us right now!"

"Bite me!"

"Mr. Knudsen," said Blades, "this is Detective Blades."

"I don't care who you are! What right do you have to assume more than is necessary!"

"Mr. Knudsen," said Stewart, "this is—

"I know—

Stewart. Stewart and Blades! Wake up and smell your coffee man!"

"No Mr. Knudsen this is a murder investigation! We have to check out all available leads! You were involved with Ms. Dubias no?!"

"Listen Guys I was involved with her like I said for just a short time! There was nothing pre-meditated about our meeting at all I just wanted to get some poontang!"

"We understand Mr. Knudsen. That's why we need to know a few things!"

"Ask away then!"

"Could you open."

"Look what's so frigging important about a frigging closed door muthahfucker!"

"Mr. Knudsen if you'll just open the door."

"Kiss my ass! You guys got some nerve showing up here! I'm a hard working mothahfucker you understand! I work my shit and don't no one need to be hassling me 'bout no bitch who can't *even* sit on no fuckin bar stool."

"So you have seen her again?" answered Blades.

I opened the door, stuck my head out into hallway space.

"Yeah. So what. What's the point. How much do you need for this case. How many people do you have to drag into this ordeal. Can't you assholes figure it out yet! What the hell do you think motivates someone like that? Where did she live? Who did she know? What does she need from her son? Is there any past information could be relevant here? Am I getting close guys tell me when I'm getting close! Have you done a background check on her husband? Have you tried to figure out where he worked what his connections were? Have you figured yet he's probably an asshole and he couldn't control his own wife and so he had to drive her crazy so she'd probably leave or vice versa? Is any of this shit getting through? Have you ever wondered what it takes for people to drive other people mad?—

Put yourself in somebody's shoes here for a change you guys are not investigating a murder you're investigating the entire city and as for the drugs why don't you leave that to the fucking *federales*. They've never gone wrong when it comes to this kind of thing. Where the hell you think that shit is coming from anyway from Poppy's scrapyard or maybe it's these nice Italian families up along Union you should be questioning. Everyone is."

"That's enough Mr. Knudsen," said Stewart.

"All we wanted to know was if you had seen her subsequent to the first meeting and we've been able to ascertain that by now. Thank you for your co-operation."

"I ain't never seen her again! Ascertain all you want muthahfuckers! You ain't know *jack* shit!"

But Stewart and Blades were on their way down the stairs. Sure, I had given myself away. But there was nothing to it. They had needed me to piece something together, something I was not privy to.

They were doing, like they said, a murder investigation. It had nothing to do with me. I could have turned into a thousand different people before their eyes and danced on my god-damned head and it wouldn't have changed the dynamic of their investigation. Apodictic knowledge versus common knowledge.

Furthermore, what was retained in that dynamic (which I did not possess?). The reason I was unable to pull myself away from the bar and Carlyle Dubias was that there was a greater magnetic at work than what I had previously perceived. Had I been a lot quicker in hunting Hippolyte down, as it were, if I had asked her out on a simple date long before the Dubias Episode, there would have been no Dubias Episode. What was it kept me from Hippolyte?

I could have gone to her and explained, that night at the bar, that I did not know Ms. Dubias in the least. I could have joined the others in making fun of, or noticing, Ms. Dubias as an "outsider." But I did not. Why had I been so congenial?

The fact is, I should have hunted her husband down *before* the police. I should have been ruthless, flat out ruthless to discover the truth about this mysterious mercury poisoning of the penis. Was she making it up? What could it possibly mean, other than something diabolical? Was she simply mad and there was no end to the madness? Why was I there, in her corrugated cardboard box, lured to stay only by the promise of a fully naked, middle-aged mother? Why did I get involved?

It was, no doubt, a kind of sexual urge that drew me to her, but not because that was my first instinct. In fact, my mind was so much elsewhere I could never have, like I told Blades and Stewart, "premeditated" any kind of meeting sexual or otherwise.

I happened to be there, and my evening was finished. I

was in a woman's apartment. I had the opportunity to see her, touch her, fondle her—
so it was there—
from the beginning?
When she stuck her pin in the padlock of the Garden-Cemetery was it the beginning of *that* involvement? And now sex was presuming its involvement.
All for some memory—
to revisit the site of a conversation.
A very important conversation. It had been the end of my life in and of this rumor men call God, as it were, for the theological and the beginning of my true life. I had seen the Cogito go down toward simple cognition as the controlling force, the controlling reason of existence. People were giving it names and all names led to this idea of God *uber alles* but there simply was only a body for each of us to step into and assume, not an identity, but a body—
and not for a few brief moments of guilt-ridden bliss but for as long as one desired to stay inside that body.
What is good then or even necessary about God if *it* is everywhere and *we* are nowhere? There is only one Being at work and it *is* God. At least it is one God among many questions or relations of Godhead. I couldn't then or now spend much more time contemplating the different worlds represented by the Cogito and the pumping blood of Cognition. It is literally too vast to handle with the small vanity of divine studies.
Whatever I meant initially by all those cards, those plays and poems, about everything inside the controlling influence of the graph paper performances and everything outside (my life and other writings and events) momentous and infini-

tisemally dull, the fact is some sort of sexual dynamic was at work behind all scenes and encounters. And the blood flows.

When will people rise up, armed with nothing but their sexual dynamic, and rout God itself from the vast and overpopulated Earth? Is the answer always a predestined and resounding *Never*? It was the center of the work long before I met Hippolyte and fell in love. It was there before Richard and Sara and their silly little theater. It was there before they decided to use nothing but graph paper to evaluate the future of the performative.

Is all life merely a part to be played out from the sexual dynamic?

And yet here I am, alone, with nothing and nobody. I have the possibility of meeting Ms. Dubias and/or being pursued by Ms. Dubias for the rest of my life. And, on the other side, I have the endless misery of memory and have no one else to thank for that but the young Hippolyte.

—

THE SURPRISE, and doesn't it always happen under the sun.

Out again in the neighborhood, to the 3rd Street bridge and wandering down the back of the recycling station. Bottle collectors and garbage men hauling containers of empties. Epiphanies?

What I did was wander down past the wire fence and found a hole that emitted me onto the literal bank of the canal.

Now, it's just like me to take such a dangerous step. Danger seems to beget the answers we've been desiring so;

nothing, or little, else will do.

There were the stories of runaways and other victims of the canal. I had, of course, heard them. They made their rounds from time to time in snippets of conversation on the street. A joke pronounced loudly across Union Street, for instance—

"Whatever you do don't go swimming you'll never come out alive!" Followed by yuks and guffaws and—

"Naw! Won't phase *me*!"

The point is, of course, the canal is palpably poisonous. Viral strains emanate from its rich black inky bottom. A body falling into it would (it had been proven) not make it another day. Pathogens of the old world—

cholera, TB, dipthyria and deadly viruses not yet named or forgotten, took hold of the swimmer and leveled his ability to go on amongst the living.

But there I was, another afternoon, walking along its banks. No one saw me. A little farther along and I could see the large, open field behind the *Casa Marble and Granite Works*. Something sang to me from the rays of the sun beating against the scattered piles of stone across the canal.

It was relatively easy to cross, however. A metal dredging ladder lay just above its surface and stretched from shore to shore. On the other side it would be easy enough to climb into the back end of the field. That is, provided I didn't fall into the water.

I think I was thinking about death, but not that consciously. Not as consciously as we do when we are imagining it. There was the ladder before me; others had used it to survey the depths of the canal for the dredging equipment, so, presumably, I wouldn't have been the only idiot to attempt a crossing. Indeed, I crossed very easily to the far bank without tottering or wavering or thinking about the ladder or my footwork over it.

Up into the field at the back of the *Casa Marble and Granite Works* and I sizzled and cracked in the hot afternoon sun. Here and there were boulders and upright huge markers of marble, unfinished sculptures baking in the field that stretched from the canal to 2nd Avenue and the elevated Gowanus Expressway, from filthy Luquer to Harrison Streets.

Maybe it was the heat, or the vacancy of the field itself, but I was suddenly seized with uncontrollable vertigo. My breath came fast and in spurts that seemed to jar my brain into thought too mental for my bodily frame to capture and recognize. It also felt like some unseen hand were grabbing hold of my intestines and rearranging my body's cavity. Every few moments I had the urge to either vomit or pass out.

And perhaps I did pass out of consciousness for somehow I found myself in the very center of the field, completely unperturbed by the bedding that some one homeless person had strewn up the backside of a piece of granite. The sun made me even more dizzy and for some inexplicable reason I wanted to look straight up into its razor-sharp rays that were falling into that field, slicing me up as I made my way through it.

Was this the personification or realization of early memory? What had I accomplished by all that in my youth now seemed to be the same field from the days of my fervent Lutheran escapades? Or was this sense of being an out-of-towner something that could drill me back in time to my earliest and most shameful memories, so that the very field I now walked of an afternoon *was* indeed the same? I was completely winded. Everywhere my eye sought to rest in that field, a new apparition as of pain and the poverty of my mortal self brought me into the uneasy depths of my own void. It was as if I were truly the most empty creature or thing that had ever existed.

The strange thoughts that snapped into my fuzzy chamber of a head now had me seeking rest on a slab of marble. And as I lay on its smooth but weathered surface, the sky clouded over. Not the kind of clouds, however, that precipitate. It was as if the entire canopy of sharp light were suddenly converted to shadow.

I *must* have passed out, because before me I thought it quite certain a figure hopped up and then quickly disappeared behind a massive slab of Granite. But when I stood to pursue the illusion the sun began its knifing once again. From the farthest edges of the field echoes of voices permeated my brain. Or it was the cavity of my head and hollow eyes playing a trick on me. How could someone live in that field? What would be an adequate sense of confidence that would allow someone to inhabit a bed behind a rock? I, being a relative stranger in this town, had no place to bring my instincts to focus? What was I missing as a human animal, as a cosmopolitan?

I began to make my way toward Luquer Street, knowing I'd be able to at least walk home, rounding corners then for a few wretched and vacant streets. The yellowed grass rasped under my tread. How despised and unwanted I felt! My shelter in this world was the front end of an old abandoned warehouse that had no material use anymore; my day-to-day existence was spent preparing meals for tourists that had no idea people actually lived in this shallow wasteland; and now the fact of actually being homeless held nothing but the prospect of empty madness, as if my body were not strong enough for my so-called mind.

I squeezed through the fence and made a way across 2nd Avenue to the children's playground that nestled right below the concrete giant legs of the Gowanus Expressway. Here and there a few kids with their parents or sitters were busy swinging or climbing or running. I sat on a bench while the traffic roared through the cemented ceiling above.

I rested, and caught my breath. I was beginning to get my strength back (probably because of the blacktop and the canopy above, shielding me from the deadly rays of the sun) when I looked around at some of the children playing on the monkey-bars. One kid in particular caught my attention, as if I had seen him before. Indeed.

It was none other than Cynthia's son. He was being helped down from the jungle gym by a man in brown canvas overalls. Squinting, I realized soon enough it was the man whom Cynthia had said was her husband. They gathered their things together and walked off toward the Luquer Street exit of the playground. From there they turned west. I followed to the fence and spied them entering a building just two doors down from the playground.

Had the man changed his identity and moved to Brooklyn to avoid the police? What were the odds he would be situated merely a half mile from my own dwelling? But maybe this was only a place of work and not where they now lived. I decided to knock on that door they'd disappeared behind and confront the mystery head on.

Back and forth in front of the building a few times to size it up. It was indeed a residence, a nice two-family walk-up with what looked to be an abandoned second story. I knocked on the door under the front stoop, the one they had used. The man who came to the gate seemed not to recognize me. I was slow to speak.

"You probably don't remember me."

"Can I help you?"

"You probably don't remember me."

"I can't say as I do no. Can I help you?"

"I'm a friend of." His face turned yellow. "A friend of Cynthia's I." His eyes glazed a bit. "I'm not really a friend just."

"Come in," he said, unlocking the gate and abruptly turning away. I followed him past another door into what would be the shell of the house, it having been, obviously, stripped bare and in the process of renovation. The kid, his son, was riding around in circles on a small bike with training wheels. He continued riding and did not look up to see us enter.

"Joel now stop that I'm getting dizzy."

The brick walls layered up with old concrete trowel slaps smashed behind two inch studs rose to a ceiling whose handhewn beams were exposed.

"My name's Hans by the way."

He held out his hand and I shook it. "Jim."

Joel continued biking around, knocking into the wall every now and again.

"Least it keeps him warm. Y'know?"

"Yeah," I said, somewhat dubiously.

"It's cold in here," and he sat down at the lone chair in the room, against the back wall.

"You must be the Father."

"I s'pose I am." He stared off at the boy now trying to go in reverse.

"I guess I'll just come right out and say it," I said, looking for a sign of recognition or reaction from him, but none was forthcoming. His arms were down along his sides, hanging there, big hands that now had no heavy labor to perform.

"I guess I'll just come right out and say Jim," and he nodded, as if to reassure me I had his name correct. "I'm guessing you're the Father and that Cynthia really has. By the way she told me her name was Carlyle."

"Yep."

I rubbed my arms. "It is a bit nippy in here."

"Joel. Joel. Joel. Joel say hello."

"Hello,' said the boy, shyly, hunched up and arms cocked over the handlebars, his hearing finally adjusted to our presence.

"How old's he?"

"'Bout 5."

"Does he know?"

"What's that?"

"Does he know?"

"What you mean?"

And I let it drop. I looked up the staircase. A burnished tier of tar-paper over red wood.

"I haven't gotten to that yet," said Jim. "I'm working my way from bottom to top. Let me show."

And we left Joel to his bike and the walls for a minute as Jim showed me the upstair's layout.

"Not too much here right now. We sleep there. That'll be a bathroom. Had to tear all the tiles out o'course. The plumbing's all got to be done new. And those windows in the far room over the street will be coming next week."

"How long you been," I began. "I mean how long have you owned this place?"

"It's my grandfather's. Bought it 1900 or thereabouts."

"Jesus."

"Yep."

We stepped our way back down to the main floor. Jim sat back in his lone chair.

"So you do all the work here or have you hired."

"Most of it. I'm a welder so," He paused and looked to make sure I was following. What was there to follow? Joel now got off his little tricycle and leaned up against his father. "I'm a welder so whatever I can do here I do but I'm so busy most of times I have to contract a lotta work out." The boy now climbed up into his lap. Jim didn't seem to mind, but he also kept his arms down at his sides, seeming not to help the small child as he ambled up onto his lap.

"Well Cynthia never."

"Did she send you?"

"No I mean what I was going to say was she seemed to have glommed onto me for some reason I," and Jim the Father's eyes grew perplexed and deepened in hue, seeming to gather the sparse light of the room into them. "I mean she. I don't know her. I only met her once it's just a coincidence I'm here I mean that I followed you."

"You're following me why?" Jim cocked his head

slightly.

"No it's not that I'm following you I'm not. You just happened to be out in the playground."

Now the boy slid down from his father's lap and went to the tricycle, crouching there to examine a small piece of plaster wedged under its tire.

"So what does she want?"

"Oh. No you don't understand I."

"Listen. Let's go out to the back," Jim suggested.

"OK. The back?"

"The yard. Joel. Joel. Joel. JOEL!" And Joel came trotting up to his father's pants, holding on. We opened a door half-hinged to a recently plated lintel and sideboard behind the back wall of the main floor. Out in the lighted yard I began to warm.

"I don't know you," I began, "and like I say I don't know Cynthia. I never really saw her before in my life."

"Then what are you doing here?" I sat on a rusted lawn chair.

"You want somethin t'drink?"

"Sure."

To my surprise he went to a small work shed with 2 X 4's sawed and spread out before it, returning with a flask.

"I keep it here just in case. Go ahead. Joel stay away from there. Joel. Stay away from there. JOEL!" I swigged and continued:

"She seems to be ill-at-ease about something. Something she told me."

"What you mean?"

I swallowed. "Well she got it into her head."

"Joel stay away from that com 'ere. Joel. Joel. Joel. JOEL

Come. 'Ere!"

"She got it into her head that you did something to the boy and now. I don't know why I'm telling you this. It's like a confession or something I don't mean to sound that way."

"What way?"

"Well I don't know exactly it's just I got the impression from her she had been put to pasture. By you. Not that it's any of my business and I really don't care it's just."

"What do you mean put to pasture?"

"Nothing really."

"Listen you seem nice and all but tell me what she wants and I'll do it." Jim took a swig, his lower lip wetly protruding, and swallowed.

"Well it's not for me to say. I mean that's none of my business."

"She's got you too eh?" Jim chuckled and his shoulders hunched and I could hear the canvas of his brown overalls shh shhoo.

"No she hasn't got me in anyway although."

Jim's eyebrows climbed his forehead. "She's got ya too," he persisted, a beam of light flashing from the whites of his eyes. "Well that's the way it goes. And you're not the first mind. Here gimme at." Up he took the flask for a bite. "Now," he said, "you 'n me seem to get along alright. Know what I mean?" I smiled, mildly. "What's this now she was tellin'?"

"Nothing really just."

He stood and we went back into the house, Joel running after him and pulling on his overalls and dashing to the tricycle once again.

"Nothing really she seems to think."

And he positioned himself back on his chair.

"She seems to think you did something to the boy." He looked down at the kid, fiddling once again with a piece of plaster. "Like I said it's not for me to say it probably is just a flight of fancy but I couldn't help."

"A flight? Ha! What's that s'posed to be?"

"I mean some bit of imagination just to play a trick on me. Nothing again like I said it's really nothing."

"What does she mean by that," asked Jim, suddenly seeming to understand what she had confided to me.

"It's silly isn't it. It's not really true. It can't be. I mean here we are talking and something like that is pretty dastardly to have."

"What?"

"It's not something you or anyone would ever really do now come on. Don't you think?"

"Maybe it's just another one of 'er tricks like you say. Let me tell you other tricks. She told me she was going for a pack of cigarettes whaddaya think about that? This was when we first met. I mean there used to be laundry left in the bathroom for months. I mean I'd take it and bag it you know and she'd return it."

"Well I don't know what's the trick I mean."

"You think there's something to it?" asked Jim, in earnest.

"Something to it. Something. No. Nothing. I don't get it I mean I."

"Then what's she mean by all that? Listen. You seem pretty good natured and all know what I mean? What's it got to be?"

"Well I don't think it means anything!"

"Nothing?" he asked, "Then why's she been at me this way for all this time?"

"It's been a long time?"

"There's the time after that when she had to get medication. Yep."

"Well I don't know it's probably nothing it's probably nothing to think about at all I wouldn't worry about it." I was looking for a verbal exit.

Jim looked down at his kid, now beginning to ride the tricycle back and forth in a slow, rocking motion. After a long silence he finally said, "But you think it's something don't ya?"

"No. Well yes."

"Then tell me!" Jim was mildly excited now and his arms came to fold in his lap. The wind was beginning to go from me, so I leaned against one of the studded walls.

"Well I like you too Jim but."

"Listen if I'd a had a conversation like this with her long time ago. Listen. Did she tell you about how we conceived Joel?"

"Of course not like I said I don't."

"Well we were in Central Park. I knew she was this you know."

"Ditz?"

"Huh?"

"Ditzy woman?"

"Yeah that's it well."

"I'm not so sure it's as simple as a conversation," I interrupted.

"What ya mean? Ain't we gettin' along?"

"Sure but."

"Go on spit it out you're alright I can see what'd she say to you?"

"It makes me kind of sick to think it could actually be true and all!"

"Probly ain't nothing I heard it all. Quick. I gotta get back to work soon."

I tried to stand on my own two feet without losing balance. "Oh hell."

"No," he gestured with his big arm, "it's not so simple is it? Like I said she's been this way for a long time." And he laughed, then smiled over at Joel who was throwing pieces of fallen plaster and cement against the corner, where the plywood floor ran up about an inch short of the studs and the brick walls.

"She said."

"What she say? Something 'bout me and my son?"

"Well it had to do with the way you're raising him I think. If I understand her correctly."

"Well *what* she say then? 'Cause she's said a lot about that. You know I set her up with that apartment?"

"Yes I know that."

"Do you? Did she tell you how? I was working on the boiler there on 20th Street a couple years ago and I got home."

"It doesn't bear repeating," I interrupted, again.

He eased himself back in his chair, as if finally giving up the ghost of the conversation. I leaned against the wall.

Plunk. Plunk. Joel was filling up the corner of the room with whatever piece of plaster or wood shim he could find. Jim slowly turned from watching his boy and averted my own gaze, staring off into the murky, undeveloped space.

"I'll tell you," I began again, "but you have to promise that none of this was her idea."

"I'd like to think that," he quickly added, "Mostly she thinks it's her idea. You know what I mean? She's great at making stories like."

"No really I don't think you believe me. I had—"

"Listen ya gotta get this off your chest. I know it killed me I mean I was litterly hanging for years with this kind of thing."

"What kind of thing? You mean lies?"

"So she *did* lie to you."

"Well it could be a lie I don't really."

"Now you're just being plain silly 'bout the whole thing."

"Did you do it?" I asseted.

"Do *what*? Y'seem to be going all over the place and still not telling me what she said. You *even* standing over there? I've heard it all before. Listen I think it's kind of nice you even thought to check on me after all you been through with 'er." His arms dangled back down the sides of his chair again.

"Did you stick the piece of mercury in his."

"Mercury?"

"Or maybe solder you're a welder you said."

"I s'pose. What's mercury got to do with anything? She's inhabiting you?" Jim sat forward a bit and gave me an examination.

"Well you stuck something in his. Abdomen."

"He eats regular if that's what you mean."

"This isn't what I've said this is what Cynthia told me!" I couldn't believe he refused to acknowledge I had nothing whatsoever to do with his whore of an ex-wife.

"Whatever. You both seem to be on the same wavelength."

"So I don't suppose you stuck anything in his. You know. His."

"His what?!" Jim was smiling, about to bust out laughing.

"His PENIS for god's sake!"

Jim fell back in his chair. Joel stopped with the filling up of the floor-crack. At first I thought the overalled father was going to rear up out of his seat and pitch me from his building. But he began to cry. Silent tears began to run a glistening groove down his high-cheeked face.

"Well," I kindly asked, "did you?"

"What can I do. But of course not but don't you see what she meant? I never heard that one before 'at's a new one. When she started on the medicine we both had a joke about the ingredient. One was a merc'ry met'nol lith-ate or some such—"

"Lithium?"

"Yeah." He rubbed his calloused hands together and then brushed them loudly over the seemingly frozen trill of moisture under each cheek.

"Why don't you tell me what she meant," I flatly, pallidly, placidly commanded.

"You gotta help me. I mean I have no idea." He held his hands together, clasping them, gathering all his strength and focus into them.

"Listen Jim I'm sorry I told you I didn't want to bring it up it's nothing. It's nothing Jim. I shouldn't have opened my mouth."

"No you're OK."

"Well so are you Jim."

"What you say your name was again?" Jim snuffled.

"Hans Knudsen."

"Hans," he began, "what should I do?"

"You're asking *me*?"

"You have some kind a connection."

"I don't have anything. I have nothing. I keep telling you but you're not."

"No not that," he snuffled again. "Not that I mean what should I do now that I know. This. Now that I know this."

"Same as before I guess."

"No really what should I do I mean," he lightened a bit, "now that I know what she thinks a me an' the kid. What you suppose I should do. Call the doctor again? I mean it's outta control outta my hand at this point don't ya think?"

"Why? You were thinking something might be required?" He didn't hear me, however, and stared off in the direction of Joel. I couldn't say another word for fear he might take me to task again. I felt as frozen in my stance as he in his lone chair.

Without turning to me he said, "I'll see ya later thanks for the information I appreciated it. Got to get to work. Ha! Thanks for stopping by," he chuckled, "you're decent folk. Thanks for the heads-up. We'll be OK though."

"OK then," I uttered, and carefully made my way out the door. My steps heavily bounded up Luquer Street to 2nd Avenue and before I knew it I was heading down Union into my valley home once again. I spent most of the rest of the day staring out my window at the little drawbridge over the canal. As the evening wore on I think I was still there, wondering about the mistakes it takes to count and add up to a single life.

How many cities, from the beginning of time to the end of time, would continue to be built only to become rubble? How many humans would continue to inhabit the rubble? How many would continue to pay for the rubble with the growing abstraction of their lives?

How many would continue to believe in the abstraction of their lives, of these cities, of all these ruins in the new-new world as if *they* were some kind of God?

I woke in the morning feeling sick. The vanity of my own rubble and ruinous abode at the end of the world, far, I used to think, from the rest of the world. Now its very and only center.

—

"Up above the Canal there's the BQE the Gowanus Expressway and you can see it elevated you know on big huge pivots or pylons what are those called the big cement T's and all the cars whizzing up there and I think it leads to."

"The Prospect?" said my waitress friend after work the other day.

"No it's not the Prospect the Prospect runs east and west doesn't it?"

"Oh brother you're asking me I'm from Queens I wouldn't know," she said, sounding a bit serious.

"No," I continued, "I mean in the other direction."

"What other direction," she asked, laughing in her usual manner, straightening her blouse having taken off her apron.

"The Belt Parkway that's it."

"No that's not the Belt Parkway that's the BQE," she said, as we made our way across the street to the bank, then past 2nd Avenue and 4th street.

"It goes *that* way?" I asked.

"Oh brother why do you think they're called the Brooklyn-Queens-Expressway and the Belt you know Parkway?"

"Don't you find it odd," she had said to me in the back of the restaurant, "that those who would want a no smoking section would come into a restaurant that has and is known for its bar and its comfort and its reputation for being a smoking-designated type of establishment?"

"I guess," I said, thinking it odd, but not that odd, considering how strange people are in general. "Maybe they just want to take back what they feel rightfully belongs to them?"

"Oh brother I think you're giving them more credit than they're due," she said, and lit another Salem Lights 100.

"Maybe," I continued, "they see the new no smoking laws as something should have happened a long time ago."

"I get the feeling," she began, "you're not talking about the same law I."

"Well Law the law the law. Open your mouth let me see your teeth," I asked.

"My what! Oh Lord you're really gone," she opined.

We sat smoking in silence for a couple of beats.

"Don't," she began, "you think it odd we're sitting here talking about each other's mouths? I mean we've only known each other through that bell that dinger in the kitchen."

"That's right," I said, sniggering. "Is that the way it works for you?"

"What do you mean?"

"You go all the way around a subject in order to find a point in time is always the same point because it's about to be thought and so it's more having to do with a sort of nakedness catches both of us off guard kind of like so forces the moment flush sort of toward a sort of kind of new vocabulary only we two will have?"

Her mouth did fall open at that. "How did you know!"

"It was a guess. But it seemed like what was happening," I said, lying.

"Anything else happening?"

I blushed. She said nothing more.

—

As my shift begins I am always walking into the restaurant past a growing clientele. They look up from their menus and, upon seeing me, recognize by my swift and purposeful movements the grace of an employee.

They are at a loss, I see in their eyes, to continue with the menu. They want to continue talking but they cannot because of the sight of one of the cooks. Maybe if I enter while busily chewing on a piece of meat I'd be invisible.

—

Hot grease in the oft-used skillet.

Pop pop.

Then into it I add a little salsify.

Pop pop. Sizzling grease.

Ding ding.

The steaming stir-fry rises from the plate, sucked in by my nostrils, and then out the kitchen.

I'm writing this having taken my shirt off smelling its sweat and sickly greasy odor.

—

Another plate. Another round plate.

Side of greens. Side of meat. Ding ding.

I was going to write about the feeling, the sudden wave of nausea that passed over me on my 30th dinner last night. It was another plate. But it was also Hippolyte's face.

It *was* Hippolyte.

I thought of all that effort I had put into the cards and the graph paper performances. All of it was for nothing because I had fallen for her. But it was also all for a kind of nothingness to begin with, and so, like my falling for her who had fallen for me without me even having to get to know her, I had also fallen into a hole of existence by willingly participating.

I had wanted to participate in theater, to make a writer's contribution, but all I'm left with are voices in my empty head, painful omnipresent reminders of Hippolyte, of Carlyle, of Sara and the excruciating intellections brought from my early flirtation with the Cogito of self and un-self—

as if even my own dreams could penetrate reality. I am left with nothing but failure as if *that* were all there ever was.

And yet as bad as it sometimes makes me feel I'm still moved by the whole pageant and realize were it not some recognizable shape it would not be of the living. I'd rather be of the living, while I'm here, than of the dead.

In this, my mental life is renewed. In this, also, it is always on the verge of falling out the window into the Canal to be lost again forever, missing among these living shades of the Valley once again.

I *can* perceive, then, and the Cogito is renewed.

—

"Oh brother," said my friend the waitress, "what's this now!"

She was leaning over a pile of photographs she had taken a while back, when she had entertained the idea of becoming a professional photographer.

She pulled one out and showed it to me from the far end of the room. "What do you make of this?"

I approached and said, "Looks like a rabbit."

"You would say that wouldn't you. Oh brother."

It *was* a picture of a rabbit.

She threw it back on her stack in the backroom and went to light another cigarette and sip her iced coffee. The fan was blowing through the kitchen window.

"How long have we had that fan," I asked.

She sighed, trying to recall. She couldn't recall. And so we spent our night after the shift resting before cleaning and then leaving the slophouse.

—

"No one's ever left the meat locker open that long before—

and I want to know who is responsible. I've talked to Walter and Enriqué and you are the only one left."

The owner of the restaurant, yesterday, when I arrived, was explaining the situation to me, trying to get me to confess to the error. Apparently one of us left the meat locker open and most of the meat spoiled. The owners (we are run by two women who started in the restaurant business Upstate) rarely interfere in the dealings of the kitchen outright and so it was a strange sight to be called into the office in the basement for the express purpose of discussing what, at this point, should have been a routine part of lock-up.

"Hans I intend to find out what happened last night and since you are the only one who was left in the restaurant and the last of the kitchen help to leave—"

"But I *wasn't* the last!" I asserted, knowing I had stayed with Walter until the bartender was ready to leave, together, with us. "When we were leaving I told Walter to make sure the bottom half was done because I had done the top half."

I was referring to the lock-up list. I usually performed the top half of the routine and either Walter or Enriqué helped with the bottom half. That is, I was saved from having to mop the floor and deal with the meat locker and some of the other lifting involved with clean up. Besides, I was responsible for set-up and creation of the menu from week to week so I had other chores that kept me busy, ordering produce, making sure there were enough preps for the night, and so on.

"I always do the top half of the list."

"What top half?" the owner asked, knowing full well there was a list and a procedure followed every night.

"The list we wrote for the lock-up."

"Oh that," she said. "But who left the meat locker open if the list was followed?"

"Well it must have been Walter then because he was doing the bottom half of the list."

"He insists you were doing the bottom half."

"He said that?" I was confused.

"That's what he told me and I have no reason to doubt him."

"What does that mean?" I smartly asked.

"It means that your behavior of late has been noticeably—

agitated—

and *weird*," she asserted, firmly, making it stick.

"Weird?" I asked. What was so weird about having to work my tail off and sweat and come up with a clean kitchen every night?

"That's right—

weird. You've been snippety with everyone and now on top of it I find you've been drinking every night from the bar before you leave—

and this must be why—"

"But everyone does that!" I blurted.

"And now you are blaming everyone *else* for an occasional drink from the bar which is allowed this is not a jailhouse."

"Listen. What do you want from me." I was getting tired of the act already.

"What do *I* want? No need to get fresh with me you're the one who kept the meat locker open and you know the policy on this."

"There's a policy?"

"It comes out of your pay fortunately there wasn't too much damage Enriqué and Walter caught the mistake in time this morning because they were early and that's another thing you have to get here on time. Hans just don't let this happen again that's all I'm saying."

"Sure."

"And lay off the booze."

"No problem."

"I mean it."

Chastisement over, I felt like a little kid again trying to do the best I could, slopping the dinners together on the plate, making sure every little detail was just—

so—

—

SITTING at the waitresses apartment on 14th Street, late, after work, wondering why I came, and suddenly it dawns on me, this waitress is very very pretty.

I found myself listening to her, watching her light a cigarette, wander over to her records and choose something to play.

That she let me into her apartment! But how did this happen?

Is this the same thing that happened with Hippolyte? Was I taken in by some kind of physical presence and then the rest of the insanity followed, loosing me into a world of nothingness?

—

WALTER swears I said I would do the bottom of the list.

This, he says, was what he heard me say the night in which the meat locker was kept open and the meat not completely bagged and put away.

"Since when do I do the bottom half?" I asked.

"Listen I don't know why you gettin' all upset— what the hell she do to you? Nothin'. You the one gettin' away with it."

"Just like you're trying to get away with something right now am I right?" I was positive there was a concerted effort on the part of the other kitchen staff to get me fired. "Why?" I said, stopping the flow of an otherwise useless conversation, "Why? Walter? What's going on? What the hell is so important about getting me skewered?"

"No one tryin' to skew you man that you own problem. Huh!" he grunted, going about his little duties in the kitchen, before the restaurant opened.

"So nothing is anyone's responsibility except me who happens to be in charge in terms of prepping and ordering and whatnot around here—"

"You think that somethin' that ain't nothin'!"

"It's *all nothing* you Jackass!"

"That it. I'm gone. You can take you motherfucking

white ass the fuck where it mattah! Dig *that*!" He threw down his apron and marched out the front of the restaurant.

Now there are not enough cooks to run the line.

The owner has an ad in today's paper and is interviewing for the position. Meanwhile, it's doubletime for me, not only because Walter quit, but because I'm responsible for him quitting.

—

I USUALLY DON'T SIT HERE AND LINGER after the kitchen is closed. I usually don't open my notebook here at the restaurant. I am waiting for the waitress. She has disappeared into the bathroom or some place.

I said I would wait for her, to walk her part of the way home. But now I see what has happened—

she has forced my notebook open. *She's forcing me to write*!

—

CAUGHT up in a moment of irreality—

I was standing behind the order station, my usual spot in the kitchen, and a series of dings on the order bell prompted me to pull down the order checks and begin preparing them. But I was, simultaneously, struck by the memory of Hippolyte. As I prepared the food I became distracted, but pleasantly so.

The euphoria began to pass as I realized what a fool I

had been to have fallen in with her. But I felt even more foolish and embarrassed to think that, now, as I stood in the hot and busy kitchen, her presence, that is, *my* presence, hovering within her, within those rising flames of what I took to be love, our connection, rising over my body, captivating and controlling me completely—

that I was still *in* her world, and not the so-called real world.

—

LEFT to clean up the bottom half again.

This is the second or third time already since the initial meat locker incident. I am being screwed by the other kitchen help.

The new kid, Alex, is not any better than Walter was. He has learned to follow everyone's lead. In other words, he has learned to follow everyone following my lead which isn't a lead but is who they want me to be?

Fuming, blood boiling, I took myself away from the restaurant as quickly as possible after cleaning up the entire list. But not without lifting a bottle of bourbon.

—

SITTING AT THE WAITRESS'S apartment on 14th Street in front of her kitchen fan.

She shows me more pictures. But this time I say absolutely nothing. She wants me to notice certain aspects of the frame. I'm not an expert on photography, I tell her.

She gets frustrated and I find I have to get out into the city to walk.

—

My friend the waitress informs me I had better pay attention.

She says the owners are about to make some changes. In fact, she says to me on my way in today, they have already got it all figured out.

"Got what figured out?" I say, in a low voice, out on the sidewalk where she had been smoking a cigarette.

"Hans watch yourself—

just—

watch yourself."

"What's that mean?" I asked as she stared back into my eyes. We turned and walked into the restaurant. The owners were in the corner talking with someone. I hoped it was about new kitchen help.

—

Just speaking with the owners, my tone of voice, obviously English, and without any accents or inflections out of sync—

just speaking with them is enough to have the other kitchen staff think of *them* in consonance with *me*—

my authority in the kitchen comes not from the detailed

description of duties that belong to my position, but within that consonance—

within that appearance of belonging to the ruling, or owning, class.

—

IT TURNS out there *was* a change at work. But I still have my job.

I don't quite know what my waitress friend was referring to. There was no big controversy. Some of my duties have been taken away. I now share my time with the new cook and do not prepare the menu nor order produce. The owners site my attitude as of late, and I couldn't help but agree with them as they assessed my performance over the last year.

I thought they were going to fire me. A demotion (if that is what you want to call this) is not bad. I still get paid and that's all that matters.

—

MY "REPLACEMENT" and I work sometimes long stretches without saying a word to each other. Not because we are angry with each other, but because nothing needs to be said. We both understand what needs to be done and when and in what order so well there's a groove of speechless communication between us the work itself occupies.

—

W̲ɪ̲ᴘ̲ɪ̲ɴ̲ɢ̲ ̲ᴍ̲ʏ̲ ̲ʀ̲ᴀ̲ɢ̲ around the edge of the plate to clean it off and then ringing the bell.

—

T̲ᴏ̲ ̲ᴛ̲ᴇ̲ʟ̲ʟ̲ ̲ʏ̲ᴏ̲ᴜ̲ ̲ᴛ̲ʜ̲ᴇ̲ ̲ᴛ̲ʀ̲ᴜ̲ᴛ̲ʜ̲ I've been drunk most every night after work so I haven't really been able to figure where I'm going, what I've done, where I should be, right now, along side the so-called facts of my days.

But now on a Sunday (my only day off) I am shedding cobwebs of work and the weather has also changed to overcast and rainy. I feel I'm under the rain clouds, sheltered by their threat. I never thought attachment to the so-called Cogito would have me seeking shelter within the elements but that's precisely what I'm faced with.

Others, it seems, have already passed this way. And yet is it only my own sense of things. I call it the *Cogito*. Keeps me in contact with the "character" of other citizens? I think I have developed a conscious sense of Being the others do not possess. It is as if I have possessed my own self to a degree to which no "other" has any need nor want to inhabit.

—

A̲ ̲ᴄ̲ʀ̲ᴏ̲ᴡ̲ᴅ̲ of people wait for me to serve them food.

—

I suppose without the need to pay rent I would have no need to work. I would have no need to come back to this valley to sleep. I would have no need, period. These walls, this window, all this room, is, properly speaking, nothing but my own need.

—

Rosita, on her way downstairs with her chair. I stop behind her. She takes a long time to get to the street, especially with folding-chair in hand.

So I'm left staring at her backside. And my eyes wander to the chair. I find myself becoming entranced by the pattern of the polyester weave. Little circles made with blue, red, and green strands.

When she's finally in her spot and the chair is opened, I'm standing there watching her go through her routine. She doesn't seem to notice me.

"Rosita that's a nice chair," I say.

She looks up as she's about to plop into it. Then when she plops she nods her head.

"I like the pattern. Did you pick this out yourself?"

"It is the—
beach section—"

"The beach section?"

"No
other—
biggest—

New York City—"

"It's the biggest store in New York City. For beach supplies?"

She nods her head.

"Uptown? Downtown?" I ask.

She motions with her hand, circling like a helicopter above her head.

—

AWAKENED by the sound of the fire hydrant being opened and the children screaming under its tap.

—

I CAN HEAR POPPY SINGING over his radio in the scrapyard. Now he's calling for his dog. Now he's feeding the kittens. There must be about a thousand kittens in that yard. Has he begun to fix even one engine during the entire time I've been here? Probably. I wouldn't know it if he did. I can only see part of his workshop when I walk by some afternoons, en route to my shift on the line. He's certainly not working late into the night when I return. All the lights are off. I'm probably the only idiot in the entire valley to get home so late and stay up so late and never, seemingly, have anything to say about anything here—

what purpose, other than raw danger, would ever come to a stranger like me?

GOWANUS CANAL

—

THE RADIO is in Spanish. But the advertisements and the songs are all echoes of what happens on the other stations.

The talk around the auto body shop, heard when walking past the scrapyard, or sometimes, especially this summer, through my windows, front and back, sounds like any other English banter and small talk.

It's as if I could speak to them and their world in Spanish because it is the same as the English version.

But then I'd be really crazy, right?

—

POPPY'S SCRAPYARD in the afternoon—

the radio playing the same songs from the same Spanish from other days that could be so much this very same summer day.

I imagine Poppy under the umbrella of that radio and those familiar songs, safe within his little corrugated shack.

Safe from the heat, surrounded by hub-caps. The memory of an entire race?

—

STRANGE LIGHT and mist this morning. Couldn't sleep for the heat and was up early.

Corner for coffee and the early morning folks in suits

and nice shoes down from the hill off to the subway or walking toward the river to plunge into a day of office—

Coming back with the coffee and a pack of cigarettes, a kind of country scene on the water, in the narrow Canal. My sight narrowed into the foggy distance. It felt like another time, another place, another country.

Suddenly I felt all destiny come flying out of that mist and penetrate me.

—

I AM SITTING IN THE SUN, rising toward noon, blazing to eliminate both Rosita and me.

The laundromat is unbearably hot. Rosita moves her jaw and says absolutely nothing, emitting some kind of strange sound that could be a baby exiting gas but this is the retarded Rosita.

She's not really retarded. Something was done to her. Something—

she is looking down at me scribbling—

see, she knows I'm writing about her—

there, another sound from her—

and the church bells up on the slope are sounding toward noon.

Time for me to begin getting ready.

—

I THINK WE ARE deluding ourselves by believing we are here, that we're civilized, that we're a civilization, here, on this land, on this continent, superior to all. Or at least equal to all. We must, I believe, get down in the shade and turn the soil of this wilderness until it resembles a wilderness and that is the only way we can confront our problems.

Most of our problems will be seen as nothing if not the flat dead that once roamed back in Europe and all the many "homes" the people of these States do come from. We are in the middle of something very wild. The least little drop of oil on the hot skillet in the greasy, hot kitchen can prove and show the dimensions of this wilderness.

I like to see myself in a car driving fast out over the land, up in the mountains, or just out, away from this city, from my apartment above this stinking sewer called the Gowanus Canal.

But one has to look at it from low down. Even the mighty were once midgets. Just as this Canal was once a real canal—

People actually traversed it.

—

A HOT, very hot day, very uncomfortable.

An uncomfortable morning, trying to move my stinking flesh into the shower. Trying to keep the sweat from driving me insane.

The Spanish music seems never to stop. How can I go to work. It will be better there because of the air conditioning but the kitchen will still be warm.

The music is non-stop and is rising with the heat.

Everyone is out in the street. Children's voices punctuate

the songs. The tinny rasp of the radios out their windows, and from Poppy's lot the people mill about, the heat having final say, the music lifting them into the afternoon of the world.

It seems I have lived a life that is consonant to the city—

and these others, the neighbors, have lived a life, are living a life according *to* the world. They follow the course of the sun. They follow the distant cries and explosions over there under the expressway and seem to take to life before these events happen.

My relationship with the Gowanus Canal is the only relationship I have. I have the waitress from the restaurant, sure. I have the memories of the theater. I have the memories of my life as it seemed to progress toward an understanding of itself. But I have nothing now but the Gowanus Canal. It measures my days and nights. I cannot follow what others follow, but somehow, privately, I do.

I *see* it in the nearness of the distance these others give their *full beliefs* to.

—

IT IS PERHAPS NOT GIVEN any of us to lead so-called normal lives.

The sister or cousin (Rosita) of the *Gowanus Laundromat* owner may see it differently, but I can't help thinking if she had had a normal existence she would have warded off her suffering so. But it was simply not given to her to have that capacity. Others have come and gone in this new-new world, and yet none have been able to survive it.

That's a fact.

But those who have been able to adapt moved out, convinced that enough is indeed enough. Or others yet concerned themselves with endless diversions, entitling them through some sort of symbiosis within the new-new world to a survival mechanism—

whether it be money or what have you—

to allow themselves to survive, to rise above the earthly predicament. I certainly wish it had been given to me.

And if Rosita had been given the opportunity I'm sure she would have taken it; but the thing is she was given nothing and she is left with nothing; a compiling nothing, a nothing that keeps her isolated from humanity and time. Maybe someone is needed to record the history of this wasteland. And given enough, myself, I might ask her for it, for something, some data, anything.

Is there anything in there you old bursting buzzard of tar and cement shoes, the bottom of the canal? I wonder if Rosita has seen any of the bodies that supposedly were dumped in the Canal, actually being tossed over the bridge's railing.

Can you hear me?

Walking past her with my bag of laundry—

that's it, there's nothing else.

How many times has she counted the people coming and going? And then I stop to think of her body, her colon, and all that has been stopped up there for years. She's *got* to be constipated. It must be true; I never see her leave her place in front of the laundromat.

But maybe Poppy Rodriguez lied to me. Maybe it's another fanciful tale. Why would someone invent something

like that, though? She's obviously *non compus mentas*. And so they have decided to pin one more sordid thing on her—
because they can't face the fact of her existence—
and by extension their own existence? This fact, compounded with all the other facts but that fact alone above all others—
that it wasn't in their power, ever, to *have* anything, anything.
And so they say she is constipated, like some sick joke on their own sick lives. Something they can share with others, without having to really come right out and say, you know I have nothing and I'm a stupid son-of-a-bitch to boot; and, we're all a family of inbred dysfunctional pariahs who can't get off our lazy asses to do anything about anything; anything.
But this still isn't fair. I know, look who's talking. Look who's sounding off. I can't even go and win the most obvious mutual attraction from the corpus of a living madonna.
My calling lay elsewhere?
This they say—
people's true gifts might lie elsewhere, but where could that be if everything is simply up front and either given or not—
what's the big mystery?
Whether I was or am still able to go get Hippolyte (or any other desirable) would it really change the habits of an entire race? Would they stop going to school to found a mechanical career? Would they stop lusting after foolish objects—
cameras, for instance? Would they want to stand up and look at the sky? It seems I learned long ago people are

exactly what they are not; and yet they persist. And that ridiculousness is what keeps the whole modern thing going under the umbrella of the old sad religions.

Why was I brought to the edge of existence merely to peer over and be told I have no option but to jump? My brain tells me to keep going, and yet the reality of my particular circumstance is that the cards and the theater I was involved with, and the entire theatrical spectacle industry in general, just has nothing whatsoever to give to me. My poems and plays and stories have gone un-performed. They have been read only by me.

And yet why would I want anyone else to see them? It occurs to me now I must not let anything deter me from the secrecy of this multitude-imposed denial—

the cards I had produced were, in effect, erased, flattened, reduced to nothing. To a lot of furniture.

And yet still I know and persist in knowing they are reduced!

—

Rosita is sitting in her chair watching heat blister into the oily wood piling of the canal and I bet even she can hear the truth (rumbling through the body-shop of the world, flushing like one big toilet all history and the entirety of race and of what once was so interesting, so mysterious—

as if now only history could be mysterious! Animate!)

It's not just my own predicament then. And it's not just Rosita, or Poppy's Scrapyard. It's the entirety of what has transpired.

It is completely unknowable?

If Richard and Sara had reduced my initial bursts of love and creativity into nothing well then what difference does that make in the long run? Everything has been reduced to nothing; everything is *bound* to be reduced to nothing. These two truths have nothing whatsoever to do with my little problem nor my existence in general?

And so, I should just forget it, plod my way through without a thought, or better yet do what they've done down at the *Gowanus Laundromat*—

pin a fabulous story onto a freak of the living to fill themselves up. Make her the idol of the human race. Make her the forgotten person of the entire human race. It makes more sense than anything, more sense than the tar and the machine parts and the rats and the garbage; more sense to them than those little bridges lining the Gowanus Colon off the East River's toilet flush.

—

T<small>RYING TO FIND</small> on a Sunday *all* the bridges along the Canal.

Starting at Union they are this new kind of wood, a green wood, unpainted. Some of the streets don't intersect, there are dead ends and I've gone down 4th Avenue and had to cut in toward the Canal in the direction of it without any idea where it would be.

Then of course under the expressway where there are seemingly no pedestrians, toward Red Hook, and then back toward the Canal again. Eventually, the new bridges cease and there are nothing but old, blackened metal and wood structures. The precursors, no doubt, to the greenwood drawbridge just out my window on Union.

—

"Do not look," says Poppy to me in the stairwell while I'm waiting for my dry cycle to finish downstairs, "do not look—
these people—
ach! You are good—
person—
an' doan care!" he says as he gets up to leave, opening the door, the August light filling the stairwell, the weekend evening, the valley's streets warm and pleasant—
"I do not care—
what you are—
you unnerstan?"
And the door closed. I went to my room. True, I thought, I do pay my rent on time. But is this the only reason Poppy talked to me this way? I'm not sure. Others might contend with him on that level but I can't help thinking he is saying something else by telling me I'm a good person. There are all kinds of good people. Most of them are invisible. We pretend to know people by how prompt they pay their bills. I have only been late with the rent once and that was because I had forgotten.

Poppy does the collecting of rent for the *Gowanus Holdings Company*. I have not bothered to ask him his "arrangement" with them. I have a feeling the *GHC* is some kind of front. But in this world where money is of necessity the creator of a "front" for servicing all kinds of things, I don't quite see where it would be any of my business to get behind that front. I've had enough of fronts.

—

IN THE DISTANT SCHOOLYARDS the cheering fillips of the little children. By the afternoon they descend toward the neighborhood and play in the street all day. Sometimes I run into them in my walks about the Canal.

I can't help but think of Carlyle's son, now nothing but his father's son, having been taken away. What is it going to be like to live one's entire existence knowing one's mother is mad?

What must it be like to have nothing but a piece of mercury deciding the direction one must take—

To proceed then toward further mercury ad infinitum up the ladder toward a career of mercury and—

—

HEADING OUT TO WORK on a Friday, lingering and late, I stopped by the Canal instead of racing directly to the subway. I took a different route, knowing I was late. I decided to merely take my time.

Crossing back over 4th Avenue near Flatbush, something in the sky (the light maybe) began to send signals. Obviously I was not used to being in the neighborhood so late in the afternoon. Then, just as I was ready to pause and take the wind's direction and continue toward the subway, hundreds of school kids flooded out the doors of the school I was standing in front of.

They rushed out the doors with their bags, all of them yelling and screaming and laughing. I had heard their noises before, but from a distance, from within my apartment. Now they were all around me and we were all proceeding in the same direction.

I tried not to be noticed and to be swept along with their tide.

—

WHEN THE APE-CHILDREN begin their march, my view from this window will have been fulfilled within the entire species and a new civilization will be sounded from the shores of what was once (also) a new world.

It will then be seen as the old world. Or like some kind of fiction.

History ceases its trickery when there are people that stand up on her to realize solid ground beneath the feet, and suspended animation in the old time mind of man.

—

THE LIGHT GOING DOWN.
    What am I doing standing on the drawbridge—
    an entire day off and there I am just lingering—
    somehow lingering doesn't make sense here.

—

THIS WHOLE Gowanus Valley swings between two things—
voices yelling from the scrapyards and lots and buildings and stoops across the street.

Family members, friends, whatever they are, have only the two walls—

One is placated with hubcaps, fenders, littered with engine parts; the other wall is a high brick façade with windows.

Between these two rallying points the voices weave their contents until, eventually, one day, they will recognize the wall that speaks—

the wall that was; the wall that is.

And it will seem like a pretty petty thing to have spent one's life being controlled by that tension.

—

AS THE LIMO DOORS SLAM these summer nights and the security men with their German shepherds enter the training facility for a late-night session, I often wake, like last night, with the idea blazing in my sleeping head that everything these people do, from Long Island over to Hoboken, is nothing if not a racial thing.

The Italians have German shepherds; the Spaniards have their music; me and the Pennsylvanian's have a clan somewhere cooking beans and investing in Wall Street; the

African's have the wood carving industry; Jews have a history in every industry; the Irish have the Horse-stables; and any other race you can think of has some trade secret germane to their underbelly of city and system.

The system, it occurred to me last night, with my temples flaming, greasy, miasmic poison and the stress of overwork and death—

is nothing if not all the different races uncrossed and unrealized.

Who has crossed any line to find out how any system works? A civic heat stews in my bed every night. Is there no escape? Can I leave this place? How much money will it take? Is any of this supposed to "mean" me? What would happen if I put it all together as one: a new system?

Am I only faced with the Gowanus Canal and this valley of cement? Am I the giant of the valley? What power does the giant have, besides infernal headaches and a low-paying, back-breaking job in an over-priced slophouse?

—

TOGETHER WE ARE NOTHING.

All that life once was becomes a center ring in the circus of nerves. Some of us go to prey on those nerves. Some of us go to that center ring. Others are left behind. But it is still nothing at the center that we've discovered?

In the final analysis, the sky above the Gowanus Canal is not there, but below, rising from fermenting and poisonous collections of sewer drainage, spilt barge oil, de-oxygenated H_2O.

Dreams are like fingers that touch the surface once and watch the delicate ripple spread forever through the earth.

I rise in the middle of the night and walk toward the Brooklyn Bridge. Standing in the wind, high in its spindled shafts of air, I decide it is too cowardly to simply jump. The city of Manhattan in the near distance; the traffic below and the East River with a few boats. The smoke is rising from here and there, light enough in the dark to see it rise. The waves of flags are all flying on the top of tall skyscrapers; the booming voice of its Being rises above the sound of the wind cupping my eardrums.

—

PERMANENT CHANGE must be just a glance away in the realization of such a place. In fact, so they say, these old buildings, these industrial spaces, unused since mid-century, where I now live, will rise in value. So it is rumored that this space will rise in value to the talents it has harbored in its poisonous piers and useless way, inward, toward the Union Street Bridge. Here I sit, a block down from the *South Brooklyn Casket Company*, the *Acme Guard Dog Training School*, the *Empire State Oil Company*. Here I sit, waiting, wondering what that old-world significance of water might hold for the new world recently and ever-presently rushing to evaluate all.

Will the draw-bridge just out my window suddenly rise with a splendor and value not yet recognized? Its gears suddenly become a thing of antiquity and amusement? Who must look to realize it and everything connected with this canal; who must be paved over and forgotten?

Will it be that moment of valuation and discovery and attendant wealth that suddenly lifts all this ruin and churning poverty into the heaven of museums?

—

HIPPOLYTE OBSESSION AS A PROPOSITION—

If she is everywhere I turn—

I mean, here above me is the window and if I stare long enough I begin to see outlines of her face, of the parts of her I most admired. Isn't this approach of reality toward me similar to the rising predicate from any proposed ideation? Especially those that most ruled my years and my head so far?

So that all my mind, that any thought or rumor ever proposed to me, now becomes nothing more than attraction I held for her? And for *her* in particular? Is she going to be easy to forget? Should I *forget* her? Should I forget everything that happened in that theater, that bar?

How could I have let one person rule me? How could I ever justify that? The world is nothing more than its various parts to me now and nowhere must it come to be one, because then I will be under the spell of Hippolyte once again?

Had she known from the beginning this was going to happen to my mind? How many of us are so composed? How is this Canal and this cement and this brick to be taken now?

It's as if I did see my descent into this urban valley as

dangerous, everything it indeed is—

a certain hell, an imprisonment, guarded by other citizens, guarded by closely watched walls and bridges and cars and noise.

And yet I was unable to listen to my senses in that panic and alarm. Why am I so purposely ignorant? Why can't I break out of this place that is now everything, that is now shrunk to the size of the whole world?

—

Cogito—
    splash—
I should write nothing but Haiku?

—

Finally, a cool night.

I can hear the populace return to something like normalcy but wonder, in the back of my brain, whether that isn't quite simply the end of everything. Change of season, change of heart, change of cement as if cement can change.

And of course it can; it contracts and expands according to weather.

Once I thought trees in the Seminary Garden were the sources of a possible dream in which Descartes had actually existed and through which he wanted to return all to—

his benefactress whom *he* taught?

But I can't bring myself to teach Rosita *anything*. She

only makes me want to throw up.

I can't think about these people here in the valley.

—

I FEEL a unitary being.

Even though all has gone out around me, the lights and the people, I am whole. And also extinguished, annihilated because of that oneness.

I don't think the deleterious effects of miasmic intervention, causing these bricks to heat like a furnace during the summer, have shown me to be anything but what I most am. My record, as invisible as it may seem to most—

a cook, an out-of-towner, a single man living with the underclasses—

has very little to do with me.

Having seen the demise of love (or what is called love).

Love has given me nothing but time?

Perhaps the world has fallen apart. For good. Perhaps there is nothing, truly nothing, in that respect, to live for. But I do not feel that; furthermore, I do not witness that. I look to the window and beyond the walls toward the Gowanus Canal and see it teeming with life—

and nothing *but* life. I cannot help but believe in life no matter the anti-bodies floating in its dark scum.

—

WEDNESDAY, 3:00 A.M.—

Explosions on the far side of the Canal, near the river.

Quiet 'til a minute ago. But it was loud enough for an explosion of some kind. It might have been a large truck on the elevated expressway. Or some large tanker at the docks. But the docks aren't really used anymore. A gas or petroleum container of some kind. Or a gun or M-80 let off in an abandoned building underneath the expressway.

It could also have been one of the drawbridges being lowered, coupling in its bed of iron, echoing through the bottom of the Canal, carried up through the buildings—

a kind of tidal wave of sound.

—

Do my thoughts really matter?

Isn't the Cogito, and my attachment to it outside any Church, that which exists already? Aren't there shoes to be filled, as always, and so we fill them, as always?

Is the world that which happened between the theater, the bar, and this home in the low valley of a territory called Gowanus?

Are these the only eyes that see?

—

It had rained today and so coming home, walking past the apartments along Bergen and Smith Streets, coming down into the valley, the coolness from the day and early evening still lingering in the late late night for the early early

morning—
 a depression in the earth itself. No time but the weather patterns that occur within their seasons. All human gesture and aspiration goes into this place as if it had nowhere else ever to have been.

—

THE LIGHT—
 The time—
 The motion—
 The sadness of the inevitable—
 The unbearable position of mere existence—
 To have been brought to mere existence by everything that already is and by nothing else no evolution but the material evolution that was set in motion before people came and will continue after they go so why are they so obsessed with God and their silly religions it's all so beyond us I mean why don't they realize they are going to die or that they are already dead that's all it's going to take that one realization and then what—
 No light—
 No time—
 No motion—
 Sadness of the inevitable—
 The unbearable—

—

BED is the only place where I am not imprisoned—
lingering in wakefulness not wanting to drown in sleep—

—

A SCREAM off in the distance.
From here it sounds like someone being violated in the middle of the late night. But it is probably only a child yelling after a friend in a faraway street. Echoed off the cement and seemed to permeate everything in this section of the valley.

—

I'M NOT THE ONLY ONE who heard that booming explosion-like sound in the distance, vibrating through the entire valley. I can't be the only one who works nights and gets home at 3:17 A.M.
Significance must be giving birth to my ear and mine alone because I could swear I also heard an answer to that explosion, as if the city were playing some kind of sonic call-and-response.
Maybe all these explosive dots and dashes will fill me in on what I've been missing.
But I haven't been missing anything have I?

—

IF INFINITY IS the *expression* of human progress, and finitude is the *place* of human progress, is the Cogito of all humanity then the self that thinks "progressively?"

Is this a different way of thinking? Compared to what?

Has thought always existed with the mass of humanity only incubating until its full exposure within a totality of the world's population?

Is this the revelation the Bible speaks of?

How trite!

—

THE WIND is whipping across the night's earth and the night's sky's clouds are being furrowed by it.

There is nothing within the world there is no human no thoughts no nothing just a walk in the park listening to the wind—

It is speaking—

a large gaping hole in a bulbous and warted old tree on the dark street up close looks exactly like a mouth.

—

IS THE COGITO CONFINED to its reference points or places or is it always free from them?

That is, am I the sum of my parts, or the *summing* of my parts?—

Rosita's wrist whirling around above her head.

—

WATCHING THE BLIPPING red light on the security system of the bakery on 7th Avenue. Each store along the street, presumably, has one also—
finally, I'm home.

—

WONDERING IF MY thoughts are not rather the hand-me-downs of others, all others.
There is not an original thought in my head?
Yet how can this be. Wasn't I an absolute originality at the Theological Seminary, the only one in recent memory who had gone on to relate, to continue relating to the world outside, and yet alongside, the dictates of that or any religion?
And yet Mickelmann had seen me go, had let me go, had even encouraged me to go. Was that the entrance of my self into the world of "no thought?" Was that the exit from any originality, any individuality, any institution ancient or modern?
And yet I continue to enter and exit my mental world. All in order to maintain originality and identity? What's the point of religion, or, for that matter anything we recognize, when, after all the heart of all goes in and out and—
and Aladdin's lamp was so buffed—

―

Is what I call the Cogito just a diversion from my true self—
    and the role that self should be fulfilling?

―

I love this hour more than the morning hour—
    finally the people's senseless voices, along with their senseless lives, have gone down to sleep the only proper place for anything at all—
    and I can hear the slight sounds punctuating night air from the safety of my apartment—

―

Somehow I was kicked out of everything that at one time or another I thought to be due me. Is this to be the way of my entire life? Is this our *essence*?

―

What does Carlyle's plight have to do with reality?
    Is there something this night as I think of her, here in the Canal, the street, the walls, my shower in the coming morning, my path to work, all the people's paths to work, all the

cars and trucks up on the elevated expressway—

the mercurial clock her husband allegedly put in her son's penis—

tomorrow and tomorrow and tomorrow—

was this a figment of her imagination or did it really happen?

I see her in the madhouse surrounded by sympathetic guards and Blades and Stewart. Will they question her with kid gloves until they discover she is insane and then throw the book at her? Or will they really want to discover what made her into the mind she is today?

Whatever it takes, I suppose, to solve the murder, and nothing more.

—

A HERD of limos at 3 o'clock a.m.

I'm coming down the hill from Smith Street when I notice a line of black cars, shiny under the street lamps on Union, wrapped around the corner to the *Acme Guard Dog Training School.*

At the bottom of the hill, standing in front of the Gowanus Canal where it intersects with 3rd Avenue, I saw all the drivers of the Limos, each with a German shepherd, make their way toward me.

I stared for a moment but only to appear as if I was looking at the non-existent street traffic. As I slowly walked toward my building's door I turned and noticed that all the drivers were then getting into their Limos, each with their own German shepherd.

SEEING the Canal in the moon's light I am ashamed to think of myself alone in my apartment, contemplating it and this valley that I have come to inhabit.

And yet that is a completely ridiculous assertion. What has made me feel this way? This is where I live! I have every right to inhabit, to think, to come to the window of my room and contemplate, at my leisure, this Canal.

—

ALL my time is spent now in the concentration of the Cogito. To get it. To get beyond the work and the summer and everything else about my life, whether it be memory or actuality, and try to understand what is happening to the Cogito.

—

NO Rosita today.

And this evening, in her place, the same group of old men. Poppy is down there now. I tried to say hello but they would not let me into their group. Even Poppy would not say hello. In their eyes I sensed an effort to not acknowledge my presence. They were just standing there smoking, talking in low-toned Spanish. They know I live here and yet they refuse to even nod in my direction.

They are whispering and my Spanish isn't very good. My Spanish isn't very good.

—

"Rents going up all ovah!" said Poppy as he tried to explain the note that was shoved under my door tonight.

It was from the *Gowanus Holdings Company*, and notified the tenant of a rent increase as of next month, when my lease expires.

"But this is expected Poppy it's in the lease agreement it goes up when renewed."

Poppy seemed concerned, as if he wanted me to understand something.

"But Rent going up all ove-*r*!"

"This is a different increase it doesn't say anything there about—"

I took the paper from him. "Poppy it's OK it's only 25 dollars I can handle it besides rent does go up it's a fact it happens everywhere the world over—"

"Rent going up all ovah the world! That—
Han—
you a good kid I like you that is true," he said, laughing and smiling and winking and wagging his finger up at me as he made his way back down the stairs.

—

GOWANUS CANAL

If I had never left the Church, the Theological Seminary, everything I know about the Cogito would simply not have existed.

The world would have been filtered down to me through a series of levels, none of which come close to *the* level of understanding which *is* the world.

Self, selves, *and* the world.

—

The world is surrounded by a ring of fire—

Letting go after work, pushing my senses into the night, imagining the Canal sleeping along its length toward the River then along the coast and out to sea.

—

Will I now up and walk?

Have I been completely forgotten? Who would ever have remembered me anyway?

Was I to have been in the bosom of some God forever?

—

Footsteps—

A thousand footsteps tramping off to work. All their beat must have been the concentration of one point out of time last night the stillness which I call my "thought."

—

History is sleeping in the stillness of cement—
in the stillness of buildings?

—

My own sickness turns out to be the reason my head is swimming. Though I made it in to work today.

—

Someone is talking to the owners.
They suspect, and have a new system of inventory for the bar.

—

Somehow I know I'll get through—
but my explanation, my fulfillment, will be nowhere near the mark others center theirs upon.

—

SHE UNTIES HER APRON-STRINGS and then turns and notices I've been watching her and she says "What? What are you looking at?"

—

RAIN rushing down flooding the street the only motion any water has in this valley.
    The Canal is actually rippling with waves.

—

IT'S NOT THAT I REALLY WANT to, because of the hangover, like this morning—
    but reaching over to that freshly poured straight shot of bourbon, especially after I haven't had any in a long time, brings me back to my senses.

—

    ALL ALONG UNION STREET they say the money is going to run. All the way down into this valley they say the real estate is going to rise in value—
    as if in changing its existence its rotten essence will change.

—

MAYBE IT WAS THE BOOZE AGAIN—
   I leaned over and by the whirring of the kitchen fan—we kissed.

—

A LARGE PIECE OF METAL maybe a fender being bent and hammered and sharply shaven by some kind of electric grinder.

—

THE COGITO and *my* Cogito are one and the same in that I think it and therefore all my thoughts then merge, flatten and become clear and all is clear within the brain made that way by the Cogito itself. Flattened.

—

A LARGE RAT startled me as I was coming down from Smith Street into the center of the valley.
   It trundled out very slowly from under a black plastic garbage bag and strutted right in front of me. It had to be about two feet long. Honest to god, I was ready to crap in my shorts!

—

SOMETIMES I'm absolutely absorbed by my routine. Other times I can't be bothered.

—

I FOUND A TABLE on the street and brought it back to the apartment. Small enough to fit next to the one I already have, yet big enough to actually be of use.

—

ANOTHER 200 DOLLARS and I should have enough for that plane ticket to the Virgin Islands. If I can stay there for three weeks—
    can't think about that yet—

—

KIDS THROWING STONES against a brick wall covered with graffiti. Behind it a large and blackened and obviously unused building. On the other side of the Canal, on the other side of the Expressway.

—

STANDING in the middle of the trees at the edge of Prospect Park while it thunders and rains.

Eventually I ran out of there but it was no use I'm soaked to the bone.

—

IT DOESN'T MATTER if we forget; it doesn't matter if we change; *it doesn't matter if we die*.

—

IN THE NIGHT, listening for distant sirens to bellow forth into the valley, I moved a chair. It creaked and scudded on the kitchen floor. It was as if I had never really heard that sound before. Or it's another night, a new night.

—

WHAT AM I MISSING? So what, everybody's missing something.

Is this true? I'm not sure.

Obviously something is being missed if I can't apply this moment's quandary to anything other than the Canal. It is situated outside my window. I've had a couple of night-caps. I'm just about done for the day. The night.

Yet I can't help feeling I'm missing something.

GOWANUS CANAL

—

TELEVISION next door and I can hear it very plainly as if it were just the next room of the same apartment. But it is sounding through a double wall of brick and cement. The valley is so still and quiet tonight it's as if the entire surrounding city has left for the duration of the summer.

—

DEAD tired. A splash—
    as if the water in the Canal had stirred. How many times have I thought about—

TOD THILLEMAN moved to New York at the age of 18 and worked for a brief period with Pace Editions. He is the author of numerous poetry collections including *Three Mouths*, also from Spuyten Duyvil. From 1991-1999 he was editor of *Poetry New York: a journal of poetry & translation*.

SPUYTEN DUYVIL

1881471772	6/2/95	DONALD BRECKENRIDGE
193313223X	8TH AVENUE	STEFAN BRECHT
1881471942	ACTS OF LEVITATION	LAYNIE BROWNE
1933132221	ALIEN MATTER	REGINA DERIEVA
1881471748	ANARCHY	MARK SCROGGINS
1881471675	ANGELUS BELL	EDWARD FOSTER
188147142X	ANSWERABLE TO NONE	EDWARD FOSTER
1881471950	APO/CALYPSO	GORDON OSING
1933132248	APPLES OF THE EARTH	DINA ELENBOGEN
1881471799	ARC: CLEAVAGE OF GHOSTS	NOAM MOR
1881471667	ARE NOT OUR LOWING HEIFERS SLEEKER THAN NIGHT-SWOLLEN MUSHROOMS?	NADA GORDON
0972066276	BALKAN ROULETTE	DRAZAN GUNJACA
1881471241	BANKS OF HUNGER AND HARDSHIP	J. HUNTER PATTERSON
1881471624	BLACK LACE	BARBARA HENNING
1881471918	BREATHING FREE	VYT BAKAITIS (ED.)
1881471225	BY THE TIME YOU FINISH THIS BOOK YOU MIGHT BE DEAD	AARON ZIMMERMAN
1881471829	COLUMNS: TRACK 2	NORMAN FINKELSTEIN
0972066284	CONVICTION & SUBSEQUENT LIFE OF SAVIOR NECK	CHRISTIAN TEBORDO
1881471934	CONVICTIONS NET OF BRANCHES	MICHAEL HELLER
1881471195	CORYBANTES	TOD THILLEMAN
1881471306	CUNNING	LAURA MORIARTY
1881471217	DANCING WITH A TIGER	ROBERT FRIEND
1881471284	DAY BOOK OF A VIRTUAL POET	ROBERT CREELEY
1881471330	DESIRE NOTEBOOKS	JOHN HIGH
1881471683	DETECTIVE SENTENCES	BARBARA HENNING
1881471357	DIFFIDENCE	JEAN HARRIS
1881471802	DONT KILL ANYONE, I LOVE YOU	GOJMIR POLAJNAR
1881471985	EVIL QUEEN	BENJAMIN PEREZ
1881471837	FAIRY FLAG AND OTHER STORIES	JIM SAVIO
1881471969	FARCE	CARMEN FIRAN
188147187X	FLAME CHARTS	PAUL OPPENHEIMER
1881471268	FLICKER AT THE EDGE OF THINGS	LEONARD SCHWARTZ
1933132027	FORM	MARTIN NAKELL
1881471756	GENTLEMEN IN TURBANS, LADIES CAULS	JOHN GALLAHER
1933132132	GESTURE THROUGH TIME	ELIZABETH BLOCK
1933132078	GOD'S WHISPER	DENNIS BARONE
1933132000	GOWANUS CANAL, HANS KNUDSEN	TOD THILLEMAN
1881471586	IDENTITY	BASIL KING
1881471810	IN IT WHATS IN IT	DAVID BARATIER
0972066233	INCRETION	BRIAN STRANG
0972066217	JACKPOT	TSIPI KELLER
1881471721	JAZZER & THE LOITERING LADY	GORDON OSING
1881471926	KNOWLEDGE	MICHAEL HELLER
193313206X	LAST SUPPER OF THE SENSES	DEAN KOSTOS
1881471470	LITTLE TALES OF FAMILY AND WAR	MARTHA KING
0972066241	LONG FALL	ANDREY GRITSMAN
0972066225	LYRICAL INTERFERENCE	NORMAN FINKELSTEIN
1933132094	MALCOLM AND JACK	TED PELTON

1933132086	MERMAID'S PURSE	LAYNIE BROWNE
1881471594	MIOTTE	RUHRBERG & YAU (EDS.)
097206625X	MOBILITY LOUNGE	DAVID LINCOLN
1881471322	MOUTH OF SHADOWS	CHARLES BORKHUIS
1881471896	MOVING STILL	LEONARD BRINK
1881471209	MS	MICHAEL MAGEE
1881471853	NOTES OF A NUDE MODEL	HARRIET SOHMERS ZWERLING
1881471527	OPEN VAULT	STEPHEN SARTARELLI
1933132116	OSIRIS WITH A TROMBONE ACROSS THE SEAM OF INSUBSTANCE	JULIAN SEMILIAN
1881471977	OUR DOGS	SUSAN RING
1881471152	OUR FATHER	MICHAEL STEPHENS
0972066209	OVER THE LIFELINE	ADRIAN SANGEORZAN
1933132256	PIGS DRINK FROM INFINITY	MARK SPITZER
1881471691	POET	BASIL KING
0972066292	POLITICAL ECOSYSTEMS	J.P. HARPIGNIES
1933132051	POWERS: TRACK 3	NORMAN FINKELSTEIN
1933132191	RE-TELLING	TSIPI KELLER
1881471454	RUNAWAY WOODS	STEPHEN SARTARELLI
1933132035	SAIGON & OTHER POEMS	JACK WALTERS
1933132167	SARDINE ON VACATION	ROBERT CASTLE
1881471888	SEE WHAT YOU THINK	DAVID ROSENBERG
1933132124	SHEETSTONE	SUSAN BLANSHARD
1881471640	SPIN CYCLE	CHRIS STROFFOLINO
1881471578	SPIRITLAND	NAVA RENEK
1881471705	SPY IN AMNESIA	JULIAN SEMILIAN
1933132213	STRANGE EVOLUTIONARY FLOWERS	LIZBETH RYMLAND
188147156X	SUDDENLY TODAY WE CAN DREAM	RUTHA ROSEN
1933132175	SUNRISE IN ARMAGEDDON	WILL ALEXANDER
1881471780	TEDS FAVORITE SKIRT	LEWIS WARSH
1933132043	THINGS THAT NEVER HAPPENED	GORDON OSING
1933132205	THIS GUY	JAMES LEWELLING
1933132019	THREE MOUTHS	TOD THILLEMAN
1881471365	TRACK	NORMAN FINKELSTEIN
188147190X	TRANSGENDER ORGAN GRINDER	JULIAN SEMILIAN
1881471861	TRANSITORY	JANE AUGUSTINE
1933132140	VIENNA ØØ	EUGENE K. GARBER
1881471543	WARP SPASM	BASIL KING
188147173X	WATCHFULNESS	PETER O'LEARY
1881471993	XL POEMS	JULIUS KELERAS
0972066268	YOU, ME, AND THE INSECTS	BARBARA HENNING

All Spuyten Duyvil titles are available
through your local bookseller via Booksense.com

Distributed to the trade by
Biblio Distribution
a division of NBN
1-800-462-6420
http://bibliodistribution.com

All Spuyten Duyvil authors may be contacted at
authors@spuytenduyvil.net

Author appearance information and background at
http://spuytenduyvil.net